R.L. PEREZ

THORN & ASH

Willow Haven Press

Acheron
The Undead
Aidoneus's
Penthouse
Forest of Thanatos
Sty...
Oceanus
Erebos

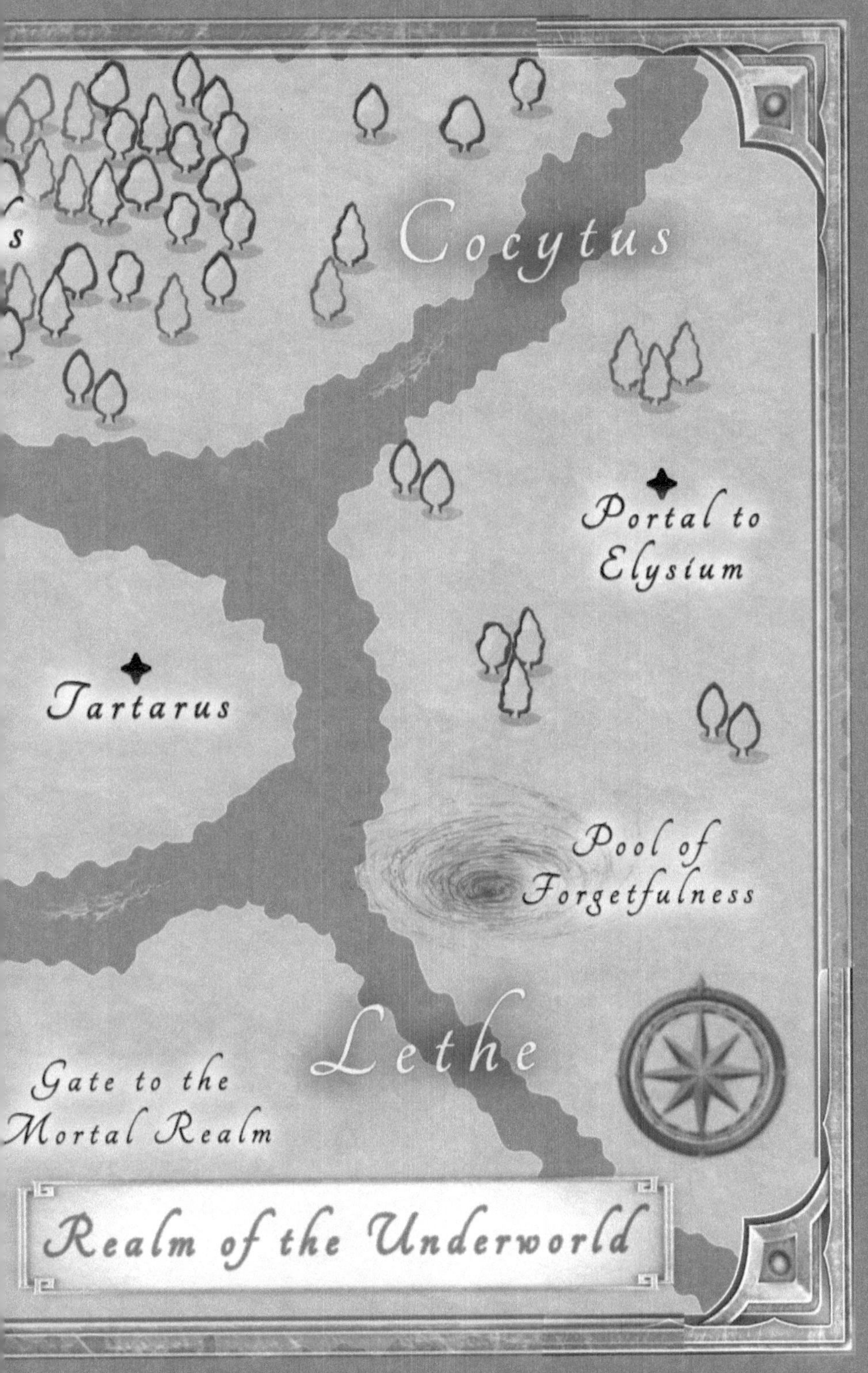
Cocytus
Portal to
Elysium
Tartarus
Pool of
Forgetfulness
Lethe
Gate to the
Mortal Realm
Realm of the Underworld

CONTENTS

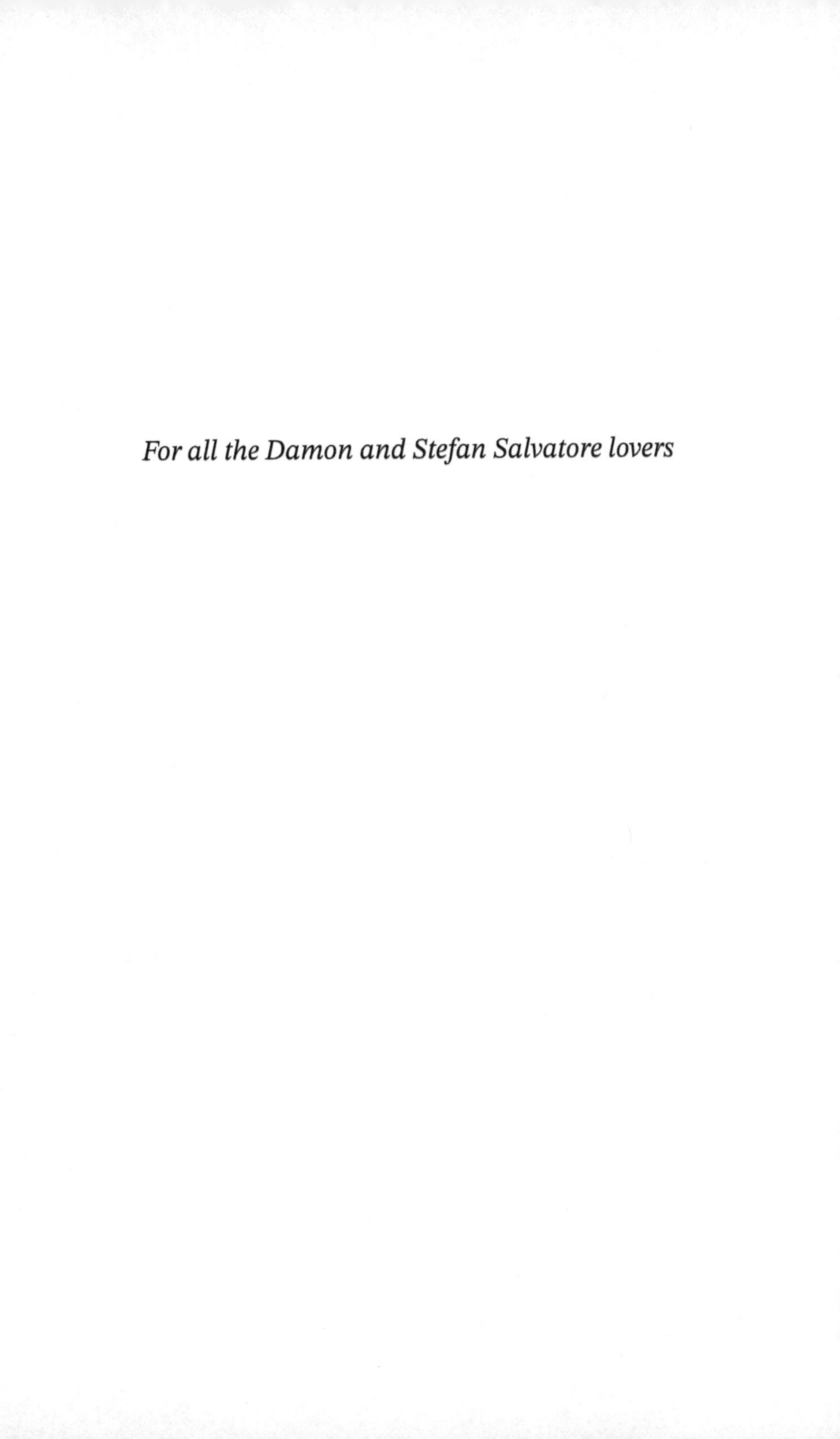

For all the Damon and Stefan Salvatore lovers

PROLOGUE
PRUE

THE SHACKLES CLANGED ALONG THE CAVERN wall, grating against Prue's ears. Her wrist ached, now raw and blistered from her useless attempts to free herself.

She wasn't sure how long she'd been chained up in this dank cave, but it felt like days. The darkness pressed in on her, making her wonder if she was actually alive or if she was rotting away in Hell itself. Had she died, and this was her eternal punishment? She couldn't make out any of her surroundings but the cold, moistened stone beneath her and the rock wall at her back, to which her chains were attached.

Occasionally, a horned or scaled demon brought her a plate of stale bread. The first few times, Prue peppered them with questions, desperate to know where Cyrus was and when she could see him. But every time, the demons were stoic and silent, refusing to respond to her. Once they deposited her food, they left without a word.

Prue wasn't sure why they bothered feeding her. It was clear Cyrus wanted nothing to do with her. She'd been a means to an end. He'd only needed her to provide passage to the Underworld.

Now that she had, he had no use for her anymore.

So, why was she still alive?

Her mind was too numb with fatigue and hunger to properly put the pieces together, but she had to try. She couldn't believe Cyrus had deceived and betrayed her now that they'd finally crossed into the Underworld together. As cruel as he could be, she didn't think him capable of putting on an act for that long—during all their travels across the mortal realm, through everything they had fought for.

No, something had changed during the attack with Gaia and Vasileios. She'd noticed it in the strange murkiness of his eyes, lacking their usual luster and brilliance that captivated her so easily.

This was not *her* Cyrus. This was... something else.

Footsteps echoed nearby, and Prue stiffened, sitting up straighter, the chain scraping against the rocky wall. She expected another demon servant bringing her sustenance, but to her surprise, it was Cyrus himself. He wore a long black cloak with a matching dark tunic underneath, gold buckles gleaming from his belt. A dagger was sheathed at his waist, and atop his head was a crown made of bones.

He looked positively regal. And terrifying.

A shiver swept over her as his dull, muddied gray eyes locked onto her. Her dress was torn and dirty, and she hadn't bathed in days. She probably smelled awful.

Good. Maybe her foul stench would bring him back to his senses.

"Why not just kill me?" Prue spat. If Cyrus was truly himself, she would demand answers from him. She was tired of waiting. "Why keep me here?"

Cyrus cocked his head at her, his expression unsettlingly blank. He resembled a bird of prey assessing its next meal, and it made her shudder all over again. "You are of no use to me dead."

"What use am I alive? I won't be your plaything, if that's what you think."

Cyrus laughed, flashing his teeth, but the sound was harsh and cold. "No. Trust me when I say I won't be getting any closer to you than I am now." Something flashed in his eyes, and if Prue hadn't been staring in horror at his irises, she might not have noticed.

For the briefest of seconds, it was a flash of silver. A glimpse of the Cyrus she used to know.

She frowned, scooting closer, and he took the tiniest

fraction of a step backward. Again, so subtle, she might have missed it.

Interesting. Not only was he afraid of touching her, for some reason, but at the mention of toying with her body, the real Cyrus emerged for half a second.

"Are you afraid of me?" she taunted, unable to help herself.

In a flash, Cyrus stood before her, his hand gripping her neck. She gasped, her lungs straining, her body going stiff under his unrelenting grasp.

"I fear no one," he snarled. His fingers squeezed, making her throat burn, before he released her and stepped back, his face a mask of fury.

She had struck a nerve. That much was clear. She rubbed her neck, her throat on fire. Each swallow felt like hot knives raking along her insides, making her shudder in agony.

But she wouldn't give up. She'd provoked him somehow. This was progress.

"Why are you here?" she asked carefully, noting he carried no food. Was he here just to taunt her? It hadn't escaped her notice that he'd avoided answering her question: *What use am I alive?*

Cyrus straightened, lifting his chin. "I have come to see if you are properly subdued. I see now that that is not the case. There is still fire in your eyes that would likely cause me trouble if I were to free you."

Prue let out a harsh laugh. "You were considering freeing me? I highly doubt that."

"Would you give me your word you would bring me no harm if I were to release you?"

Prue was silent. She could lie and promise him anything just to get out of her situation. But after what they'd been through together, she found she couldn't lie to him.

She owed him that much.

She almost agreed right away, knowing she would be unable to harm Cyrus, no matter how cruel he'd become.

Because she loved him with all her soul.

But *this* Cyrus didn't need to know that. Better he think her dangerous and volatile than weak and submissive.

Prue reached for her magic, summoning that reserve of power deep within herself. But, like every attempt, her body felt nothing but cold emptiness. Her third eye remained closed. There was no magic to be conjured. No spells to cast.

Her magic was gone.

She didn't know if it was Cyrus's doing or because she was in the Underworld, but whatever the reason, she was powerless.

"I don't enjoy seeing you like this, Prudence," Cyrus said softly. "Show me you can be a loyal and obedient subject, and you will be rewarded for it."

Prue's eyes narrowed. "I am not your subject. I am your wife. Your queen. I bow to no one."

Cyrus's lips curled into a smirk. "The Underworld has no queen. It never has, and it never will."

Prue shook her head sadly at the bitterness in his voice. "You are mine, Cyrus. And I am yours. That will never change."

They had sealed their bond the night they consummated their marriage. Cyrus had warned her that connection was permanent; never to be broken.

They were tethered. For all eternity.

With a snarl, Cyrus turned away from her... but not before Prue caught another glimpse of that striking silver in his eyes. Stunned, she watched him leave the cave, his cloak swishing with each step.

Her Cyrus was still here. Barely. Her words had drawn him out for only a moment.

She clung to that hope, vowing to do whatever it took to bring him back.

WHIRLPOOL

MONA

THE WIND RAGED, THE SPRAY OF THE SEA DOUSING Mona's already soaked form as she clung to the rails of the ship. Dark clouds swirled in the sky, the large vessel tossed about with each wave. Mona's grip on the rails tightened. She couldn't fall in.

Not yet.

She gazed down at the emerald ring she wore on her finger, now flecked with water droplets. According to Evander's specific instructions, she needed an emerald on her skin to keep her alive when she passed through the portal to the Underworld.

She also needed to be *alive* when she crossed over, otherwise she would just be another spirit drifting among the rivers. She had already played that role. After sacrificing her life to save her sister and her village, Mona had died, traveling to the Underworld as a spirit.

That was where she'd met Evander.

But after Prue had resurrected her, Mona had watched her sister vanish into a portal to the Underworld alongside the god of the dead.

Mona couldn't just sit there and let Prue live out the remainder of her life bound to the Underworld. She had to bring her sister back and free her from the realm of the dead. Prue needed her.

And yes, a small, heated part of her yearned to see Evander again. Their conversation during her communication spell had been... stilted. His voice always had a kind, soft timbre to it, but after spending an inordinate amount of time with him in the Underworld, she had learned to differentiate his cordial voice from his passionate voice.

It had definitely been the former.

Did that mean he wasn't glad to hear from her? Had he hoped to be rid of her forever?

Mona shook the thought from her mind as another splash of water hit her in the face. Even the ocean was chastising her for her superficial thoughts.

It didn't matter what Evander thought of her. Prue was in danger. And Mona had to save her.

Wear the emerald at all times, Evander had told her. *It*

is the only thing anchoring you to the mortal realm. Without it, you won't survive.

He had then encouraged her to travel across the Manos Sea toward the dreaded whirlpool that most seafarers avoided. Only after Mona had shown a rather impressive bit of magic had the captain agreed. And even then, he only agreed to get her close enough for a rowboat to take her the rest of the way.

Mona couldn't blame him. The crew were risking their lives to bring her here. Thank the Goddess they were pious enough to believe her blessed by the deities.

In a sense, she was. Gaia was her mother, after all.

Mona flinched at the reminder. Her entire life had been a lie. She'd believed herself to be an ordinary witch living in a coven on the small island of Krenia. As it turned out, Gaia had just been hiding her daughters away, waiting to use them... but for what purpose? What had the goddess been waiting for?

She had obviously been hiding from someone. But who?

Add this to the long list of questions I have, Mona thought bitterly. She'd spent most of her life buried in the pages of books, seeking answers to her mind's endless supply of questions. But no matter how much she had researched the gods and goddesses, nothing could tell her the truth of what happened to Gaia except the goddess herself. Books contained histories, but only as people penned them. And if Mona's suspicions were correct, then her mother wanted to keep her history hidden from the world.

Mona had left Gaia, bound and gagged, in the village of Faidon. Her bitterness and anger had overwhelmed her, along with her sense of urgency in finding Prue.

"This is as far as we go, lass!" bellowed a voice nearby.

Mona jumped, whirling to find the captain clutching the wheel, his hair and beard a ragged, soaked mess about his face.

"Take the lifeboat and go!" he urged. "May the Goddess bless you on your quest!"

Mona clutched her shawl tightly around her, though it did no good since it, too, was drenched. "Thank you!" she cried, though the howling wind drowned out her weak voice. On feeble legs, she staggered toward where the lifeboat was tied to the ship. One of the ropes was frayed, ready to snap, so she didn't feel too guilty about taking this boat. It would not return.

She hopped inside, and two crewmen lowered her onto the raging sea below. Fear twisted in her heart, tightening in her throat and making it hard to breathe. She clutched at the ring on her finger, twisting it in circles.

I am not a coward. I am not a coward.

Prue had once said the words to her, trying to snap her out of her crippling fear. Now, Mona chanted it to herself, a reminder of why she was doing this.

For her sister. Prue had sacrificed everything to bring Mona back. Mona couldn't just leave her in the Underworld forever.

I'm coming for you, Prue, she thought. *And I'm bringing you home.*

Mona lurched forward as the boat met the sea, immediately rocking violently with each wave. She gripped the edges, determined not to fall in just yet. She had to be right on top of the whirlpool before she jumped in. Squinting against the salty spray around her, she made out an eerie mist funneling into a circular cloud.

The whirlpool.

Goddess above, she was really going to do this.

Her terror intensified, numbing her chest into a hard block of ice. For a moment, she sat there, stunned and immobilized.

I am not a coward.

She thought those words again and forced her limbs to move. Her trembling fingers gripped the oars and attempted to steer her toward the whirlpool, but there was no need; it was drawing her forward. Behind her, the *Dreamer* was already sailing in the opposite direction, and Mona heaved a sigh of relief in knowing the crew was escaping the maw of the whirlpool.

If she'd been responsible for their deaths, she would've never forgiven herself.

Dive into the heart of the whirlpool, Evander had said. *But you must be alive until the very last moment, otherwise you will only cross over like the rest of the dead.*

After everything Prue had gone through to bring Mona back from the dead, now Mona was about to risk it all. The irony almost made her laugh.

For you, Prue, she thought. The boat lurched again, jostling her from side to side as it careened toward the roaring whirlpool in front of her.

Mona's heart jolted as a shadowy shape took form underneath the waves. It must've been her imagination. Her fear playing tricks on her, surely.

But there it was again. A dark presence lurked just beneath the surface.

Nausea roiled in her gut. What manner of creatures lived alongside a whirlpool? Perhaps drowning was not the only danger here...

With a mighty splash, a massive tentacle emerged, stretching high toward the sky before falling with an earsplitting *thwack* against the sea. Water gushed over Mona, filling her small vessel and lapping over the edges, threatening to drag her under.

Almighty Goddess, what the hell *was* that? The tentacle had been bigger than any creature Mona had ever heard of. Certainly no ordinary octopus or squid.

A low groan rumbled from beneath the sea, making the boat and Mona's very bones quiver.

Then, a voice echoed from within the whirlpool.

"You are not like the others." The speaker was female, but her voice was deep and powerful, somehow resonating loudly enough to be heard over the roaring waves.

Mona clutched the edges of the boat so tightly her fingers began to throb. Her wide eyes remained pinned on the whirlpool, convinced she was imagining things again.

"Ah. Daughter of a goddess. Well, this is a first."

The whirlpool... was *talking* to her.

"It is no mere accident that you are here, then," the voice continued. "You are here for passage. And I am the gatekeeper."

A startled breath left Mona in a whoosh as her thoughts caught up with her. Of course this wasn't a sentient whirlpool. It was a creature living *within* the whirlpool.

The pieces connected in her mind like a puzzle, and now that she had a mystery to solve, her clever mind shed all sense of fear in favor of her curiosity.

A creature living within a whirlpool with huge tentacles. Her thoughts spun as she considered each and every book she'd studied on mythical sea monsters.

After a moment, she had her answer. "Charybdis," she said.

A soft laugh reverberated against Mona's small boat. "You are certainly a smart one. Very few know me by name."

"If you are Charybdis," Mona said, her voice gaining confidence, "then you require a price for passage."

"Indeed I do."

"What is your price?" Mona gripped the emerald ring on her finger, praying the beast didn't ask for jewels.

"My price... is your memories."

Mona froze, her insides chilling at the beast's request. Her memories? "All of them?"

"Yes. All but one. You may keep one thing you treasure most. One thing to remind you of who you are. But everything else will belong to me."

Mona swallowed hard, eyeing the gem around her finger. How could she save Prue if she forgot everything? Gaia, Cyrus, Mona's own death...

Evander.

No. She wouldn't give that up. She couldn't! When she had died, Evander was the only one in the Underworld who helped her. He discovered her unbound state and was kind to her. How could she sacrifice her memories of him? It would be as if they'd never met...

"Make your choice, little goddess," Charybdis crooned. "I grow impatient. If you do not decide soon, I will take you to the depths of the sea like all my other victims."

Mona closed her eyes, anguish claiming her, tightening her chest like a vise. She would pay any price to save her sister. After all, Prue had paid the ultimate price to do the same for her.

I can't save Prue if I don't remember who she is, Mona thought, the truth of those words gutting her like a knife. There was no other option. If she chose anything else, she might forget her entire mission to bring Prue home.

Which meant she had to do it. She had to give up Evander.

Hot tears streamed down Mona's face, momentarily warming the chill of the salty sea air. As she swung her legs over the rim of the boat, she pictured Evander's face. Those silvery eyes claiming her, just as his hands and lips and tongue had.

Goddess, she would miss him.

A memory resurfaced in her mind, as if her thoughts were bidding him farewell. Evander, with his body molded against hers, his mouth hot on her neck, his hands roaming her body and tearing at her dress. The growls and moans of his throat making her toes curl. The scrape of his teeth against her skin...

Enough. This was too painful. Mona had to let him go. This was for Prue. Even if Mona might fancy herself in love with a prince of Hell, her sister was more important.

Eyes still closed, Mona said in a choked voice, "I accept. I will give you all memories... but those of my sister, Prue."

The beast laughed as if it found this funny, but Mona had no idea why. "The price is paid. Dive in, little goddess, and I will grant you safe passage to the Underworld."

With a deep breath, Mona sucked in as much air into her lungs and chest as she could before plunging into the sea. The spinning vortex captured her immediately, spinning her about, her body twisting and flailing. The icy water seeped into her, freezing her bones and numbing her flesh. She closed her eyes, fearing she would be sick if she watched the churning water.

Then, she felt something brush against her ankle, and her eyes flew open. She caught sight of the massive beast, its jaws open wide, rows of jagged teeth gleaming as Charybdis drew nearer...

The vortex sucked Mona through, and her scream was lost in the sea. A heavy force slammed into her, flooding her with memories of when she entered the Underworld for the first time. Before her resurrection, before Samhain, when Prue had summoned Cyrus. Before *all* of this. Her final thought was of Evander and how they had first met, just as the darkness overtook her and swallowed her whole.

PART ONE

"To die is landing on some distant shore."

John Dryden

UNBOUND
EVANDER

BEFORE MONA'S RESURRECTION

EVANDER CROUCHED ALONGSIDE THE RIVERBANK, breathing deeply. The air held the faintest smell of pine and evergreen—the only sense of reality the charmed atmosphere could muster, thanks to his father's powerful illusion spells. Frankly, Evander was impressed the magic included scents at all. The vision of the forested landscape was delightful enough.

But beneath the familiar smells was the sickly odor of death magic. The sharp scent stung Evander's nostrils, and he subconsciously ran his fingers over the smooth surface of the moonstone he wore on a leather cord around his neck. He never took it off.

He shuddered, ignoring the stench of the powerful and deadly magic he tried not to think about on a regular basis as he looked for something else. Something new.

He hadn't shepherded a new soul in days. Yet the river continued to flow smoothly. Evander wondered if perhaps he was doing something wrong, or if he was neglecting his duties. He liked patrolling the river Cocytus. It was peaceful out here, and he didn't want to lose his position.

Cyrus, his younger brother and the ruler of the Underworld, had once been a friend to Evander. But with his mighty rise to power, he had become something corrupted. Something dangerous. Something Evander couldn't trust at all.

Again, Evander's hand went to his moonstone necklace. *I will never become like him,* he thought grimly. The magic contained in his necklace made certain of that.

The beast within him surged forward, sensing where his thoughts had turned. But Evander willed it to remain caged.

Not now, he told it. Soon, the beast would be free. But not now.

His brothers were too dangerous and volatile to be around, which meant Evander's only companions out here were the grieving souls in the river. Between his curse, the beast inside him, and his godly responsibility, Evander would likely spend an eternity alone.

But it was worth it.

If constant loneliness is the price I must pay to be free of darkness, then so be it, he thought. The alternative was allowing himself to be warped and twisted into something evil and uncaring like Cyrus.

Never, he vowed.

Evander couldn't trust that Cyrus would spare him from the same torment he had inflicted on their other brothers, regardless of how cautious Evander was around him. He strived to keep his head down, to avoid drawing attention to himself. But power called to everyone in many disturbing ways. Friends became foes. Love became a weakness, something to despise. Any sign of affection bled away in favor of a cruel, hungry need for more.

It would never be enough. And it would never satisfy.

Deep inside him, the beast rumbled its assent. *Never enough.*

Evander sighed, determining that there were no new souls in his river today. The purest of souls traveled to Elysium, and the remainder were sorted in the rivers of the Underworld, each one monitored by a prince of Hell. The majority of souls here went straight to Tartarus.

Evander's river, Cocytus, was certainly not a prison for the damned, but also not a refuge for the innocent, either. It was somewhere in between; a small space with very few occupants to keep Evander busy.

It certainly made for a dull lifestyle, but Evander couldn't complain. His suffering was nothing compared to the souls in the river. They might not be tortured by the woes of Tartarus, but they were still in constant pain and turmoil.

He rose to his feet, only to stop, his body going stiff as he sensed someone approaching behind him. His skin prickled, and quiet footsteps drew closer. Slowly, he turned, his nostrils flaring as he recognized two of his brothers.

Marcellus, the older of the two, had short-cropped black hair with a thin streak of silver and a beefy, muscular frame he enjoyed showing off. Beside him stood Leonidas, taller and leaner, though still deadly and dangerous. His silvery eyes glinted with mischief, his gaze shrewd and calculating. His own black hair curled at the nape of his neck, also streaked with silver.

"Gods, Evander," Marcellus said with a laugh, crossing his bulky arms over his chest. "You look even more miserable than Leonidas these days. What's your excuse? Is Cyrus forcing you to shovel shit now?"

Leonidas snickered, though a flicker of darkness flashed in his eyes. He had the worst assignment of them all—tending the river Acheron, which housed the most anguished of souls.

Evander arranged his expression into something apathetic. Almost bored. But inside, his chest flared with alarm. *Why are they here? They need to leave...* "Don't you two have your own duties to tend to?"

Marcellus snorted and nudged Leonidas with his elbow. "He says 'duties' as if he knows what that means. As if he's ever known a day of hard work in his miserable life."

"I have a funny feeling he wants us to leave," Leonidas murmured, a smirk playing on his lips. "Almost as if he doesn't care for our company."

Marcellus cracked his knuckles. "Why wouldn't he? We are clearly the most superior of all our brothers. He should relish our company."

Leonidas idled closer. "Perhaps we should punish him for his offense. Remind him how lucky he is to have brothers like us."

Evander sighed, closing his eyes briefly. Occasionally, his brothers bullied him, eager to assert who was more powerful. And Evander could do nothing but let them overtake him. Because if he fought back, if he risked unleashing the beast... he risked losing himself to the dark magic completely. And all would be lost.

He was fortunate. Ordinarily, Vasileios, his oldest brother, joined in as well. Today it was just two of them.

He could endure their torment. It was only a few moments of pain and humiliation, and then it would be over.

Evander turned to fully face them, then spread his arms. "Go ahead. I'm ready."

Marcellus's eyebrows lifted. "Oh, trying to be brave, are you? Imagine that, our feeble brother trying to prove something."

Leonidas barked out a laugh. "I don't believe it for a second. Look, he's practically trembling with fear."

Evander clenched his fingers into fists. He *was* shaking, but not out of fear... out of fury. His fingernails dug into his palms as he tried to keep his rage at bay.

Don't let them see it. This means nothing to you. Just get past this moment and move on.

The glee on Marcellus's face told Evander he wouldn't let up easily. He wanted to keep teasing. To find more flaws to poke at.

If Evander didn't give them a reason to end it, he might do something they would all regret.

"It's really rather childish," Evander said with a long-suffering sigh. "I wish you would just leave me be. I have better things to do."

Leonidas pressed a hand to his chest and offered a look of mock horror. "You *wound* us, Evander."

Evander only shrugged. "If you aren't strong enough

to make the first move, then that's fine. I'd rather be working anyway."

Anger flashed in Marcellus's eyes, and Evander knew his strategy was working. If there was one thing Marcellus wouldn't stand for, it was an attack on his pride.

"You're an insolent little shit, you know that?" Marcellus spat. "Cyrus should've thrown you into Tartarus with the rest of the scum. I don't know why he bothers to leave you here when you offer *nothing* to this realm. You're a waste of space."

Evander swallowed hard as Marcellus drew closer. Evander was taller, but the rippling muscles on Marcellus were intimidating all on their own.

"I'll make you wish you were in that pit," Marcellus growled. Behind him, Leonidas approached, looking eager.

Evander closed his eyes as the first punch struck him. As always, the blinding pain was a shock to his body, the agony rippling over him in sickening waves. He staggered backward, his jaw burning, just as Marcellus hit him again, this time in the stomach.

Evander doubled over, wheezing, his ribs feeling like they had been shattered completely.

Leonidas jumped in, striking a blow to Evander's nose. The hit wasn't as forceful as Marcellus's, but it still slammed into Evander, rattling his bones and making his head spin. Silver blood trickled from his nose, and he choked on his breaths.

Another punch to the gut had him on his knees. When Evander collapsed, his two brothers crowded him, exchanging kick after kick, their attack relentless. Evander tried to raise his arms to cover his face, but the pain roared inside him, consuming him. White stars danced in his vision, and the monster within him lurched, eager to be unleashed, to end this attack once and for all.

Evander channeled all his energy into keeping the beast at bay. He allowed his brothers to beat him, to smash him as if he were nothing more than a caged animal.

He couldn't risk it. Unleashing his power would have deadly consequences. And with his brothers, he didn't dare expose that side of himself. Everything was a weapon to these two, and they would easily exploit it if they knew.

He had worked hard for eons to keep this part of himself shackled forever. This was a small price to pay to keep his mind and body intact. He would never give in to that darkness. Ever.

He had to keep this secret. Keep the beast bound. Even if it meant enduring his brothers' cruelty for a few more moments.

When the two finally stopped, they laughed,

mocking the way Evander remained curled up on the ground like a child. They left without preamble, their jeering echoing in the forest long after they vanished from view.

Evander remained huddled on the ground, the pain so blinding and intense that he knew the smallest of movements would amplify it. So he remained where he was, struggling to breathe through the blood in his throat.

He was immortal. He would heal from these wounds, as he always did. But that wasn't the point. The point was, his brothers had the power to render him weak and powerless. And they often sought to remind Evander of that fact.

After what felt like hours, Evander finally rose, his muscles burning and his head throbbing. The blood had dried on his face, and he hastily scrubbed at it, causing silver flecks of it to fall to the earth. His hands ran along his forehead and cheeks, searching for more wounds. But there was nothing else. Either his immortal body had already begun healing, or most of his injuries were internal. He could feel it as he staggered to his feet, his insides burning and scorching a path of fire through his blood that he endured with every step. He gritted his teeth, telling himself this was worth it. His brothers would leave him alone for a while. He'd bought himself more time.

And his secret was still safe.

He sat by the edge of the river, resting his back against a large pine tree as he struggled to control his breathing. The silence of the forest surrounding him, lulling him into a calm and peaceful mentality. Slowly, the trauma of his beating faded, and he focused on the solitude he loved. The tranquility of this secluded space.

He wasn't sure how much time passed—perhaps hours—before he finally climbed to his feet and dusted the dirt off his clothes. A few flecks of silver blood had stained his tunic, but he buttoned his jacket, covering the blemish. His ribs still ached and his muscles protested his movements, but the worst of his injuries had already healed.

He would overcome this. Just like he always did.

He turned toward the forest, then froze with the realization that there was something else lingering nearby. For one horrifying moment, he thought his brothers had returned. But as he inhaled, he realized it was something new. A magic he had never smelled before.

Evander faced the river and breathed in more deeply, allowing the hunter within him to sift through the foreign fragrance in hopes of identifying it.

Salt and seawater. The faintest hint of roses.

Evander frowned. None of those things belonged here. This was a freshwater river, and he had never seen roses in the forest before. Eyes narrowing, he scrutinized the depths of the river, peering at the glowing silvery orbs of the souls floating within. Nothing seemed amiss. Except...

There it was. Several paces away, farther upstream, was a faint, transparent fog that Evander might have missed if he hadn't been looking for it. Heart pounding, Evander edged along the riverbank, drawing closer to the strange mist. Whatever it was couldn't be good. This was a strange magic—a *new* magic—which meant it was dangerous.

Like all forms of magic.

As Evander drew nearer, he realized the fog was taking shape. It slowly solidified until it formed the semi-transparent embodiment of...a woman.

Evander stopped short, his mouth falling open in surprise. Wariness crept into his thoughts. He trusted women about as much as he trusted magic. Both Aidoneus and Cyrus had been tricked and betrayed by women in the mortal realm. Even if this mist belonged to a wayward soul, Evander still didn't trust it.

Something whispered in the air, making the hairs on Evander's arms rise. He wore a black tunic and jacket, much more modest than what some of his brothers wore, and yet a chill skittered along his body, making him feel as cold as if he stood stark naked in the forest.

"What are you?" Evander asked, his soft voice ringing clear over the babbling river.

The eerie whispers continued, intensifying and rising, and only then did Evander realize it was... music. A haunting melody sung from a grieving soul. He'd only heard a handful of souls sing their grief; most screamed or wept or wailed.

But this... This was beautiful. Striking. Each note triggered something powerful inside his chest. He drew in a breath, his eyes stinging, though he didn't know why.

"Let me help you." Evander drew closer, his feet now planted on the very edge of the bank. Any farther, and he would have to wade into the stream itself. He extended an arm, and the singing abruptly stopped.

The disembodied woman solidified further until she resembled a rippling silver statue. She wore a thin gown, almost as sheer as a nightgown, and her long, dark hair floated around her. Her eyes were luminescent enough for Evander to believe she probably had blue or green eyes in her mortal form, though he couldn't make out the color in her spirit form.

But he didn't need to. Even like this, she was quite lovely.

Or perhaps it had just been too long since he had seen a soul's body. Most of them were spherical orbs, making it easier for him to keep to his task of shepherding them onward. If he had to look upon their mortal countenances like this, it would make his responsibilities that much more difficult.

Especially if they were all as beautiful as this one.

Something inside Evander stirred at the sight of her... Some desperate hunger, an aching yearning, like a sensation that had been there his entire life but he'd only just now identified it.

A low hum resonated inside his chest, and after a moment, Evander realized it came from the creature that dwelled within him. Almost as if it were *purring* with contentment.

Whatever energies this spirit radiated were *soothing* to the beast. Evander had never felt anything like it before.

The woman—who was younger than he expected, likely around twenty or so—fixed her gaze upon him. Her lips parted, and Evander thought she might sing again. He even hoped for it.

But instead, she said, "Who are you?"

"My name is Evander. I am the overseer of this river. I'm sorry to tell you this, but you have passed on to the next life. Your mortal life has ended." He had rehearsed this speech several times. Most of the souls lived in their own spaces, ignorant of everything around them—including Evander. But occasionally, a soul had questions for him, and he was always prepared.

"Did it work?" the woman asked urgently, her eyes wide.

Evander, momentarily startled by her sudden question, only cocked his head at her.

"My sacrifice," she clarified. "Did it work? Did the souls stop attacking the village? My sister, my mother—are they all right?" Her voice broke as if she were holding back tears. "Please tell me they're alive."

Evander shook his head, helpless to offer her any consolation. The desperation shining in her eyes made him wish he could access her realm, just to see if her loved ones were safe. "I'm sorry," he said earnestly. "I have no way to reach the mortal realm."

Even if he wanted to, the dark magic festering inside him wouldn't allow him to transition to other realms. It was bound to the Underworld. And so was he.

"There's no way to send word?" the woman pleaded. "Nothing at all you can do?"

Gods, this was torture, having to disappoint her again. Ordinarily, the souls were nothing more than orbs who didn't even register his presence at all. But this, seeing a dead mortal face-to-face and having to explain this to her? It was almost too much.

"This is your home now," Evander said quietly. "All who live in the Underworld are destined to remain here. There is no way back, and there is no way to communicate with other realms."

This wasn't entirely true. Some souls, when they completed their journey, would transition to Elysium, but those were rare instances. And Evander knew his father, Aidoneus, had traveled to Elysium before to convene with other gods.

So it wasn't impossible. But for a mortal soul? This woman had no say in the matter. Her soul would travel wherever the river would take her.

Or rather... that was how it *should* be. But she wasn't moving. She was merely hovering above the river, her feet not even touching the water.

"So, this is the Underworld?" The woman gazed around as if just noticing her surroundings. "I'm truly dead?" Her brows knitted together in confusion.

"Yes," Evander said.

The woman stared at him, her face a mask of shock. "I don't understand."

"I know this is hard to accept," Evander said gently. "And I'm so sorry for the loss you have suffered. But you are dead now, and there is no way back."

"No, that's not it," the woman said quickly. "I knew I was going to die. But this... doesn't feel right."

Evander cocked his head at her. How would she know what death felt like?

"I've visited the other side," she went on, her gaze distant. "Once or twice. I'm a witch. We perform rituals, and I have sensed death before. It isn't this."

That same wariness crept into Evander's thoughts again. Witches couldn't be trusted. They were the worst form of humans, capable of deceit and lies and manipulation. But as he studied her, he couldn't deny something *was* wrong. She wasn't an orb, for one thing. And for another, she carried a strong fragrance with her, a fragrance that usually faded with death.

Realization swept over him, and he drew in a sharp gasp.

This woman was unbound. Her soul must have been separated from her body at the time of her death.

No. This couldn't be happening. Not *here*, at Cocytus. The only detached souls were those who dwelled in Tartarus and who had earned a gruesome punishment. Because to be separated from one's mortal form was an unspeakable torture that most souls did not deserve.

Especially not this woman.

"Oh, Goddess." She moaned, hunching over, her form flickering slightly as a breeze drifted along the river, making the waters ripple.

On instinct, Evander reached for her, even knowing he wouldn't be able to feel her solid form. As he did so, her spirit vanished, leaving an empty silence in its wake.

Stunned, Evander stared at the space where she had been, horror turning his stomach. Where had she gone? Where *could* she go? If she was part of Cocytus, then this river was her home. She had no other connections.

Evander turned, thinking she'd perhaps floated farther down the river. He hurried down the river bank, occasionally peering into the waters to search for her. Panic erupted in his mind. He thought of Cyrus finding out about this. Would he punish Evander? Would he re-assign him? If Cyrus imprisoned him, he would find out about Evander's dark secret...

Oh, gods, no.

Evander froze when that same haunting melody pricked his ears. He turned, and there she was, taking shape in front of him once more. Panting, Evander dropped his arms and sagged with relief. "What happened?" he asked.

The woman blinked slowly. "I saw my sister. She pulled me back. Just for a moment." Her eyes sparkled as if with tears.

"That's not possible," Evander said. "As I mentioned before, once you pass on, you cannot return."

"I'm not lying," the woman said.

"I know." His tone was gentle. "I am only conveying the laws of the Underworld. It's clear something has gone wrong with your transition into death." He scrutinized her, but her gaze was distant, seeing past him. He imagined she was thinking of her sister. "What's your name?"

"Mona. Pomona Donati."

Even her name sounded like a song, rolling off her

lips like a soothing melody. "Mona, I will do everything I can to solve this mystery and ensure your safe passage through my river. Did you have any control when you were pulled to your sister?"

"I—I don't know. Once I was there, I didn't know how to get back, but... I didn't *want* to come back." Guilt creased her expression, but Evander couldn't blame her. Death had ripped her from her life. Of course she would want to return to her loved ones.

"If it happens again, will you test your strength? See if you can go back and forth at will?"

"Do you want me to try now?" Her voice was eager, as if she yearned for the challenge.

Evander's mouth quirked into a small smile. "You don't have to. Most souls are weak when they first cross over. I don't want to push your limits, especially if you are unbound."

"Unbound?"

"It's the term we use for souls who are disconnected from their mortal forms. Most of them transform into orbs, and their bodies become dormant, absorbed by the soul. They will reunite with their mortal forms later once they have fully processed their journey through death. But for now, they are content with floating along this river." Evander gestured to the river's depths. As he did so, a faint cry of agony drifted from the waters, echoing in the air.

Evander winced. "Well, *mostly* content. Some are still grieving the loss of their life, which is to be expected."

Mona looked at him then, her silvery eyes spearing right through him. Evander shifted uncomfortably on his feet, uneasy with this strange sensation of a soul looking directly at him. He was so accustomed to them being shapeless orbs, unable to interact or pry or *do* anything.

And yet, this woman was here, inspecting him. He felt laid bare before her as if he could hide nothing from her pensive gaze.

"Why would you help me?" she finally asked.

"It's my duty as overseer of the river Cocytus," Evander replied immediately, the response instinctive.

"Yes, but... if one soul is hurt, it's not your job to mend them, is it? That seems like a rather complicated task."

Evander heard what she wasn't saying: *You don't seem powerful enough to handle this situation.*

She wanted someone else to help. Someone more capable.

Perhaps someone like one of his brothers.

He straightened, defiance blazing in his chest. "I assure you, I am perfectly equipped to manage this. And I'll prove it to you." Just because he wasn't frightening and overbearing, like Marcellus or Leonidas, didn't mean he was weak or incompetent.

Not all strengths paraded loudly for all to see. Some were quieter, lingering just beneath the surface.

Mona's expression softened. "I'm sorry. I didn't mean to offend you. It's just—this is not at all what I expected."

Evander wasn't sure if by *this* she meant death, or her unbound state. Both were startling and traumatic. She must have endured quite an ordeal to wind up here at such a young age.

"Why can't I see the other souls?" Mona peered down into the river, squinting. But Evander knew she wouldn't be able to see the others. Only a god or goddess had such an ability.

"You are not meant to," he said. "Each soul must journey along their own path to peace in the next life."

Mona's brows furrowed as she stared hard at the water. Something like surprise flashed in her gaze, her lips parting slightly. Then, she quickly looked up at him, her mouth clamping shut.

Evander stared at her. What had she seen? Surely, she hadn't seen another soul. It was impossible.

Then again, many things had occurred today that were impossible.

It made Evander wonder—was this strange situation with Mona an isolated incident, or was it a sign something larger was affecting the Underworld?

"Can you—are you able to descend into the water?" Evander asked. "Perhaps that would help heal you."

Mona shifted, her form rippling once more. Her jaw clenched from the effort, and she sighed, shaking her head. "No. I can't move at will."

Evander nodded, trying not to feel discouraged. This had never happened to him before. What must it be like for her to hover there in mid-air, unable to move freely?

What if this started happening to other souls, too?

He stretched out his hand again, this time the motion deliberate. He drew close enough for his fingers to brush against her, but no closer. He didn't want to frighten her away or trigger another disappearance.

"What are you doing?" Mona asked sharply.

"I'm trying to see if you are corporeal. Most souls are not, but... you are not like most souls." He smiled. "Only if you are comfortable, of course."

Mona hesitated, her eyes guarded. After a moment, she nodded.

Evander took a step, submerging his left foot into the river. An icy chill bit into him, his trousers now damp as the current brushed past him. Ignoring the cold waters around him, he brought his hand closer until his fingertips met the edges of her skirt.

Mona gasped, and Evander felt it, too. A bolt of heat scorched his fingers so intensely that he jerked back in alarm, his skin throbbing from the contact. He cradled his hand, inspecting the injury. Two angry red splotches appeared on the spots where his fingers had touched her. They faded quickly, the pain vanishing along with it. But that didn't change what had happened.

This soul had *burned* him.

CONFESSIONS
MONA

BEFORE MONA'S RESURRECTION

"TELL ME ABOUT YOUR MAGIC. MAYBE THAT WILL shed some light on your situation."

Since his first attempt to touch her had gone badly, Evander seemed to keep his distance. He sat on the edge of the riverbank, his arms propped on his knees as if he and Mona were simply sharing a picnic by the water. Instead, Mona felt ridiculous, merely hovering above the water's depths like a lost and confused ghost.

Being around this otherworldly man still unsettled her, too. He wore a plain black tunic and trousers, but his silvery hair and eyes kept drawing Mona's gaze. He had a thin spread of facial hair and an intriguing stone hanging around his neck on a leather cord. At times, he seemed the picture of ease, nothing but calm and polite. Other times, a brief darkness crossed his features, making Mona wonder where his thoughts had turned. But those moments never lasted long.

All in all, Evander was a mystery Mona wanted nothing more than to solve.

"Don't you want to hear about how I died?" Mona asked, thinking this would be the first thing souls should talk about.

"Not necessarily. And, since you appear young, I presume it was a tragic death. Sometimes facing the circumstances of your death too soon can trigger unexpected reactions. Given the circumstances, I think it's best if we stick to safer subjects for now." Evander offered a pleasant smile.

Mona sighed. "Well, I'm an earth witch. My grace is rose vines."

"Grace?"

"It's a magical affinity. Something that comes naturally to you."

Another smile spread across his face, this one much softer. "And you could effortlessly summon roses? That sounds quite lovely."

Though she couldn't feel much, Mona felt her cheeks burn. "Yes, I really did love it." She couldn't keep the sorrow out of her voice. Goddess, she missed her magic. It had been a part of her, and to be stuck here without it was like losing a piece of her own soul.

"Are all the witches like you? Is their grace the same?" Evander asked.

"No. My sister's is ivy. It's different for everyone. But for earth witches, it is usually some kind of flora." She looked at him then, assessing his expression. A deep longing filled his eyes. He tried to mask it, but she'd already seen it stark in his gaze. "Why are you so curious about my magic? This is more than just resolving my complex situation, I can tell."

Evander gritted his teeth, averting his gaze. Frustration creased his brow, and Mona could tell he was angry he'd revealed so much to her. "I... am fascinated by light magic."

"Light magic? I'm only aware of the elemental magicks." She knew of blood magic, of course, which was the darkest form of magic. Her coven had forbidden the use of it because of its addictive nature and capacity to alter a witch's aura.

Evander huffed a sigh, looking as if he'd rather be anywhere but here. "We don't have much magic down here, but the powers that do exist are... dark. Unnatural. Demonic, even."

Mona's gaze fell to his moonstone necklace, and he went rigid. She did notice his hand often went to the moonstone dangling at his throat. Even as a spirit, Mona could sense power from this trinket.

There was something to it, she was certain. But based on Evander's evasiveness, he certainly wouldn't tell her outright.

"From my experience," she said cautiously, "it isn't always the magic that's evil. It depends entirely on the caster."

"You do not know death magic, then," Evander said, his voice lethal and quiet. "It is alive. It consumes everything without restraint."

A chilled silence fell between them. Mona's eyes remained pinned on him as she longed to pick apart the secrets he was hiding.

He changed the subject. "Tell me of your home."

Mona's brows knitted together in agitation. She didn't want to talk about something else, but she knew she wouldn't get much out of him right now. "I'm from the island of Krenia."

Evander furrowed his brow. "I've never heard of such a place."

"Not many have. It's quite small."

His eyes turned wistful. "Will you tell me about it?"

Mona offered a gentle smile at the pure interest in his tone, like that of a child wanting to hear a story. "The climate is warm and breezy, the air always smelling of the sea. You can feel the power of the earth beneath your feet, like a constant thrum of energy. The village is so small that everyone knows who you are and where you came from. They are more than neighbors; they are family."

"That sounds... quite nice." Evander's voice was strained, but his eyes turned wistful.

"It is, but it comes with its challenges. For instance, it's hard to leave. I often dreamed of the places I was missing out on by being stuck there. And also..." She paused, her cheeks heating again.

"Also what?" Evander prompted.

Mona shook her head slightly. The logical side of her brain told her to stop talking, but she felt inexplicably safe here with Evander. Like she could tell him anything and he wouldn't judge her for it. "I never felt like I could find a deep, passionate love like the ones I've read about in stories. Not in a village full of people who've known me since birth. It's silly, I guess, but it made me feel... lonely. Even when surrounded by people I loved, I was lonely."

Evander went perfectly still. So still that the air around them seemed to grow tense with anticipation. For a moment, Mona feared she'd crossed another line and he would refuse to speak. But instead, he said in a soft murmur, "I feel the same way. Day after day, I am surrounded by souls eager to tell their story and lay their grief on me. But I am never truly... seen. I can never live freely. I merely exist."

Sadness tightened Mona's heart as she considered how lonely Evander must be. It would be far worse to live forever in eternal loneliness than to live as Mona did, with a family who loved her. Even if she had never found *true* love, at least she had that.

But Evander, it seemed, did not.

"Do you have a family?" Mona asked.

"Brothers," Evander said, his voice monotonous. "Five of them. And a father."

Judging by his impassive tone, he did not have an affectionate relationship with them. The thought made Mona's heart twist further. "Do they live here, too?"

Evander nodded, his gaze falling to the blades of grass he twisted between his fingers.

"They don't understand you, do they?" Mona asked.

Evander looked at her then, his glowing silver irises locked onto her. The haunted devastation in his face was answer enough.

"My family didn't, either," Mona went on. Somehow, she knew that Evander wouldn't talk about this, so she felt it might help if *she* shared something. Something he could relate to. "Prue always wanted to climb trees and explore hidden places. But all I wanted to do was read. To bury myself in knowledge and stories and the vast enormity of secrets our library contained. The possibilities were endless, and that was enthralling to me. It still is."

"You miss it," Evander said. "Reading."

"Yes. I mean, of course I miss my sister and my home. But without my books and my magic, it doesn't feel like I'm really here at all. Like I'm dreaming and I'll wake up soon and be able to resume my life."

Evander gazed toward the forest, his mouth pressed into a thin line. "I understand that, too. My duties here feel... temporary. Like I am waiting for something bigger to come along. This cannot be *all* that's in store for me. And yet, every day, it is the same. Nothing changes."

Mona had nothing to say. It was startling, how much she resonated with this stranger. Trapped on her tiny island, unable to leave and see the world for herself. Waiting for her life to begin.

"If you could change things, what would you change?" Mona asked.

Evander didn't answer for a long time. His gaze was still fixed on the forest, and something hardened in his expression. The openness she had enjoyed with him now seemed closed off, like whatever connection they shared had ended. "I don't know," he said, dropping his gaze.

It was a lie. He knew, he just didn't want to tell her.

It's all right, Mona thought. *He can keep his secrets. We are still strangers, after all.*

But to her, it didn't feel like they were strangers.

Perhaps it was because he was the overseer of her soul that she felt this way. He had a special bond with the souls here, and that's what she was feeling. Surely that was the explanation for it.

But this knowledge didn't stop the sting of rejection from working its way through her.

Evander looked at her with a softness in his eyes that lessened the ache in her heart. "You are a kindred soul, Mona. I feel if we had lived in your small village together, we could've been great friends."

Mona found herself smiling. "I think so, too."

Evander's expression turned grim as he stared at the setting sun. "It's an enchantment, you know," he said suddenly. "Everything here. The forest. The sky. The weather. Even so, it helps me measure the days. To feel more alive." He shook his head and rose to his feet, dusting the grass and dirt off his trousers. "I must leave you now, Mona."

Discomfort wriggled inside her at the thought of being here alone. "Why? Where are you going?"

Evander said nothing. He merely glared at the sunset as if it had mortally wounded him.

More secrets, Mona thought sadly.

"Evander," she whispered, and he finally looked at her, his eyes so full of torment it made her want to weep. "You aren't alone. I see you. And I understand you."

A sad smile spread across his lips. "Ah, yes. That is

true. But you, like all the others, will one day leave as well. And then I will be truly alone once more." The gentleness in his gaze told her he didn't blame her for this; he had merely accepted his fate.

Mona's throat constricted with agony as she watched him turn away from her and stride into the forest.

LAGOS
PRUE

STILL CHAINED IN THE DANK CAVE, PRUE FADED IN and out of consciousness, her mind foggy and weak from hunger. It felt like days since anyone had brought her food. Perhaps her last encounter with Cyrus had angered him so much he'd decided to starve her.

What am I doing here? she thought. Frustration crept into the corners of her mind, but she was too frail to allow it to consume her completely.

She couldn't surrender. She forced herself to sit up, though her head throbbed from the movement. "I am an earth witch," she said, her voice hoarse. "The Maiden of the coven. The daughter of a goddess. And the queen of this realm. I will not be defeated." On unsteady legs, she rose to her feet, the chains rattling from her movement. "If Cyrus wants to kill me, he'd better do it himself."

Every inch of her ached, the pain rippling along her limbs and spine. Goddess, she was so weak. Her head was spinning.

"I will not be cowed," she forced herself to say. She had once been powerful enough to summon the god of the Underworld to the mortal realm. Surely, she could muster enough strength to overcome these flimsy chains.

She dragged her finger against the cavern wall behind her, her fingertip coming back coated with dust and ash. In her coven, ash was a powerful, magic-inducing substance. Maybe she could use that.

Her thoughts traveled inward, seeking that familiar warmth of her magic. But all she felt was a hollow emptiness in her chest. She swept her ashy finger over the middle of her forehead, hoping to coax open her third eye. The skin on her forehead twitched slightly, something faint quivering from within. But that was all. Nothing happened.

"*Incantare*," she whispered, sweeping her hand through the air.

A puff of air brushed against her ear like a whisper. A faint breeze drifted along her skin. There was certainly power here. But something was stifling her magic, keeping it from fully surfacing.

Suspicion prickled along her skin. The sensation of being watched crept over her like a dark shadow.

Someone was here. Was this why her magic wasn't working? Was there a powerful presence blocking her?

"*Excito,*" she said, her voice gaining strength. "As queen of this realm, I command you to reveal yourself." It was a feeble attempt, especially since anyone who could see her would know she was a prisoner. No one would believe she was a queen.

Queen. Goddess, even she couldn't quite believe it. As Cyrus's wife, yes, she was queen of this realm. But it felt like a delusion. A fantasy. Something she had dreamed up.

It didn't feel real at all.

Footsteps shuffled nearby, followed by a deep, feral growl. Prue tensed, alarm slamming into her. Was this some sort of creature, waiting to devour her? She scanned the darkness, fruitlessly trying to make out whatever was approaching.

"Who's there?" She forced a note of authority in her voice.

No one answered. Prue waited, her heart slamming against her ribcage. The longer the silence stretched on, the more her fear melted into curiosity. If the creature hadn't shown itself by now, it likely wasn't here to harm her.

Gradually, a figure came into view. It wasn't a creature, but a human. Or rather, a being with human parts. He had the torso and legs of a man, but from the neck up, he had the head of a bull with horns protruding from his temples. In his human hands rested a bowl of stew. His dark, beady eyes assessed her as he growled again.

Prue resisted the urge to back up a step. She'd seen demons like this before; in fact, she was certain this particular demon had brought her food earlier.

"Why were you lurking in the shadows?" Prue asked, grateful her voice didn't shake. Her eyes dropped to the stew, and her stomach rumbled audibly.

"I wanted to see what you would do," the demon said, his voice low and gravelly. Prue was surprised to hear him speak so clearly, given he had no human mouth. "For a moment there, it seemed as if you might conjure magic."

Prue's eyes narrowed. "Were you the one blocking my powers?"

The demon cocked his head at her. His animal-like features were unnerving; Prue couldn't make out facial expressions or sense any indication of his mood. Was he angry? Curious? Amused?

"Something has been blocking the magic in this realm for... a long, long time," he said at last, his tone sorrowful. "I was hopeful that you had found a way around it. But alas, you, like the rest of us, are rendered powerless."

Prue went still at the utter devastation in his voice. There was something ancient in his words, as if he had been alive for a very long time and witnessed all manner of tragedies.

"What's your name?" she asked.

The demon said nothing for a long moment, as if he were considering whether he should reply. "Lagos," he finally said.

"And what is your position in the Underworld, Lagos?" Prue asked.

"I'm a warden of Tartarus."

Prue inwardly cringed. She remembered what Cyrus had once told her—that the task of torturing souls was normally given to lesser beings like demons. Was Lagos in charge of torturing the souls of Tartarus?

"You are the Queen of the Underworld," Lagos said. It wasn't a question.

"I am." Prue huffed a dry laugh, gesturing to her chains. "I know it may be hard to believe."

"I heard the authority in your voice," Lagos said. "You commanded me to reveal myself, so I had to obey."

Prue stared at him, her chest thrumming with anticipation. "You—you are forced to obey me?"

Lagos fixed his dark eyes on her and said nothing. She had the distinct impression he was testing her somehow.

"But how?" Prue shook her head. "I have no magic here."

"It's not your magic. It's the magic of this realm. It

recognizes you as the rightful queen because of your bond with our king."

If only Cyrus would recognize that bond, she thought bitterly.

Lagos straightened. "So, what do you command of me, my queen?"

Prue's eyebrows lifted. "What?"

"I am yours to command." The words were stiff, as if rehearsed. Those dark eyes wouldn't meet her gaze.

Prue frowned. She *could* order him to release her. But with Cyrus possessed by that strange darkness, she had no one on her side in this realm. No allies. No friends. If Lagos freed her, she would no longer be chained up, but she would still be utterly and completely alone. How hard would it be for Cyrus to send someone to lock her up once again?

"No," Prue said slowly. "I won't force you to do anything against your will."

Lagos was silent for a long moment. "Why not? You are in chains. Surely, you wish to be freed?"

This is definitely a test, Prue thought. But was it Lagos who was testing her, or Cyrus? Was Lagos here on Cyrus's orders?

"Of course I do," Prue said. "But not that way. There's enough darkness and evil deeds going on down here. I don't wish to add to that. That's not how I would rule."

Lagos snorted. "Perhaps when you've lived for thousands of years as I have, you will feel differently."

Prue chuckled. "Perhaps." She squinted at him, assessing him. "What would *you* do, as ruler of this domain? Would you order your subjects to obey you?"

Lagos considered this, his eyes narrowing slightly. "Maybe some of them. Not all subjects are the same. Some of the more rebellious ones might require a firm hand. But... no. I would not compel *everyone* to obey."

Interesting, Prue thought. "Would you help me identify these more rebellious subjects you speak of?"

"Is that an order?"

"No."

Lagos hesitated again. "You wish for me to be your advisor?"

Prue almost laughed at the word. Here she was, starving and sitting in her own filth, plotting ways to rule this kingdom. As if Cyrus would allow her to do that.

Allow me? He does not allow me to do anything. I make my own choices. Determination rose up inside her, quelling all weakness and exhaustion, squashing her doubts and uncertainties. She *was* the Queen of the Underworld. Even if Cyrus wouldn't recognize it, there were others here who would.

"Yes," Prue said firmly. "If you help me get out of here, you will be named my most esteemed advisor. I will release you from your position in Tartarus and you can work alongside me instead. That is, if you accept. I will not force you."

Lagos stared at her, motionless, for several moments. Prue resisted the urge to fidget under his gaze, her nerves twisting inside her as she feared he would reject her proposal. What would she do if he turned and walked away? She had no other options.

"If I accept," Lagos said, "it will anger His Highness."

Prue smirked. "Yes, it will. But you would be under my jurisdiction. Surely, the magic of this realm will recognize that?" This was speculation, of course. Prue had no idea what the magic here would do. But she had to have a contingency plan; if Lagos worked for her, she couldn't risk Cyrus punishing him for it.

"It will. But we will have to forge an agreement in blood."

Icy coldness crept into Prue's chest. Another blood bargain? Her insides churned at the thought.

But what choice did she have? She needed allies.

"All right," she said. "I'll see that it's done."

"Then, I accept."

Lagos strode forward and set the bowl of stew in front of her. Prue's stomach rumbled again, but she held back as Lagos jammed something into the lock of her chains. She flinched when the metal cut into her just before the cuffs sprang open, clattering to the floor.

Prue exhaled with relief, rubbing her raw and bleeding wrists. "Before we do anything else," she said, pointing to the bowl in front of her, "do you mind if I eat that?"

Prue could've sworn Lagos's mouth twitched in a smile, making him appear more human. "Of course, my queen."

FADING

CYRUS

CYRUS WAS A SHELL OF WHO HE ONCE USED TO BE. The only thing he could compare it to was that hazy state between sleep and consciousness, when his brain was muddled and he couldn't quite think straight.

Of course, thinking about this state of mind made him think of Prue. It was only with her that he had ever slept. As a god, he generally had no need for such mortal weaknesses. But around her, it didn't feel like a weakness at all, but something private to be shared just with her.

A sudden bolt of clarity speared through his mind at the thought of his witch bride, and the dark cloud of his mind began to clear. He sat atop his throne in Styx, overseeing Tartarus. The crown of bones rested upon his head. He could barely make out the horned demon who stood before him—Abraxos was his name. He was tasked with keeping the tormented souls in line, ensuring they wouldn't escape.

Cyrus had no control over his motions or his voice, but whatever magical being held Cyrus's body captive was using him to yell obscenities at the demon overseer.

Cyrus had tried raging and thrashing against the death magic that had trapped him. But his fight only seemed to empower it. And upon further reflection, Cyrus realized this made sense. His anger, his rage, always fueled his power. It fed it like tinder to a flame.

He needed a different tactic. So for now, he lurked in the shadows of his mind, watching. Waiting.

Cyrus had never been particularly patient. But when his consciousness had emerged to find Prue shackled and starving—yet her pale purple eyes as fierce and determined as ever—something inside him broke. He would do anything—*anything*—to free her from this prison.

Even if it meant biding his time until he found a weak spot in his magic.

He paid close attention to the words coming out of his traitorous mouth. Sifting through the violent curses, he made out words such as "careless" and "dangerous" and "escape."

Gods above... Had a soul escaped from Tartarus?

Cyrus strained, his mind already beginning to fog once more. *Focus,* he urged himself. *Just a bit longer.*

Finally, he could make out the mumbled response of Abraxos.

"My king, no one has escaped," the demon growled. "We are being cautious."

"Not cautious enough!" Cyrus screeched in a voice that sounded nothing like his own. "I felt the souls at the edge of the barrier. They should never be allowed that close."

Cyrus grew more alert at this. There was genuine panic in his captor's mind. It bled into Cyrus's own thoughts, leaking through as if this magical being were so enraged—or frightened—that its defenses were wearing down.

Something in Tartarus had his death magic terrified.

This was interesting news indeed.

Perhaps he could use this panic to his advantage. How much could he get away with when the death magic was so distracted?

Carefully, tentatively, Cyrus pressed his consciousness forward, trying to reach his body. *A finger. Just move a finger. That's all.*

The air went perfectly still, and Cyrus stopped.

But it was too late.

A dark force slammed into him, crushing him, dragging him back down into oblivion. Foul curses filled his mind as the death magic chained him once more, bringing everything into darkness.

What are you? he demanded into the darkness. How could he fight this foe if he didn't even know what it was? Until recently, he believed his magic to be something non-living. Something he could wield like a weapon.

But it was so much more than that. It had thoughts and fears. It was alive.

A deep chuckle resonated in his mind, and the voice answered: *I am Kronos.*

PROGRESS
MONA

BEFORE MONA'S RESURRECTION

REST WHEN YOU'RE DEAD WAS SUCH A STUPID phrase. Because, as it turned out, Mona *couldn't* rest when she was dead. Her soul remained hovering meaninglessly above the stream alongside a very quiet river guardian who watched her tirelessly as if she were a rare specimen to be observed instead of a soul to be saved.

At first she tried to engage him in conversation by asking such questions as, "Where did you come from?" or "What do you do in your spare time?" or "What's the most remarkable soul you've ever come across?" But Evander only answered in cagey half-truths or avoided the question altogether. It seemed that their open conversation earlier had made him more cautious, and now he didn't want to share anything with her at all.

The thought stung her more than she cared to admit.

When Mona tired of her fruitless efforts to talk, she strived to move, even just a small part of herself. She knew she didn't have her body and that was part of the problem, but she was still here, still looked like herself, even if it was a whisper of who she once was. Surely, she would have *some* kind of control. She'd been a fairly capable witch in her lifetime, and now seemed as good a time as any to practice her abilities and see what she could do.

Her insides twisted at the thought of Prue, who often practiced alongside her—albeit begrudgingly. It made the experience so much more enjoyable.

But Prue wasn't here. Because Mona made the choice to die instead. And she never once regretted it.

Mona was determined to make her sister proud. So, she tried everything... to no avail. She strained her nonexistent muscles, willing her limbs to move with the strength of her mind. She managed to blink her eyes, even close her eyelids. Her head could droop and she could nod and shake her head. But her arms and legs were utterly useless. She couldn't even lift a finger.

When she was too tired to attempt movement, she merely observed, just as Evander did. She watched him stride up and down the river, his gait perfectly at ease. Sometimes he even had his hands shoved in his pockets as if he were simply on an evening stroll instead of over-seeing a river of dead souls. His manner, his posture, even his expressions were nothing but calmness and cool calculation.

But based on what he'd told her before, she knew a riot of emotions and sadness swarmed inside him. It was all a facade.

Mona couldn't stand it.

She much preferred someone with Prue's demeanor—passionate, quick to anger, but fiercely loyal. Someone she could read easily.

But Evander—he was full of secrets. And these secrets only made Mona more curious and wary.

For instance, when the sun set—even though Mona knew there was no true sun here, since it was just an illusion—Evander disappeared. Every day. She watched the dark forest, trying to convince herself not to be afraid of demons or beasts that might roam nearby because, well, she was already dead, so what could they do to her?

But Evander remained absent until the sun rose once more, and he emerged from the trees as if nothing were amiss. He passed underneath a pair of pine trees, two towering forms that marked the edge of the forest.

Mona was grateful she had enough control to scowl at him as he approached. She hoped her fearsome expression would frighten him into telling her all his secrets.

But, of course, Mona had no such luck.

"Where were you?" Mona demanded when he said nothing, just crossed his arms and gazed at the water like he always did. It had been three days of this, Evander avoiding her and then disappearing with the setting sun, only to return and infuriate her once more.

Evander blinked as if just realizing she was there. "Excuse me?"

"You've been gone all night. For three nights." Her tone was full of accusation. "Don't you have a solemn responsibility to monitor the river at all times?"

Evander's expression remained calm and unreadable. "The river was in no danger. I was watching."

Mona scoffed. "You were not. I watched the forest the whole time, and I couldn't see you."

"Just because you could not see me doesn't mean I wasn't there."

Mona opened her mouth, then closed it because he was right. Was it possible that, even as a spirit, she still couldn't see well at night? Prue always had better vision than she did.

Did Evander have perfect vision? Could he see well in the dark?

"What exactly *are* you?" Mona asked.

Evander tensed as if she'd just thrown a nasty insult

at him. His silvery eyes flashed for the briefest of moments before his expression schooled itself once more. "I'm not sure what you mean."

"Are you human?"

He relaxed slightly. "No."

"A demon?"

Evander said nothing, his gaze straying to the river as if he were bored with the conversation.

"Perhaps you're a guardian angel?" Mona tried again.

His face darkened. "I am no angel." The words rumbled deeply in his throat, causing a chill to ripple over Mona's form. "But... you could say I am the guardian of your soul. And all the souls of this river."

"Are you the devil?"

Evander smiled, but it didn't reach his eyes. It was a small curve of his mouth that made Mona wonder what a *true* smile looked like on his face. "No. My brother holds that title."

"One of your five other brothers?"

"Yes. The youngest."

The youngest is the devil? Mona thought. *How strange.* "Any sisters?"

Evander sighed, finally shifting his gaze to her. "You said you watched the forest all night. Does that mean you did not travel to any other realms?"

Mona shook her head. She'd tried that, too. She'd focused so intently on Prue that her eyes crossed and her vision blurred. But she'd remained in the same spot. All night.

"Maybe if you told me more about you and what role you play in all this, we might be able to figure something out," Mona said. "After all, I told you about *me* and my magic. For instance, do *you* have any magic?"

"No," Evander said quickly. Too quickly. Mona's eyes fell to the moonstone around his neck.

There is definitely magic at play here. But she decided not to push the issue. Not yet, at least.

"Okay, well, do you have any kind of power over the souls or over the river? Maybe we can work on that. I've struggled for three days, and I don't think there's anything in *my* power alone to fix this mess I'm in. But maybe with the two of us together, we'll have more success."

Evander watched her for a long moment, his expression unreadable. Mona resisted the urge to drop her gaze, finding his pensive look quite unsettling. Why did he have to look at her like she was a puzzle to be solved? It made her feel strangely... inhuman.

Evander closed his eyes briefly. "I originally thought perhaps your soul needed more time before the transition set in. This does happen occasionally, though not like... this." He gestured toward her with his hand, and Mona knew he meant her disembodied ghost form.

She disagreed with this—time was not the issue here —but she waited for him to continue.

"But as I've watched the river flow, the other souls moving on as they should be, it's clear to me there is something unique about *you*, Mona." His otherworldly eyes fell on her once more, and a delightful shiver crept through her from the way he said her name. "It is not natural, given that it has not affected any other part of this river. But I fear if this problem goes unsolved, it will spread to the other souls, too."

Mona couldn't help but frown. So, he was only going to help her because she was diseased, and he didn't want the contagion to spread? What a lovely thought. Once again, she felt like nothing more than some scientific experiment gone wrong.

"You seem upset," Evander observed.

Mona blinked. Damn. He'd been watching her again. She smoothed her expression. "Of course I'm upset. It's quite a predicament, isn't it?" When he continued to stare at her, she said, "You *did* say you would help me. And you haven't done much, to be honest."

"What would you have me do?" Evander seemed unaffected by her accusation.

"You tell me!" Mona fought to keep her frustration at bay. How was he so *calm* about all this? "This is *your* domain, after all. If you see a soul in distress, what do you do to help it?"

"Sometimes I speak to them. Help them process their death and work through their grief and acceptance."

Well, he certainly hadn't done that with *her*. Mona wasn't sure why that thought stung. They'd talked, yes, but they hadn't once discussed the circumstances of her death. Perhaps he was worried her strange virus would spread to *him* and that was why he kept his distance.

"Other times, I sing to them," Evander went on.

Mona's eyebrows shot up. Goddess, she hadn't been expecting *that*. "You... sing?"

Evander nodded. "Grief manifests itself in many ways. Souls have a unique melody that they often sing to work through their emotions. It's quite beautiful, really." His eyes met hers once more. "Especially yours."

Mona blinked. "Mine? I don't—I can't sing."

"No, but your soul does. I heard it when you first arrived. It was... unlike any melody I've ever heard." His gaze grew distant and full of an emotion Mona couldn't place. It made her insides feel warm. Too warm.

Suddenly uncomfortable, Mona clung to the one thing that helped her think clearly: curiosity. "What is my melody like? Could you sing it for me?"

Evander's shoulders grew tense. "Well, I—"

"You sing for other souls," Mona argued. "Why not me? Maybe that will help with this situation."

Evander ran a hand through his hair, and Mona stared at it. The strands were mostly silver, but inky black streaks lined them like stripes. His hair was long but didn't quite fall past his chin. Mona had the insane urge to run her fingers through his hair and determine if it was as soft as it looked.

Stupid, she chided herself. Not only was that wildly inappropriate, but she couldn't even *move* her hands, so the thought was altogether foolish.

"Yes," Evander said at last with a heavy exhale. "You're right. We should exercise every avenue to determine how to solve the problem."

Mona's mind perked up at his assessment. It felt like when she sought answers in books. The process of elimination was a sure way to prove if a theory was correct or not.

She tried to stifle her excitement at the prospect of Evander singing to her. She'd heard songs before, of course. Some witches in the coven performed during seances or rituals, and it was a really beautiful experience.

But she had never heard a *man* sing before. Not really. There was Erasmus, the elderly man who lived next-door and sometimes sang whimsical songs for the children. But that was nothing serious. His wizened voice was endearing, but nothing breathtaking like the female voices Mona had heard.

Male witches were rare, and on a small island like Krenia, they were nonexistent. As such, Mona never had opportunities to enjoy a proper male vocal performance.

Her insides thrummed with anticipation.

But Evander didn't move. His brows were lowered as he stared hard at the river.

"What's wrong?" Mona asked.

He shook his head as if she'd woken him from a stupor. "Nothing. Nothing. It's just... been a while since I've done this." Color stained his cheeks. Goddess above, was he *blushing*? It was... strangely adorable watching this enigmatic man act flustered. Mona couldn't help but smile.

Evander drew closer until his feet rested on the bank. He paused, then stepped into the river, drawing closer to Mona.

"What are you doing?" she asked.

"It helps if I'm close to the soul so I can sense your aura."

My aura? Mona didn't like the idea of him probing even further into her soul, but she didn't object. Her insides squirmed, and she longed to fidget or shift around, but of course, she couldn't. So instead, she settled with working her jaw back and forth and gnawing on her lower lip. At least she could manage these little actions.

And then, quite suddenly, Evander was singing.

Mona stopped her restless movements and stared

open-mouthed at him. His eyes were closed, his eyebrows lifted, and his expression fully relaxed as a haunting melody poured from his lips. His voice rang out, echoing in the forest and sending a whisper of power against Mona's skin. She sighed with part contentment and part awe as his voice washed over her like a gentle breeze. The song stirred something deep within her, something familiar and yet lost. Something long since forgotten.

Her throat tickled, and then Mona found herself singing along with him, her voice blending perfectly with his. The notes changed, and she followed a harmony, the counterpart to his melody. Their music weaved together, hers rising as his fell, and then back to the middle once more. Their tunes crisscrossed like two dancers twisting about. He moved, she followed, and then they moved together.

Mona's eyes closed as the song encompassed her, filling her very soul with energy. The melody sang of sorrow and distress, of loss and grief. It filled her with an aching yearning, a pit of agony. Her voice climbed higher and higher, the final note ringing out and echoing vastly in the space around them.

Even after their song stopped, the final note still rang, burning in Mona's ears. She opened her eyes and gasped to find Evander's hand clasped within hers.

Her solid hand, made of flesh and bone.

His skin felt soothing against hers, filling her with strength. Her skin warmed, her blood heating from the close contact. Evander stood only a breath away, gazing at her with the same wonder and surprise that she felt. His scent enveloped her, something between pine and evergreen, with the hint of musk that was so distinctly masculine that it made her toes curl. Her breaths turned sharp, and she marveled that she could breathe at all. As she gazed downward, most of her body remained a wispy translucent form... but her *hand*. Her hand was really here. Touching Evander.

She thought of the last time he'd tried to touch her, when she'd burned him. Now, the opposite had occurred: his touch had grounded her.

"It seems you're right," Evander said in a soft murmur. "It appears your song *is* the key to this problem." His mouth quirked slightly with the ghost of a smile, and Mona's breath caught in her throat.

Just as suddenly, Mona's hand slipped free of his, all warmth leaving her body. Icy coldness replaced it, and Mona was a floating spirit once more. She shifted and strained, but she couldn't move her arm, as much as she longed to take his hand in hers once more. Despair filled her, but Evander's eyes were full of hope.

"This is good," he assured her. "We have a clue to follow."

Mona's heart lightened at his words. *A mystery is*

nothing but unsolved clues. A collection of puzzle pieces to assemble. It was something her mother, Polina, always used to say.

Mona opened her mouth to respond when a voice echoed in her mind. She froze, glancing around for the source of the voice. Evander's eyes were on her, his expression curious.

"Do you hear that?" Mona asked.

Evander frowned and shook his head. "What do you hear?"

"I can't—I don't—" She broke off as the voice continued, growing stronger. She closed her eyes to focus on it.

It was a deep, male voice. Similar to Evander's, but gruffer. The voice muttered something like a spell.

Mona stiffened, her eyes flying open. "Someone's performing magic."

"Are you perhaps hearing the mortal realm?" Evander asked. "Is it trying to pull you in?"

Mona shook her head. "There are no male witches in my coven. If this is the mortal realm, it's not my home." She paused when the voice went completely silent. "I think it's—"

Something jerked her forward, and the world tilted. Mona's head spun as her surroundings shifted, the river and forest vanishing from view.

She found herself standing on the beach of Krenia, the waves lapping toward her bare feet. Her toes were buried in the sand, and for a moment, she felt completely at home, as if she'd never died or gone to the Underworld.

Wait a moment. She shifted her legs, feeling each grain of sand. A gasp tore from her throat. She was *corporeal*! She had her body! Shuffling forward, she dipped her feet in the water, laughing at the brisk cold liquid rushing over her toes.

Stunned, she looked around, confusion taking over. The last time she'd come here, she was a ghost, and Prue had been next to her. But she was utterly alone.

"There you are," murmured a voice.

Mona whirled and found an unfamiliar man approaching. He had inky black hair that curled at the nape of his neck. A single stripe of silver lined his hair. Two small black horns protruded from his head. And the look on his face was positively feral.

He was a prince of Hell. One of Evander's brothers. He had to be. Mona's insides went cold at the dangerous glint in his silver eyes.

"Who are you?" she asked. "And how are you here?"

The man glanced at the horizon and smirked. "Oh, we aren't really on a beach. We are between worlds. The surroundings change based on the soul's preference." He waved a hand toward her. "That would be you."

Mona's chest tightened as she gazed at the rippling waves. This wasn't real. She wasn't really in Krenia.

She was *between worlds.*

She'd been in this middle realm before during seances with her coven. It was dangerous to linger, since the space between worlds wasn't meant to be occupied for long.

"Send me back," Mona said, her voice shaking. "Now!"

The man chuckled as he drew nearer. "Not until you tell me where your soul resides."

Alarm pulsed inside her. "What? Why?"

"Because, my dear, your blood belongs to *me.*" A wide grin spread across his face. "As soon as I join your soul with your body, you will be my bride. And we will wield untold power."

TRIVIA
PRUE

To Prue's surprise, Lagos agreed to show her the palace and help her get situated in her rooms before they struck the blood bargain. She would've thought he would insist on doing it at once, just in case Cyrus discovered them and lashed out before Lagos was under Prue's protection.

But Cyrus had left her in that cave for days at a time, so assuming he didn't come back to check on her right away, they had a bit of time before her escape was discovered.

Apparently, forging a blood bond with a demon was a huge and meaningful occasion. No other god or goddess had done such a thing before. And Lagos insisted that a ceremony be held for it.

Prue couldn't object. In fact, this was the perfect opportunity to establish herself as queen of this realm. If the other demons and subjects saw her as a ruler, Cyrus would have no choice but to treat her as such.

She was his prisoner no more. And that knowledge made her smile with satisfaction.

The winding caves were a labyrinth of twists and turns, but Lagos knew the way as he easily led Prue through narrow passages and chambers. Eventually, the cavern opened up to a wide expanse of rocky terrain about the size of a massive crater. And in its center stood the grandest castle Prue had ever seen.

A shimmering chrome edifice towered over her. Prue's gaze drifted over the grand outer wall surrounding the castle, then lifted to take in the six towers, their sharp spires piercing the sky. Onyx stone covered each tower, a brilliant contrast to the glistening silver that coated the structure. The tallest of the towers had balconies that wrapped around the apex, along with stained glass windows that no doubt looked into the most ornate of suites. Solid stone pillars supported the archway at the entrance, each one crafted with elaborate carvings Prue couldn't make out from here.

It was even bigger than the castle of the Thanassian Empire, where she and Cyrus had been held captive for a short time. Briefly, she wondered what had happened to their monarch now that Vasileios, the prince of Hell who had stolen the throne, was dead at Cyrus's hand.

For a moment, Prue stood there, her jaw slack with awe as she drank in the magnificent architecture. It was no wonder Cyrus often spat at the drab human cities when he was accustomed to *this*. It looked like something from a fairy tale. Despite the stony surroundings and the murky gray sky, the palace still glistened as if it had been recently polished. It seemed... *magical*. Not at all like the dismal throne Prue had pictured Cyrus claiming as his own.

In her mind, a prince of Hell would live in a cold, blocky fortress, something dismal and uninspiring.

But *this*? This castle was beautiful and yet mysterious, the silvery walls just as intriguing as Cyrus's eyes.

"We'll enter through the back to avoid His Highness," Lagos said, gesturing to the left.

"Right. Good idea."

Prue followed him around the castle, still craning her neck to gaze up at the tallest towers. "Magnificent," she whispered.

"Only the finest for His Highness." Lagos's words almost sounded bitter.

Prue clamped her mouth shut and forced herself to face forward. She hadn't even considered *how* this palace had been built. But now that she thought about it, it was likely through the hard labor of demon servants.

A sour taste filled her mouth. Cyrus might have been possessed *now*, but when the palace was built, he had been himself. He had made those choices on his own.

You knew he was like this, she reminded herself. *You knew he wasn't perfect or good. You fell for the monster within him.*

Still. It didn't sit well with her. And she vowed to change things, even if it infuriated Cyrus.

They approached the back entrance of the castle, and Lagos swung open the door to let her through first. He led her down a narrow hallway through which various demons were bustling. Some looked like Lagos—part beast, part man—and some looked mostly human, but with small horns or fangs or even tails. The demons paid them no attention as they strode past, no doubt assuming Prue and Lagos were ordinary servants. That was probably for the best, considering Prue's grubby attire. She didn't want to announce herself as queen when she looked like this.

Lagos led her up a winding spiral staircase that seemed to climb forever. Prue had to pause often to catch her breath, her head spinning from fatigue. Though she had just eaten, her stomach was growling again, her body still suffering from her time in chains.

When they finally reached the top, a grand hallway stood before them, carpeted with a plush silver rug and lined with ornate vases perched atop elegantly crafted mahogany tables. They passed by several rooms, the massive double doors stretching all the way to the ceiling, before Lagos gestured to the one at the end of the hallway. The carvings on these doors were grander than the others, depicting a scene of satyrs and dryads dancing in the forest. The curved golden handles were smooth and shining under the candlelight.

"This is the queen's chambers," Lagos informed her.

Prue looked at him in surprise. "Cyrus had a queen's chambers built?"

Lagos's mouth twitched into what must've been his version of a smile. "No. But his chambers are on the opposite end of the hall. For a sense of symmetry, an identical chamber was built on this end to keep everything balanced. It isn't quite as exquisite or well-furnished as His Highness's chambers, but it will suit you just fine."

Anticipation buzzed inside her as she pushed open the door, revealing a room twice the size of her small home in Krenia. A four poster bed sat on one end of the room, with sweeping white drapes and plush pillows, along with a gold embroidered quilt on top. Massive floor-to-ceiling windows lined the room, bringing light into the large space. Though it was still cloudy outside, the light was enough to keep everything properly illuminated, even without candles.

On the opposite side of the room was a small sitting

area with a fireplace, plush sofas, and a long, narrow table between them. A tray was already there with sandwiches, fruit, and an assortment of cheeses.

Prue raised an eyebrow at Lagos. "You had food brought up here?"

"I imagined you'd want to eat more, given your... situation." Lagos dropped his gaze as if abashed.

Prue laughed. "You mean my basic human need for food? You are very considerate, Lagos."

"The bathing chambers are through there." Lagos gestured behind the sitting area. "I can send someone to help you bathe."

"No need. Just show me where the gowns are." Prue popped a grape in her mouth, relishing the way the juice flooded her mouth.

"Are you sure? You are a queen, and you should have a maid at the very least."

"I will," Prue said, avoiding his gaze. "But I want you to be the first in my court."

Lagos stared at her, his face revealing nothing. At long last, he bowed his head. "That is very kind of you, my queen. I would be honored to be the first member of your court." He turned his head, then changed his mind, and smoothed his palms along his trousers. If Prue didn't know any better, she would say he was flustered. The thought made her smile.

"I'll... give you your privacy," Lagos said, his voice a bit gruff as he exited the room.

After devouring every scrap of food on the tray, Prue took her time in the bath, allowing the soapy water to soak into her skin, removing days of grime and sweat and excrement. Her hair was a filthy, matted mess, and it took her the better part of an hour to finally scrub it clean.

When she emerged, she wrapped a towel around her body and strode into the bedroom, only to find someone already there.

She was a woman Prue had never seen before, with waist-length dark red hair and luminescent gold eyes that glowed with an otherworldly gleam. Prue scanned the newcomer for horns or fangs or a spiked tail of some sort, but aside from her eyes, she looked... human. She wore a blood-red dress that brought out the color of her hair, and she leaned casually against the wardrobe as if she belonged there.

"Can I help you?" Prue asked, trying to sound regal despite her nudity.

The woman smirked. "Well, Cyrus's strange behavior

makes more sense now. You certainly are something to behold."

The casual way this woman said Cyrus's name sent a bolt of fury through Prue's chest. Was this one of the many demon women Cyrus had slept with?

Focus, Prue told herself. *Now is not the time for petty jealousy.*

Even so, if she found out this woman had shared Cyrus's bed, Prue wouldn't hesitate to rip out her spine.

"His strange behavior has nothing to do with me," Prue muttered.

"Believe what you want. It's true. He seems... conflicted about you."

Prue met the woman's stare. "How so?" What did this stranger know?

"He's oddly protective of you, but he also seems to loathe you. Maybe even fear you." The woman cocked her head, clearly puzzled. "And I can't make out why. You clearly have no magic." Her eyes fell to the pomegranate necklace still hanging around Prue's neck. Something dark stirred in the woman's gaze, but it was gone in a flash.

Prue's eyes narrowed at the woman's odd reaction to the necklace. She wound her fingers around it as she trailed closer. "Right. So, who are you?"

The woman grinned, revealing a smooth row of

perfectly straight teeth. "Most call me Hecate. Goddess of the moon and protector of pathways and crossroads."

Prue continued to stare at her as her thoughts slowly came together. Familiarity pricked at the corners of her mind until she finally placed where she'd heard that name before. "You're Trivia. The goddess of three paths." She could picture the book Mona used to shove under her nose depicting the various goddesses their coven prayed to. Trivia was one of the most revered because of her relation to the Triple Goddess. Anything that came in threes was sacred.

"Yes. The Underworld, the Realm of Gaia, and Elysium. I help shepherd souls to all three." The woman's mouth quirked into a surprised smile. "Trivia. Wow, I haven't heard that name in ages."

"I can call you Hecate, if you prefer."

"No, please. I like Trivia."

A faint clacking sound made Prue tense, searching for intruders. But Trivia only laughed.

"Pay no heed. That's just Cerberus."

This did nothing to soothe Prue's fear. The legends of Cerberus painted a horrifying and bloodthirsty hound that guarded the gates of Hell.

But as the clacking drew nearer, accompanied by panting, a dark shape emerged from the other side of the bed. Prue blinked at the very ordinary black dog, his tongue lolling happily and his tail wagging to and fro. He drew closer and licked Prue thoroughly on the arm. She winced at the sticky moisture now coating her skin, but a smile pulled at her lips.

"Hello, Cerberus," she said, scratching under his ears. Cerberus nuzzled closer, clearly pleased by the show of affection.

"He likes you," Trivia said. "That's pretty rare. He doesn't take well to strangers."

"Why are you here?" Prue said abruptly, tired of this woman avoiding her question. "These are my chambers. And you are clearly not a servant."

"I came to pledge myself to your court," Trivia said.

Prue's eyes narrowed. This *goddess* wanted to serve *her*? This had to be a trick. "I don't believe you."

Trivia laughed. "I thought not. But you are the first female ruler this realm has *ever* seen. And lesser goddesses like me aren't treated very kindly here. Given what Lagos has said about you, I thought serving you might benefit me more than serving Cyrus."

"And what is it you *do* for Cyrus?" Prue couldn't keep the bite out of her voice.

Trivia smirked as if she could sense where Prue's thoughts had turned. "I mostly serve as a messenger between realms. I also oversee the village of Erebos."

Prue frowned. She had never heard of *Erebos* before. "And what position do you seek in my court?"

"I was thinking a Countess might be fun." Trivia grinned.

Prue stared at her. Was she being serious?

Trivia waved a hand. "Honestly, we can discuss the particulars later. If you feel strongly about a certain position, I can be flexible. So, what do you say? Will you accept me in your court?"

Prue eyed the woman over once more, trying to read her. But she was an enigma. Her confident posture and expression revealed nothing. It unnerved Prue and made her believe this woman was keeping secrets. So how hard would it be for her to lie about wanting to serve Prue?

Even so... This goddess had a reason for wanting to work with Prue. And she wouldn't find out what that was unless she played along.

Plus, it might be beneficial to add more allies to her court.

Forcing a smile, Prue nodded. "All right. I accept."

"Wonderful." Trivia clapped her hands eagerly and turned to the wardrobe before flinging it open. "Let's get you dressed."

"No, no, I can dress myself," Prue said quickly.

"I know you can. But I say we dress you like the goddess you are and knock Cyrus on his ass when he sees you. That would be a sight I'd love to see."

Prue found herself chuckling in bewilderment as

Trivia sifted through several satin ballgowns. "Aren't you... afraid of him?"

Trivia laughed, but this time it was harsh. "Of course not. He's the devil and the ruler of this domain, yes, but he's just another arrogant deity like all the others."

Prue frowned. "But *you're* a goddess, too."

Trivia snorted. "Only on a technicality. No one gives a shit about me like they do all the others."

"We do. The witches, I mean."

Trivia's expression softened. "Yes. I know."

Silence fell between them as Trivia dug through the wardrobe, finally pulling out a deep purple dress and laying it on the sofa in front of her. "This will do nicely. Come, there's a shift on the bed for you."

Prue approached the bed and found a lacy shift waiting for her. She raised an eyebrow at Trivia, who chuckled before turning away. Prue dropped her towel and slid the shift on, then approached the sofa with the dress on it.

Without preamble, Trivia grabbed the gown and slid it over Prue's head before fastening it up her back. It was just a few shades darker than Prue's eyes and cascaded to the floor in sweeping rivulets that reminded her of a rushing river. The gown was sleeveless, and the neckline plunged almost all the way down to her stomach. The fabric clung to her every curve, feeling like a second skin. This dress left nothing to the imagination.

It was a bit revealing for Prue's taste. She was hoping for something more regal and elegant to announce herself as queen. Then again, if she was hoping to rattle Cyrus, this gown would certainly do just that.

Prue sucked in a gasp as the bodice tightened around her chest, making it hard to breathe.

"I know," Trivia said with a chuckle. "But it'll be worth it, I promise. Your bosom will be impossible for the great king to ignore."

"What is he to you?" Prue asked, trying to distract herself from the pressure along her ribs. "I mean, why are you doing all this?" She tried gesturing to the dress, but Trivia slapped her arms back into place.

"I'm doing this for the good of the realm," Trivia said tightly. "I may not be able to change who rules this domain, but everyone can agree we are better off with someone who gives two shits what happens to the people here. And as of right now, Cyrus—or whatever is controlling him—does not." She cocked her head at Prue, considering. "But I have a feeling *you* do."

So, Prue wasn't the only one who noticed Cyrus's altered behavior, then. She wondered if Cyrus's brothers had noticed, as well. Would they try to take the throne from him while he was in this state? Mona had warned her that the Underworld was in danger, and Prue expected to find walls crumbling and volcanoes exploding, screams echoing around her... But so far, the Underworld had been quiet.

"What do you mean by *the people here*?" Prue asked. "What kind of people? Demons, you mean?" She thought of the rebellious subjects Lagos had mentioned.

"Some, yes. Others are souls who have fully transitioned to the afterlife."

"You mean they don't go to Elysium?" From Prue's life among a coven of witches, it was understood that evil souls went to Tartarus while righteous souls went to Elysium. But something told her it wasn't that simple.

"Some do. It depends on a lot of factors. One being the nature of the soul. The other being the soul's choice. We do not force souls to go where they do not wish to go."

Prue's eyebrows lifted at that. Souls could *choose*? Surely, all of them would choose to go to Elysium rather than Tartarus, right?

Before Prue could ask another question, Trivia stepped back and heaved a breath. "Let's have a look at you."

Prue turned, her skirts swishing against the floor. Trivia smirked, her gaze drifting up and down as she scrutinized her. "Perfect. The king will leap out of his skin at the sight of you."

Prue resisted the urge to fidget to ensure her dress didn't expose one of her breasts. One swath of violet fabric draped over each breast, gathering together behind her neck and crisscrossing down her back in an elaborate pattern of lace. A chill swept over her, prickling along her skin. Instinctively, she reached for her magic, only to remember she couldn't access it.

"Do you have magic?" Prue asked.

Trivia stilled, her expression sobering. "None of us do, except the royals." She spat the word like a filthy curse.

Royals. Meaning the princes of Hell.

Trivia waved an idle hand at Prue. "By that, I mean, the royals born in this realm. Not you."

"Why is that?" Prue asked.

Trivia eyed her as if trying to determine how much to reveal. "This realm is cursed. It has been ever since Aidoneus stole the realm from the gods of Elysium."

Prue's head was spinning. How had she not known any of this? Then again, the coven's knowledge of gods and the afterlife was puny compared to the vast existence before her.

She remembered what Lagos had said: *Something has been blocking the magic in this realm for a long, long time.*

"Aidoneus," Prue repeated, trying to keep up. "Cyrus's father, right?"

"Yes. He's here somewhere, licking his wounds."

"Wounds from what?"

"Whatever war you and your husband invoked up there," Trivia said, pointing to the ceiling, "spread to this realm, too. It stripped Aidoneus of his power and sent half the Underworld crumbling."

Prue's blood chilled. The devastation she'd thought would be waiting for her when she arrived here had actually happened when Prue and Cyrus had been fighting Vasileios. She thought of the souls screaming in the sky, the ground rumbling, the violent storm raging... *Of course* it would've spread to other realms. Especially with the way Cyrus's magic had unleashed itself.

"Is everyone all right?" Prue asked, clutching at her necklace as concern rippled over her.

"The princes are fine, of course. Some of the demons took a beating. But the souls living here were protected by the enchantment in place, thank the Goddess." Trivia straightened. "But enough talk. It's time to present you to Cyrus."

She took Prue's elbow and led her forward. Before they could exit the chambers, however, hurried footsteps echoed nearby. Someone pounded fiercely on the door.

"Enter," Prue said at once, too startled to consider ignoring it.

A female demon entered, panting. Her skin was wrinkled and brown, and small white horns protruded from her head. "Forgive the interruption," she gasped, sketching a brief bow. "But the Lady Trivia is needed in Erebos."

Prue looked at Trivia in alarm. The goddess's eyes flashed, her expression hardening. Then, she sighed. "Apologies, my queen. It looks like we'll have to make a quick detour before we see your king." She flashed a smile that didn't quite meet her eyes. "Would you like to meet some of your subjects?"

CAGED

EVANDER

BEFORE MONA'S RESURRECTION

AFTER SHARING MONA'S SONG—AND DISCOVERING one of his brothers sought her soul—Evander couldn't stay away from her. He wasn't sure if it was the urgency of it all or the power of her song that called to him. But he was determined to keep trying. After all, her hand had become corporeal after their shared song. That had to mean something.

And he couldn't risk his brother finding Mona. Just the idea of her trapped with one of them made him so enraged he couldn't see straight.

Days passed, and Evander was by her side almost

nonstop. He asked her questions about her death, making note of anything that might have affected her transition. Her death had been tragic, a sacrifice at the hands of dark magic. That would certainly have caused issues if the magic was powerful enough.

And when it seemed like she was fading, being pulled to the mortal realm or between worlds, Evander would sing for her. She would watch him with that awestruck look in her eyes, and then, after a moment, she joined in. The harmony and melody intertwined, echoing down the river and resonating among the trees. He had never heard anything more beautiful than Mona's voice. Her song cut straight through him, right to his core, making his very bones tremble with awareness.

It called to him in a way no one else's did.

For those brief, blissful moments, the realm seemed like heaven itself. Not the Hell Evander knew it to be.

Unfortunately, the more they sang together, the more Evander felt a stirring inside him. The dark presence within him yearned to come out. And Mona's song called to it, beckoning it forward.

It took great effort to hold the beast at bay. Evander was torn between healing Mona and keeping the monster caged. Every time they sang, another part of her became corporeal. First her hand, then her forearm, then her upper arm. At this rate, it wouldn't be long before her entire body was restored.

But the beast clawed closer to the surface, threatening to unleash itself.

Several days later, when their singing had freed Mona's entire left arm and shoulder, Evander had to stop mid-song, his body shuddering with the imminent release of the dark power festering inside him. His hand unconsciously went to the moonstone around his neck. It burned hot against his palm.

"What dark magic has claimed you?" Mona whispered, her eyes sad as she stared at him.

Damn. This woman missed nothing. She *had* implied she'd been a powerful witch in the mortal realm. It seemed even as a spirit, she could still sense strong magic.

Evander could lie to her, but he didn't want to insult her intelligence. Instead, he said softly, "It's my burden to bear. Do not trouble yourself, Mona. You have enough to worry about."

"Without you, I have no hope of moving on," Mona protested. "If this dark magic claims you, that will affect me as well. Please, Evander. Tell me."

A shiver rippled through him, and he hunched on all fours with a groan. *No, no, no...* It was too soon!

How was this happening? He never unleashed the monster during the daytime. This was unfounded. How was it growing stronger?

Evander willed the beast to remain inside, to stay

put, but he couldn't stop it. Now that it had begun, the transformation swept over him.

Claws emerged from his fingertips, and he hastily hid them under the shadow of his torso. He had to leave. He had to *get out* or else the beast would try to claim Mona, too...

"Evander." Mona's voice sounded panicked now. He could feel his hair changing, the horns growing along his head.

"I—I'm sorry, Mona." With a gasp, Evander fled to the cover of the forest, allowing the beast to emerge fully. A roar escaped him, echoing in the air and making the trees and the ground quiver.

He didn't understand. This had never happened to him before. How? How had the beast gained such control over him?

And how long before it overtook Evander entirely?

When Evander came to, he found himself in Vasileios's domain: the River Lethe. Across the river, he could make out the churning depths of the Pool of Forgetfulness.

What the hell am I doing here? Evander wondered. His skin felt itchy, as it often did when he transformed. Just to be sure, he ran his hands up and down his body, assessing. He was back in his black suit, and no horns sat on his head. His hair was short, his fingers no longer clawed.

Thank the gods. But he had to get back to Mona...

"Evander," whispered a voice.

He stilled, his skin prickling from the otherworldly presence that called to him.

And then he heard it. *Her song.*

"Mona?" he breathed, glancing around. Impossible. She was bound to Cocytus. She couldn't possibly be here.

Then, he heard another voice—a voice he knew well. It was tinged with laughter and triumph.

Vasileios.

Evander crept forward, using the trees to obscure his presence as he peered down the river. Vasileios sat perched along the riverbank, his hands swirling together as black magic twisted itself around his fingers. The magic plunged into the water, and Mona's song intensified, blaring against Evander's ears and making him wince. No longer a mournful song of grief, it was now a wail of agony, much more similar to the pained and tormented souls he encountered.

It was Vasileios. He was the one who sought Mona's soul.

Rage filled him, making him see red. Whatever Vasileios was doing was causing Mona *pain.* And Evander would tear him to shreds. The beast roared inside him, thirsty for blood. He strode forward, prepared to rip Vasileios limb from limb, but what he saw next made him freeze.

It was... *Mona.* In the flesh. She stepped out of the river as if she had been born of the water. She was completely naked, her black hair flowing down her back. Her eyes, a luminescent green, shone brightly.

But it was her face... Her expression was eerily blank, devoid of any emotion. Even her transparent specter held more emotion than this echo of her.

Whoever this was, it wasn't truly Mona. But it would certainly explain her unbound state; Mona's body was *here*, and her soul was elsewhere.

"Ah, my beautiful queen." Vasileios bent low, pressing a kiss to Mona's hand. But the woman didn't react. Her eyes remained fixed blankly ahead. She was nothing more than a doll. A statue.

What dark magic was Vasileios dabbling in?

A low rumble climbed up Evander's throat, reminding him of his fury. The urge to slash his claws straight through Vasileios was too powerful to ignore.

Easy, he urged the beast, willing it to remain hidden. He couldn't afford to unleash it here. None of his brothers knew of his secret, and he needed to keep it that way.

But it was hard to differentiate his own anger from the monster's. In this moment, they were one and the same. Both wanted to tear Vasileios apart for what he was doing to Mona.

The calm, logical part of Evander had to know *why*. Why Mona? What was so special about her soul that a power-hungry being like Vasileios would be drawn to it?

She is special, Evander thought, remembering the song they shared, the way her eyes lit up when she spoke of her magic and her home in the mortal realm. *But not to a creature like Vasileios.*

Vasileios only knew power and battle strategy. He desired demon women for carnal pleasures and nothing more. Mona was a powerful witch, yes, but plenty of witches came through their rivers.

Vasileios cupped Mona's face in his hands and smirked down at her, his eyes full of triumph. Evander's blood turned hot, and he bared his teeth. If Vasileios didn't get his hands off Mona's body this instant, Evander wouldn't be able to control himself.

Thankfully, Vasileios was pleased with the woman before him. He stepped back and nodded. "This will do perfectly. Come, my dear. We have plans to put in motion." He strode away from the river, and, like an obedient pet, Mona's body trailed after him, her long legs moving with ease.

Horror and despair roiled in Evander's gut. This was unnatural. It was a violation of everything that fueled the Underworld's power.

Whatever the cost, Evander had to get to the bottom of this. Or else Mona's soul could be lost forever.

The thought sent a roar of pain ripping through him, tearing apart his flesh and bones. Before he could stop himself, the monster was unleashed once more, taking hold of Evander and smothering him in darkness.

AWAKENED
MONA

Before Mona's Resurrection

For the next few hours, Mona found herself completely alone. With the threat of the dark-haired prince of Hell looming over her, as well as Evander's strange disappearance and transformation, her solitude was no comfort. Especially since she couldn't *move*.

She hadn't missed the way Evander's nails had lengthened to claws or the horns that grew from his forehead. Whatever magic he was caught up in was sinister. She remembered what he had said about the magic of the Underworld: *We don't have much magic down here, but the powers that do exist are... dark. Unnatural. Demonic, even.*

Was Evander's magic turning him into some sort of monster?

The thought gripped Mona with fear, but not for her own safety—for Evander's. She had seen what dark magic could do to a careless witch. She didn't want Evander to suffer the same fate.

Or worse.

He'll return soon, she told herself. *He always does.*

Was this why he often disappeared for hours at a time? Because this... *thing* took hold of him?

Mona huffed a sigh, knowing she had to shift her thoughts to something more pleasant, otherwise her mind would start spiraling. She missed her sister. Prue always knew how to lighten the mood, how to distract Mona from her woes.

Let's go to the town square for dancing! Prue would say. *Maybe you'll catch someone's eye...*

Mona almost laughed. There were *no* eligible bachelors under the age of fifty in Krenia. And every time Prue suggested Mona flirt with someone, she laughed then, too.

Goddess, Mona missed it. All of it—the beach, the villagers, the narrow winding dirt path leading up to their home, the sound of Sybil and Polina laughing together in the kitchen as they cooked, Prue's teasing...

Mona closed her eyes, the heat and pain of her loss rising up inside her, so intense it overwhelmed her. She unleashed a dry sob, knowing she couldn't weep in her current state. But her wails echoed in the forest, fueling her with a strange sense of empowerment. She couldn't move. She couldn't cast spells. But she *could* shout. Another anguished cry poured from her mouth, more vibrant and resonant than before. She was reminded of her haunting melody when singing with Evander. Singing it had brought her the same strange sense of liberation she felt now.

Let the entire realm hear her sorrow. She would give anything to be home right now. *Anything.*

The air shifted. An eerie wind whispered over her skin. Mona opened her eyes to find herself on the beach in Krenia.

A gasp tore from her throat. She was here! Joy filled her chest, followed immediately by unease. Wait a moment... Was this *really* Krenia? Or was she between worlds with the prince of Hell who wanted her soul?

A quick glance downward told her she was a spirit. A ghost. Just like with Evander. Which meant she had to be truly *here* in Krenia, right? When she'd been between worlds, she'd been corporeal.

But she *had* transitioned to the mortal realm once, just briefly, right after arriving in Cocytus. It had only been for a few seconds, and then she'd been pulled back to the Underworld.

Had she managed to travel again? Was she truly home?

"M-Mona?" breathed a voice.

Mona glanced around and stifled a cry of longing. Prue stood next to her, her eyes red-rimmed and her cheeks sticky with tears. Shock and hope flared in her gaze as she stared at Mona's form.

A hard lump formed in Mona's throat, and she couldn't breathe. She couldn't even process a coherent thought. "Prue." Her voice was strained.

Prue rushed forward, obviously intending to embrace Mona, but her hands fell right through her, causing a shiver to ripple over Mona's form. Prue stilled, tears leaking from her eyes. "What—what is this? Are you truly here?"

"I'm still dead," Mona said quickly, not wanting to give her false hope. "But… it seems I can still visit you." She offered a weak smile.

Prue raised her hands to her face and wept openly, her shoulders shaking. Mona longed to touch her sister, to hold her while she cried. Heat stung her own eyes, and she marveled at these human feelings, this sensation of being alive even when she wasn't. Perhaps being here —being *home*—had that effect on her soul.

"I need you back," Prue sobbed. "I *have* to get you back. It was a mistake, all of it."

"I know," Mona said, the sorrow twisting painfully in her gut.

"Please, Mona. You know more about powerful magic than I do. It must be possible. Can I bring you back?"

Mona started to object, but stopped herself. What if Evander couldn't find a way to heal her? What if her soul was in danger of being torn apart?

What if Evander's brother managed to find her and trap her forever?

Singing had seemed to help, but whatever magic possessed Evander was definitely growing stronger.

If it claimed him, Mona would be alone, with no way out.

But... if Prue brought her back, that might solve everything.

Mona swallowed hard before she said, "All right, Prue. I'll tell you everything I know about raising the dead."

Mona was yanked back to the Underworld far sooner than she would have liked. She collapsed with an ungraceful "oof," her hands meeting dirt and the scent of pine overwhelming her. She'd talked with Prue for hours, outlining every spell and every ingredient she could think of to resurrect a lost soul. And afterward, Prue had poured out her heart, expressing her grief and sorrow. And Mona just listened. Because that was what Prue needed.

Before Prue had finished, however, something pulled Mona back to the river. She gasped, disoriented from the shift, and shook her head before rising to her feet.

The familiar babbling of a river met her ears. Around her spread the expansive forest she was so accustomed to gazing at while Evander roamed up and down the river. Her eyes latched onto the towering twin pine trees that marked the edge of the forest.

Everything was the same. Except...

Hold on. Her hands drifted over herself, and she let out a half sob, half laugh. She was real! Solid. Just like when she was between worlds. She stood here, in the flesh, as if she had indeed been brought back to life. Her skin, her hair, it was all *real.* She pressed a hand to her heart, and her joy faded.

No heartbeat. So she was still dead, then.

No matter. Her body had been reunited with her soul. Whatever Evander had been doing must have worked.

Another laugh bubbled up her throat, and Mona covered her face with her hands, overjoyed to feel the sting of tears in her eyes. The salty moisture coated her fingers, and she laughed again. Everything was a marvel. The dirt against her bare feet, the wind in her hair, the smells around her...

Mona's gaze fell to her dress. It was emerald green, flowing around her like the gown of a princess. It was certainly nothing she'd ever worn in Krenia. Where had it come from?

Twigs snapped from within the forest, and Mona stiffened, looking up. Was it Evander? Or was it... something else?

A pair of silvery eyes shone from the darkness, followed by a tall, lean form she recognized immediately. It *was* Evander.

And yet... it wasn't.

Mona's breaths quickened, her stomach churning with unease as the figure emerged fully. She felt everything acutely. The unease swirling through her. The fear tightening in her chest. The prickles of awareness raising bumps along her arms.

The man's face belonged to Evander—the same silver eyes and hair, the same handsome features. But his eyes were rimmed with red. Long claws protruded from his hands, and huge wings extended from his back, a mixture of red and black, like leather. The wings were skeletal, the bones and tendons visible beneath a sheer layer of skin. Sharp talons extended from the points of the wings as they flared behind him.

Without thinking, Mona turned and ran from him. Branches and shrubs whipped past her as she fled, and the heavy footsteps behind her indicated he was chasing after her. A pained cry broke from her throat as she pushed onward, but rocks and sticks scraped at her feet, slowing her pace. Heavy breathing sounded behind her, and Mona knew he would reach her any moment.

The forest grew thicker the deeper she went, each step slowing her down as the trees blocked her path. She could no longer hear the river behind her; there was nothing but the dense wood, caging her in, blocking her escape.

Hands gripped her, turning and pinning her against a tree. Mona's head slammed into the bark, and she screamed, eyes shut tight against whatever monstrous thing she would find in Evander's face.

The dark magic had indeed consumed him. And he belonged to someone else now. Some*thing* else.

A low groan echoed around her, and she flinched, expecting his claws to shred her to pieces. But nothing happened.

"Mona."

Mona gasped, her eyes flying open. Evander stood only a breath away from her, his chest pinned against hers, his arms braced on either side of her, caging her against the tree. He was panting as if the chase had winded him, but energy lit up his gaze. His great wings spread behind him, shading them from the sun.

A whiff of pine and river water filled Mona's nose, and she realized it was Evander's scent. It smelled like… her song. It smelled like something familiar and safe.

"Evander," she said uncertainly. "What—what happened to you?"

Evander leaned forward, pressing his forehead against hers. "Mona," he repeated.

But his voice sounded different. It was deeper and more feral. She felt a rumble in his chest, reverberating against hers.

Somehow, amazingly, she wasn't afraid. He could've attacked her. He could've wounded her. But he seemed… oddly protective of her. Something deep inside her resonated with this dark being in front of her.

She *knew* him. And he knew her.

"Evander," she said again, bringing her hand up to his cheek. Evander went perfectly still, his eyes closing from her touch. "You're still here."

Evander bared his teeth, exposing long fangs, but Mona still wasn't afraid.

"You don't frighten me," she said. "I know you."

He opened his eyes, the red bleeding into his irises now. He shook his head as if trying to convey something important to her. His gaze drifted down her body, and he scrutinized her dress as if just now noticing she was corporeal instead of a spirit.

Hunger and desire flared in his eyes, and before Mona could react, he pressed his mouth to hers.

She froze as his lips roved over hers, claiming her, his hips grinding against her. She knew she should push him away. This was her first kiss, and it shouldn't have been like this—some dark, possessed demon crushing her against a tree.

But as she felt his hot breath mingle with hers, something awakened inside her. A roar of delight, a bolt of pure longing. With her newfound body, she could sense every tendril of heat coiling tightly inside her, fueling her with a desperation she couldn't contain. Every part of her flesh ached for him, to be touched, to be held. Goddess, she wanted to feel *all* of it. And the taste of his tongue awakened that need deep inside her.

She moaned and clutched his face in her hands, returning his kiss with violent urgency. Her teeth captured his lip and tugged, and his tongue filled her mouth, ravishing her entirely. His hands found her hips, hiking up her skirts, and she let him. Because no logical voice of reason could break through the desire pounding through her blood.

Perhaps it wasn't just Evander who had changed. Mona had, too. She was not herself. She had morphed into this raw, feral creature.

And she liked it.

Her skirts lifted higher, and heat burned through her. She wrapped her legs around his middle, bringing him closer, sensing the bulge in his trousers that made her toes curl with anticipation.

She had never felt such heat before. And she wanted to feel *more.*

Evander's mouth left hers, his tongue trailing down her jaw and her neck, making small circles along the hollow of her throat. Mona threw her head back and groaned with pleasure, her hips writhing against his. Her hands feverishly pushed off his jacket—which had already ripped from the wings outstretched behind him—and then worked at the buttons of his shirt. He ripped his clothes off without another thought, discarding the shredded clothing onto the forest floor. He unbuckled his trousers and slid them off, pressing every inch of his glorious length against her.

"Goddess above, I need you," Mona rasped.

Accepting her invitation, Evander tugged at her dress until it, too, ripped down the middle, exposing her breasts. The fabric fell on either side of her, the wind tickling her bare flesh. But it didn't stop the all-consuming heat from boiling inside her.

Evander cupped her breast, running his thumb in slow circles around her nipple. A wave of delight washed over Mona, fierce and powerful. She needed to have him. All of him.

She didn't know what she was doing, but she wanted to touch him, to make him feel what he did to her. On impulse, her hand found his cock and rubbed up and down its length.

A bolt of satisfaction filled her as Evander roared, his wings flaring, his head bowed as he arched against her. *More,* he seemed to say. *More.*

Something ruptured and exploded in Mona's chest. The ground quivered, and cracks split in the earth. Her magic flared to life, her third eye flying open as power burned inside her. She summoned her grace, her magical affinity. But instead of the roses she expected to spring up from the ground, brambles and thorns crept forward, prickly and pointy. The barbs were alarming, but they didn't quench Mona's desire. If anything, they aroused her further.

I am no longer innocent and gentle, she thought. *I am coarse and full of fire. Sharp and honed to a point.*

She ground against Evander, desiring him fully inside her, ready to ride this wave of power alongside him.

Then, he arched backward, a pained cry ripping from his throat. This wasn't the sound of a man enraptured; this was something anguished. It chilled Mona to the bone, and she went still, staring at him in shock. He staggered away from her, and her feet dropped as she leaned against the tree, unsteady. "Evander?" she asked.

Evander clutched at his temples, groaning in pain, his eyes crammed shut. With a cry, Mona's hand flew to her mouth as she watched his wings recede, vanishing into his shoulder blades. His claws withdrew, and when his eyes opened, they were the same pure silver she was accustomed to.

A chill swept over Mona, all heat fleeing from her body. "Evander?" she whispered hesitantly.

Evander's face paled as he glanced from Mona's naked body to his own. "Gods above," he choked. "What have I done?"

EREBOS
PRUE

Trivia led Prue out of the palace and through the network of caves where Prue had been imprisoned before. The winding tunnels were so confusing that Prue's head was spinning as she struggled to keep up. Eventually, she gave up trying to memorize the route and simply followed Trivia.

The soft babbling of water met her ears as they entered a large chamber. A gentle glow illuminated the space, allowing Prue to clearly see the winding river that cut through the rocky earth. Then, she realized the glow was coming *from* the river.

It was a river of souls.

Awestruck, Prue drew nearer, but a voice stopped her.

"You won't want to come any closer."

She turned and found a man standing alongside the river. His black hair was short, though it curled at the nape of his neck, and a dark goatee covered his face. She knew by the silver eyes that he was one of Cyrus's brothers.

"That's Romanos," Trivia said. "He oversees Styx."

The River Styx. Prue had heard legends of this river of Hell. Though she yearned to get a closer look, Romanos's warning was probably valid. This was one of the lower levels of Hell, and Prue didn't want to get close enough for that darkness to latch onto her.

"I'm Prue," she said, looking up at Romanos. From what Cyrus had said about his brothers, none of them could be trusted. But this one looked rather harmless. His expression was almost bored as he gazed at the river's depths. "Cyrus's wife."

That made his gaze snap up at her. "His *wife*? Damn... I had no idea."

"Why would you?" Trivia asked. "You always keep to yourself."

"For good reason. Have you *met* my brothers?"

Trivia snorted and waved a hand. "I'd love to stay and chat, but we have business to attend to."

Romanos inclined his head. "Carry on, then." Without waiting for a response, he turned away to fully face the river.

Prue frowned as Trivia led them away from the river and down another tunnel. "What's his story?"

"Romanos? I'm not quite sure. He prefers to be alone. But from what I've noticed, he doesn't cause any trouble, so I'm not too bothered."

Prue considered this. She didn't remember Cyrus mentioning Romanos by name—it was usually Marcellus or Vasileios he complained about.

Still, it seemed like a rather dull and lonely existence, to remain by that river, all day every day. Was it because of Cyrus? Had he threatened Romanos into submission?

That certainly *did* sound like something Cyrus would do. The thought put a sour taste in her mouth.

They continued through the tunnels until they emerged in a vast pine forest. Prue gaped at the scene before her. Lush green leaves and shrubs surrounded her, and a deep blue sky gleamed overhead. The afternoon sun winked at Prue as if mocking her confusion.

"What... what is all this?" Prue asked, taken aback by how *real* it all felt. Was she even still in the Underworld?

Trivia smirked. "It's the Forest of Thanatos. Convincing, right? Aidoneus's enchantments have only improved with time. It helps, being so close to his penthouse." She gestured behind them, where Prue could barely make out the tall peak of a narrow building.

"This is an enchantment?" Prue asked weakly.

Goddess above, it was flawless! She couldn't imagine the power it must've required.

"The smells are new. That's my favorite touch."

Prue inhaled, her eyes closing. Pine, oak, moss, and the slight hint of sage. In the distance was the gentle babble of another river.

"Come on, let's make this quick," Trivia said. "Your king awaits."

Prue nodded, remembering the task at hand. Her stomach was in knots at the thought of meeting the residents of the Underworld. What would they think of her? Would they despise her? Would they even know who she was?

And who am I? Prue thought bitterly. *A rejected queen? A scorned lover?*

But no. She was so much more than that. Cyrus loved her. She knew that. She just had to get him back.

Somehow.

Prue and Trivia pressed onward along a forest path. Despite how comfortable she felt barefoot, Prue was grateful Trivia had forced her into a pair of shoes. The pebbles and stones on the ground would be cutting into her feet by now.

Before long, they emerged from the wood and stood at the edge of an enormous, churning river, its frothy depths bubbling with vigor. They crossed a wide bridge that carried them over the river. Prue couldn't help gazing over the edge as she crossed it. Within the depths of the river, glowing orbs floated in the water.

Souls. The souls of the dead.

Swallowing down a knot of unease, Prue faced forward and followed Trivia. On the other side of the bridge was an expanse of grass, framed by a sparse line of trees. The great pines thinned out with each step Prue took, leaving her feeling exposed and out in the open.

She stilled when something thrummed in the air around her. An eerie fog hovered to her left, stretching so wide that Prue knew whatever was contained within had to be something powerful.

"What's that?" she asked.

Trivia stopped, too, and followed her gaze. Her expression hardened. "The gate to the mortal realm."

Prue sucked in a sharp breath, turning to look at the mysterious fog once more. One step through that, and she would be home. With Mona.

But then she wouldn't be able to come back.

She shook her head. *I have to save Cyrus first.* She couldn't just abandon him to whatever dark forces had claimed him.

And even if Cyrus *was* healed, if he was in control once more, could Prue really leave him forever? Even if it meant living a life with Mona once again, she wasn't sure if she could do it. In spite of everything, she still loved Cyrus deeply. And the idea of severing herself from him permanently made her chest ache.

"Here we are," Trivia said, snapping Prue out of her thoughts.

She blinked and looked up. They had just crested a large hill, and below them rested a tiny hamlet, the buildings reminding Prue so much of her home in Krenia that her stomach twisted into knots.

"Is this Erebos?" Prue whispered.

"It is indeed," Trivia said. "The only village in the entire realm."

A village. Here in the Underworld. The thought was so jarring that Prue had to take a moment to catch her breath. She had no idea what to expect.

"You'll be fine," Trivia said, misreading her apprehension. "They'll sense your power. They won't touch you."

"Do you live here?" Prue asked as Trivia led her down the hill.

"Yes." Trivia's voice lifted with pride. "Anyone who isn't royal lives here. Demons, lesser gods and goddesses, and even the mortals who have transitioned to the afterlife. At least, those who choose to stay."

Prue nodded, remembering what she'd said about giving them the choice. She found herself appreciating the system they had here, giving mortals the option of where they would like to go. It gave Prue a modicum of comfort about her own afterlife.

Will I end up here, too? she wondered. She was the queen of the realm, yes, but would that matter? What would happen to her if she died here?

Trivia and Prue reached the small gates, already thrown open wide to receive them. A throng of people awaited them, all grim-faced and stony. Most of them were demons, some with tails, and others with long horns and fangs. One had the head of an ox, and another had gleaming red eyes and a forked tongue.

Prue tried not to shudder away from them, knowing many couldn't control their appearances. She thought of Cyrus and his ram horns. She had never found his appearance disturbing or horrifying. In time, she'd even grown to appreciate his otherworldly beauty.

With this perspective in mind, she found herself looking at each demon with keen interest, wondering what their story was and why they were here. Did they have jobs? Did they serve Cyrus, or one of his brothers? One demon inclined his head toward Prue, and she repeated the gesture, feeling warmth bloom inside her.

Trivia approached the tallest demon, a bald, scrawny fellow with leathery black wings. "Another incident?" Trivia asked.

The demon nodded slowly, his glittering black eyes fixing on Prue. She met his gaze, her chin lifting slightly.

A smile curled at the corners of his lips, but it felt far from friendly.

"Show me," Trivia said.

With one last smirk at Prue, the demon turned and strode toward the center of the village. Trivia and Prue trailed behind him, past worn buildings and dusty shops. The area as a whole looked abandoned and neglected, a shell of the vibrant village Prue was used to in Krenia. With each step, her heart sank further in her chest. Broken windows, doors hanging off hinges, demons crouching in alleys and digging through garbage for food...

"What happened here?" Prue whispered in horror.

"Shockingly, the royals here don't really care about the commoners," Trivia said, her voice full of venom.

Ire and indignation flared in Prue's chest, and she heaved an angry, shuddering breath. *Cyrus* let this happen? He let this village wither and waste away, let his subjects starve? Cyrus could be cruel, but she never thought him capable of *this*.

Perhaps he's not the man you thought he was, said a small voice in her head.

Resolve coursed through her as she vowed to find out. Part of her wanted to argue that if dark magic had possessed Cyrus, then perhaps whatever happened here wasn't his doing. But it was clear this misuse had been going on for much longer than Prue had been here. Years, perhaps.

What was Cyrus's excuse? He certainly had enough power to go around. And yet, he would allow this neglect to continue...

Rage boiled inside her, and Prue clung to it, letting it bleed out any fear or uncertainty lingering in her mind. If she couldn't save Cyrus, she would do everything in her power to save this village, no matter the cost. She couldn't simply stand by and do nothing when these people were suffering.

Trivia stopped at the village square where a demon child was bound with her hands behind her back, her all-black eyes wide as they fixed on Trivia. The child's small white horns poked through her matted blond hair. Her thin, malnourished body quivered with fear.

Trivia stopped short and went rigid. "A child?" she accused the bald demon next to her.

The demon nodded somberly.

"What?" Prue asked, her eyes glued to the restrained child. "What's going on?"

"There has been a darkness seeping into the village as of late," Trivia murmured. "It's starting to claim demons. This is the first time it's claimed a child."

"How can you tell?" Prue asked, scrutinizing the child, who appeared normal, as far as demons were concerned.

"Watch," the demon said, gesturing to the child.

Sure enough, the child's body began to seize and tremble, her back arching as she cried out.

Prue jumped. "Do something!" she shouted, panic rising inside her.

The child thrashed so violently that several demons drew closer to restrain her. Inky black shadows oozed from the child's hands, staining the ground and running along the concrete like blood.

The crowd of demons jerked backward, away from the shadows. Prue surged forward, not sure what she planned to do, just knowing she had to do *something* to stop this...

But before she could, the child went still. The shadows receded inside her, and her body went limp. Hushed and terrified whispers rippled among the crowd.

Prue could only stare, horrified. *Possession.* Even the demons here in the Underworld were susceptible to this strange darkness. It was trying to overtake their bodies, just like it had the villagers in Krenia.

Prue's mind snagged on those horrifying memories she tried to keep buried. Black liquid, oozing along the road, creeping toward its victims. Each one it claimed was killed almost instantly.

"Death shadow," she whispered, her blood running cold. The same strange black mist had attacked her and Cyrus in the mortal realm.

Trivia whipped her head to stare at her. "What did you say?"

"It's death shadow, isn't it?" Prue's voice gained strength as she glanced from Trivia to the bald demon.

Stunned, the demon nodded. "I—yes. It appears so. We weren't certain before, but…"

"Death shadow comes from wraiths, correct?" Prue asked, addressing the demon directly now. Cyrus had told her as much in the mortal realm.

"Yes, my lady."

"Find all the wraiths in the area. Track them down and bring them to me in the palace, unharmed."

The demon opened and closed his mouth, then glanced uncertainly at Trivia. She waved a hand. "Do as she says."

The demon bowed. "Yes, my lady."

More murmurs swept through the crowd. Prue stood a little straighter and addressed the crowd at large. "My name is Prue, and I'm the queen of this realm. I vow to uncover the truth behind these attacks and put a stop to them." She frowned as she glanced around at the starving and haggard demons. "And I promise to send barrels of food to you as soon as I'm able."

Surprised gasps rippled over the crowd. Some demons looked skeptical. But others were grinning broadly, a few even bringing their hands together in excitement.

Trivia sighed, her form drooping as she gestured for Prue to follow her. The two were silent as they weaved down the street and back toward the gates. Trivia muttered something to the demons standing sentry before they left the village.

"Why did you do that?" Trivia hissed when they climbed the hill, leaving Erebos behind them.

"Do what?"

"Announce yourself. To them, there is no queen. There's barely even a king. They're on their own out here."

"It shouldn't be that way," Prue said sharply. "I intend to change that. This was the first step."

Trivia shook her head, her eyes burning with anger. "You can't change generations of tradition in a single day. I know it's shocking to imagine your beloved capable of something so callous, but the royals view the commoners as less than worthless. They are only concerned with themselves and their rivers of souls. They don't care what happens after the souls leave the river. It's been that way for thousands of years, and that's not about to change."

"But aren't... aren't the demons here immortal?" Prue asked, remembering what Cyrus had told her about not needing to sleep or eat.

"Demons are half-breeds. They contain mortal blood, which keeps them weak. The divine gods made them this way on purpose, to ensure they were inferior." Trivia's face twisted in a foul sneer, and Prue understood why she despised the gods so much.

"I'm sorry," Prue said softly. "I'm sorry your people are suffering so much. And I'm sorry I didn't speak with you first before addressing them. I know they are part of your domain, and I overstepped. Please forgive me. I only wanted to help."

Trivia's expression softened. "It's all right. After all, I volunteered to serve your court, didn't I?" She offered a small smile. After a moment, her gold eyes flashed as she looked steadily at Prue. "If you truly want to help, the first thing you can do is wake up your husband. Then, once he's accepted you as his queen, the real work can begin." Trivia jerked her head. "Come on, I'll show you to the throne room. I'm sure he's waiting for you."

A flare of hope filled Prue's chest. Perhaps she could do some good here after all. With this optimism, she hurried after Trivia, eager to put their plan in motion.

FIGHT
CYRUS

Cyrus had been pushed so far into the recesses of his mind that he had no sense of where he was or who he was speaking to. Kronos had completely overtaken his body and mind, leaving only the narrowest of cracks for Cyrus to inhabit.

He should have known. How could he not have *known*? Kronos was renowned in this realm as the most deadly of all the prisoners of Tartarus. And somehow, his consciousness had escaped and taken hold of Cyrus. Who else was in danger? Were his brothers possessed by the same magic? Or was it only Cyrus, because he was bound to the Book of Eyes?

Was Prue in danger because of her bond to him?

The thought of Prue—his wife, his lover, his whole soul—being subjected to the whims and horrors of

Kronos sent a bolt of awareness through Cyrus. For the briefest of moments, he could see. Kronos had him perched atop his throne, speaking with one of the higher-ranking demons about the security of Tartarus.

Ah. Kronos was deathly afraid of something within Tartarus. Another prisoner, perhaps? Or was it the prison itself?

Was Kronos afraid of being sent back? Was that the key to Cyrus's salvation?

His curiosity piqued, Cyrus's awareness grew more and more until he could make out words and sounds.

"We do not have the resources to double security, my lord," said the overseer, a winged creature named Lannis. "But with your magic, we *can* seal it shut. This would prevent us from sentencing any other souls to Tartarus, but it would effectively keep everyone contained as well."

Alarm rippled through Cyrus. *Seal Tartarus shut?* He couldn't... If they couldn't send souls to Tartarus, it would be chaos. No consequences for wayward or disobedient souls. No punishment or fear.

"Find me the spell," came Cyrus's cold voice. "I'll see that it's done."

No! Cyrus roared within himself, but of course, he was silenced. Ignored. Cast aside.

Lannis bowed and departed, and Cyrus heard a low chuckle echoing around him.

Kronos was laughing at him and his pitiful efforts to revolt.

Because, truly, there was nothing Cyrus could do.

Footsteps echoed nearby, and Cyrus, feeling the usual darkness crowding his mind, threatening to drag him back under, thrust his awareness forward, determined to hold on a bit longer.

The doors swung open, and all of Cyrus's senses sharpened, zeroing in on his visitor and drinking in every detail.

It was Prue.

She wore the most scandalous dress he'd ever seen. Two swaths of violet fabric barely covered her breasts, leaving the sides exposed for all to see. The skirt fanned out around her, swishing with each step. Her arms were bare, revealing the smooth brown skin he craved constantly. Her luscious black locks were half pinned up, the remainder tumbling down her back in delicate tresses.

And her luminous lavender eyes were blazing with fury.

Behind her, the doors banged shut. Cyrus caught a glimpse of a red-haired servant bowing before vanishing from sight, leaving him alone with his wife.

"Prue," Cyrus said, straightening at once. At that moment, it was *him* speaking. Not Kronos. A dozen emotions flitted across his mind. Shock at seeing her...

like *this*. Shock at seeing her *at all* because, as far as he knew, she was still chained up in a cave somewhere. How had she escaped? And who had given her such a tantalizing dress? Cyrus's skin burned just looking at it.

Prue lifted her chin in defiance, appearing every bit the radiant queen she was. "Tell me about Erebos."

Cyrus faltered. "I—what? How the hell did you get out of that cave?" He was half amused, half impressed that she had managed it. He'd yearned to go to her and free her himself, but each time he'd gotten close, Kronos had taken over and made the situation worse.

"Don't change the subject! Tell me about Erebos, the village you've left to starve and waste away while you sit atop your glorious throne," Prue spat, waving a hand at him in accusation. "There are people there! *Children.* Death shadows are attacking them, and you're just *sitting* here! What kind of ruler are you?"

Cyrus felt Kronos shrinking away from her fury, but he was too baffled to process any of this. *Erebos...* The name was slightly familiar to him, but there was no *village* in the Underworld. Not that he was aware of.

"Don't you dare," Prue seethed, drawing closer to him. He could feel the waves of anger rippling off her. "Don't pretend. Not with me. I need the truth, Cyrus. Is there a good reason for your neglect? Or are you truly heartless?" Her eyes bore into his, and she growled, "And I want the *real* you. Not this imposter."

Cyrus sucked in a shaky breath, everything around him sharpening into perfect clarity. Prue scrutinized his gaze, her face slackening in surprise as she saw something different in his eyes. Could she tell it was really him? He was grateful the throne room had emptied of all guards; Kronos hadn't wanted any witnesses to his conversation with Lannis, which left Cyrus and Prue alone for the time being.

"The truth," Cyrus said slowly, "is that I don't know what Erebos is. My father mentioned it eons ago, but it was an insignificant piece of land, something we don't have need for. The truth is that I'm unaware of a village in my domain, nor am I aware of the suffering of the people who inhabit it. If there is a village here, please show it to me so I can see for myself."

Prue's eyes narrowed slightly, as if she were trying to detect a lie from him.

"It's *me*, Prue," he said, desperate for her to believe him.

Her jaw went rigid. To his utter surprise and indignation, she slapped him across the face. His head swiveled from the force of the blow, his cheek burning. Nostrils flared, he bared his teeth at her. "What was that for?"

"For *giving up!*" she cried. "How often have you boasted of your power and greatness to me, stressing that you were a *god* and I was *insignificant*? And yet, when your darkness rises and tries to claim you, you just *sat by and let it take you.* You didn't *fight!*"

Anger reared inside him. "How dare you? You have no idea what I've endured, trying to overcome this and get back to you!"

"I know you're stronger than this, Cyrus! When have you ever surrendered to an enemy? When have you ever given up? Why can't you *fight this*?"

"I'm *trying!*" Cyrus roared, now on his feet, his arms spread wide. The rage bled through all the fog in his mind, and in this moment, he was here. He was in control. Kronos had vanished.

But he was too incensed to notice. All he could think of was how unfair Prue's condemnation was. Shouldn't she be relieved to finally face him? The *real* him?

"He has shut me out, Prue," Cyrus went on through gritted teeth. "He's too powerful. I've *let* him become too powerful. It was through my own neglect that this happened."

"So that's it," Prue said coldly. "Your own self-loathing is holding you back. Your guilt. Because *you* let this happen, because it's *your* fault, you think it's only fair for you to lie down and let him take over you. Is that right?"

"That's not what I said," Cyrus barked.

"Then *why*?" Prue argued. "Why aren't you *fighting*?

For you, for me, for *us*? For this *realm*? Isn't any of that worth it?"

"Of course it is!" Cyrus shouted. "Don't you think I would give up anything—*anything*—to be with you? I *love* you, Prue! And I am doing my damndest to overcome this so I can crown you as my queen!"

A deep, bone-shattering sorrow filled her eyes as she shook her head slowly. "No, Cyrus. I *don't* know what you would give up for me. Because you have always craved power. If it were between me and your magic, I truly don't know which you would choose."

Cyrus's head reared back, stung by this. How could she say that?

But as he considered her words, how could she *not*? He had *always* chosen power over all else. It was the most important thing to him. It had been for a long time.

Until now.

Cyrus took her shoulders, and Prue tensed, her ire returning. "You are more important," he said, his voice a low growl. "Always, Prue."

Always.

That word meant so much between them. He remembered uttering it to her when she seemed so surprised he would use his soul magic on her to heal her.

Soul magic. The thought sent a spike of realization

through him. He had been trying to fight off Kronos with his own death magic, but Kronos *was* death magic.

One thing he *hadn't* tried was summoning the power of the gods. The power ingrained in his body and blood; the power he was born with. Because that particular magic came at a price; it would mean giving up part of his own soul. Giving up his immortality. If he used it too much, he would become mortal. His magic would dry up and leave him nothing more than a weak human.

But he would do it for Prue.

Prue tried to shove his chest, to push him away from her, but Cyrus's grip on her shoulders was too strong. Tears filled her eyes. "Then, *why won't you fight?*" she hissed, her voice wavering. "I *need* you, Cyrus, and you won't fight! Come back to me!"

Cyrus kissed her. He didn't know what possessed him to do it, but the sight of her so impassioned and blazing with intensity made the longing course through him with violent fervor.

She bit down on his lip, hard enough to draw blood.

Cyrus winced and drew back, raising his hand to the bead of silver blood welling in his mouth. "Damn," he said.

Prue shoved him again, and this time he staggered backward.

"I don't want you," she snarled, "until you are well

and fully *mine*. Until that *thing* is gone from you for good."

Rage pulsed inside him, swift and merciless. *She is mine,* he thought. *And she always will be.* He grabbed her and pressed his mouth to hers, hard and unyielding. She squirmed in his grasp, but he held fast, holding her body against him. His hands found her waist, pinning her hips to his. She thrashed and fought, but when his tongue entered her mouth, she went still. He tasted her, groaning with yearning at the rich, smooth feel of her lips and tongue. Gods, he'd missed this. He'd missed *her*. His memories of her scent, the feel of her, did not do her justice at all.

And then she was kissing him back, her mouth moving desperately over his, as if she couldn't taste him thoroughly enough. She wanted to devour him; he could feel it in her body, in her urgent movements. Her teeth caught his lip again, just as bruising as before, but this time it aroused him further, eliciting a low growl in his throat. Her fingers tangled in his hair, tugging and clawing at it as if she were a feral beast finally unleashed from its cage. When her hand brushed his horn, he groaned. Encouraged by his reaction, she clenched it firmly in her palm.

All his restraint snapped. His hands cupped her ass, and he hoisted her up so her legs wrapped around his middle. She ground against his arousal with a wicked gleam in her eyes, knowing exactly how she tormented him. He responded by trailing his lips down her neck and grazing his teeth along her throat. She shuddered, throwing her head back, beckoning for more. He bit down harder, and she cried out, the sound echoing in the vast chamber and driving him mad.

His mouth traveled lower, his tongue tracing circles around her collarbone and the swell of her breast. He hungrily shoved the fabric of her dress aside to devour her breast fully, his teeth capturing her nipple. A guttural moan ripped from her throat as she bucked against him. He staggered backward from the force of her thrusts until he fell onto his throne with her on top of him. The stone beneath him was cold to the touch, but it did nothing to stifle the molten heat coursing through him.

Prue straddled him atop the throne, hiking up her skirts to press herself flush against him. "I want all of you," she commanded, her eyes heady and bright with desire. She stroked the length of his cock, and even through the fabric of his trousers, he felt her skin against him like a white-hot branding iron.

Gods, he needed her. He needed her *now.*

She seemed to read the hunger in his eyes, because then her hands were on his belt, unfastening it with ease. His cock sprang free, and she writhed against it, teasing him, torturing him.

"Prue," he groaned, the sound pained.

"Tell me you're mine," she murmured. "Swear you'll be mine. That you'll fight this darkness and *be with me.*"

Gods above, he would swear anything to her in that moment. "I swear it," he vowed, meaning every word.

Because she was right. He hadn't been fighting. He hadn't tried hard enough.

She deserved better.

"I swear it, Prue," he said more fervently. "I am yours. Always. And I will fight to be with you."

Satisfaction gleamed in her gaze as she sank onto him, letting him fill her completely. Their moans mingled, bouncing off the walls. Cyrus lifted his hips, driving himself deep inside her. His hands found her ass again, and her heels dug into his back as they moved together. He drew back, only to thrust harder than before. Her hips moved in time with his, her body grinding and rocking. Her hands clasped his horns as she rode him, and he cried out her name.

The aching desire in him built more and more until he couldn't stand it. He leaned in and bit down on her breast again. She threw her head back and screamed with her release as Cyrus followed after, the tension uncoiling and cascading over him in waves of pleasure. His body shuddered as his cock spilled inside her, and she clung to him, gasping, her breaths in his ear.

He was hers. Utterly and completely hers. How could he have forgotten the claim she had on him?

For several moments, they sat there atop his throne, their bodies still joined, their heavy breathing echoing. Cyrus relished the silence in his mind, indicating Kronos had fully withdrawn. He didn't know why, but he was grateful for the brief respite. All around him, he sensed nothing but stillness and the rapid beating of Prue's heart pressed against his.

Pure bliss.

And yet... his time was limited. He had to warn her.

"Tartarus," he whispered.

"What?" she breathed, drawing back to look at him. Her eyes were dark with lust, as if she could take him all over again.

"Kronos possesses the power inside me," Cyrus said quickly, worrying that speaking his name would summon the dark presence again. "He fears Tartarus. I don't know if there's something in there or if he fears the prison itself, but that's the key to defeating him."

Confusion and fear flickered in her gaze. "And you don't know what it is?"

"Kronos was imprisoned well before I was born."

"Who would know more? Your father?"

Cyrus hesitated. The last thing he wanted to do was draw his father's attention to Prue, who happened to be Cyrus's greatest weakness.

But he'd made a vow to her to fight. And he had to keep that oath.

"Yes," he said. "Aidoneus would know more. But I don't know whose side he's on. It's possible he wants Kronos to succeed. After all, he was willing to destroy this realm in his quest for revenge against me."

Prue's mouth thinned, but determination blazed in her eyes. "I'll find a way. Whatever it takes, I'll free you from this." She brought her hand to his face, her fingers trailing along his jaw. The touch was so feather-light compared to their violent lovemaking, but it sent shivers of pleasure up and down his body just the same.

Cyrus leaned in and kissed her hard, his mouth claiming hers thoroughly. She responded in kind, her tongue twining with his and her body rubbing against him. Cyrus cupped the back of her neck, bringing her mouth closer so he could fully ravish her. He felt himself grow hard inside her once more, his desire mounting. He *could* take her right here all over again.

And perhaps she wanted it, too.

But footsteps echoed somewhere within the palace, and Cyrus knew their precious moments of solitude were coming to an end. Prue slid off him and adjusted her dress, which was moist in certain places, eliciting a smirk from Cyrus. She only sent him a coy smile in response.

"If he takes over again," Cyrus said, sobering at the

thought of parting from her, "you know how to bring me back."

"Yes, I do," she said, her eyes burning with a heat that made his stomach clench. "All I need to do is make you beg."

TRACKING
EVANDER

BEFORE MONA'S RESURRECTION

EVANDER COULD ONLY STARE IN STUNNED SILENCE at Mona, keeping his eyes firmly fixed on her face instead of wandering along her naked body. Shame and mortification filled her features, her cheeks flushed and her hair a tangled mess.

Gods, she was utterly beautiful. He had never seen the particular shade of her eyes because of her transparent spirit form.

They were pale emerald. So breathtaking.

But Evander couldn't even appreciate it. His chest burned, his stomach knotting. He could hardly breathe,

the regret and embarrassment were so stark inside him. What had he *done* to her?

"Mona, I—we—did we—" He gestured between the two of them, his face on fire.

Mona dropped her gaze and bit her lip. "We—we almost did. But we never actually... finished." A blush formed across her cheeks.

"Did I... did *he* hurt you?" Evander asked in a low voice.

"No, no, I'm fine." Mona's brow furrowed. "He who? It was *you*, Evander."

Evander shook his head, a growl of frustration escaping his throat. There was so much she didn't know. So much he now had to tell her because he couldn't leash this damn beast growing inside him. "Mona—"

When he turned to her, her form flickered, becoming transparent once more. Evander stiffened. "Shit," he hissed, just before Mona disappeared entirely.

His hand flew up instinctively, as if he could stop her from vanishing. But he knew it was fruitless.

Whatever unusual magic had granted her access to her body had now left her.

But where did that leave her spirit?

Urgency flooded Evander's chest. He *had* to find her. After what had transpired between them, her emotions, her entire soul, would be in a fragile state.

What if something happened to her? All because of Evander's damn curse...

Within seconds, Evander had thrown on his trouseres and tore through the forest, tracing the path back to the river. He thought—hoped—Mona's spirit would have returned to the same spot hovering above the waters, but she wasn't there.

"Mona?" Evander called, knowing it was useless. If she were here, he'd be able to see her. *Sense* her.

He hurried downstream, his steps quick and lithe as he scanned the river's depths, wondering if her soul had finally transitioned.

The thought left him feeling desperately empty inside. He wasn't ready to lose her. Not yet.

He told himself it was only because he wanted to explain things to her, to thoroughly apologize for what happened. But, in truth, it went deeper than that. He cared for her. Probably more than he should.

"Mona!" His voice rang in the forest, louder than he'd ever shouted in his life.

When the forest thinned and he found himself approaching the caves of Styx, he faltered. Would her soul have ended up in a different domain? Was she trapped somewhere else now? Tartarus, even?

Fresh panic bloomed inside him. No, it couldn't be. She was bound to his river. To *him.*

He turned and raced back up the riverbank, retracing

his steps. He would scour his entire river if he had to. She *had* to be here somewhere.

Unless... the mortal realm had pulled her again.

Evander's steps faltered. It wouldn't have been the first time she'd hopped between realms. Was that what had happened? Was Evander overreacting?

No, he could sense it. Deep within himself, his entire *being* roiled with chaos, warning him that something was wrong. He'd known the instant he'd met Mona that she was different, that whatever had unbound her was potentially dangerous.

And now that he knew Vasileios was involved, he was even more on guard.

Did Vasileios have her? Did he find out where her spirit was?

Evander stopped to catch his breath and ran his hands through his hair with a frustrated groan. He'd never felt like this before. Desperate. Helpless. Willing to do *anything* to solve a problem.

Even...

No. He shut that thought down. That beast was the reason he was in this predicament in the first place.

And yet... the creature could scent Mona. It was part animal. And it *knew* her. Was protective of her.

Evander gritted his teeth so hard his temples throbbed. Gods, was he really considering this?

But if Mona was in trouble...

Evander swore, gripping fistfuls of his hair in his hands. Dammit, *dammit.* With a deep breath, Evander growled, "Typhon, are you there? I need your help."

Silence met his words, and he swore again. Then, finally, a voice within him rumbled, "You despise me. And you wish for my help?"

Evander's eyes closed. Typhon had a point. "It's Mona. I need you to find her."

Rage and urgency burned in his chest, and he knew it was Typhon's response. He cared for Mona, too. Evander tried not to think about how much that bothered him.

"Let me take over," Typhon said. "I will find her."

Evander's jaw ticked back and forth. This was his last chance to refuse. All his rational thoughts told him this was a terrible idea.

But when it came to Mona, he wasn't thinking rationally.

"Fine," he said. "My body is yours."

Triumph soared through him as Typhon took full control. Evander felt his body shifting, making room for his wings and horns and claws as he transitioned fully to the beast he loathed.

UNHINGED
MONA

Before Mona's Resurrection

Still rattled by her encounter with Evander, Mona had trouble getting her bearings. She was back on the beach in Krenia, Prue standing next to her as if she'd been waiting for her.

"I'm close now," Prue said. "I just have to wait for Samhain."

Dazed, Mona could only blink at Prue. She vaguely registered that she was in ghost form once more, her transparent body clothed in the same dress she'd worn on the day she died.

Well, at least I'm not naked, she thought.

"To bring you back," Prue clarified, her tone patient. Much more patient than she'd ever been when Mona had been alive.

But so much had changed.

"How long?" Mona asked quietly.

"Samhain is a month from now."

Goddess above, only a month? Time must pass differently in the mortal realm. In the Underworld, it only felt like days.

"I'll need a distraction for the coven, though," Prue said, her gaze growing distant with thought. Planning ahead wasn't her strong suit.

Mona thought carefully. "I can help with that." During the Samhain ceremony, the veil between realms was temporarily removed. She had managed to travel between realms at will before. She could do it again, especially if her soul was still tethered to the mortal realm. And with the magical energies so potent on that hallowed day, Mona was certain she would be able to sense when it was time. The realm would call to her, and with a bit of practice, she could return.

If she could manage it, her presence alone would buy Prue some time. Mona would be a diversion for the coven—particularly her mother.

Her chest tightened with grief at the thought of Polina and the pain she must be in. Mona hated the idea of tormenting their mother even more.

But if it meant Mona could come back, it would be worth it. Polina would see that in the end.

Come back. Was this truly going to happen? Was Mona going to return to her mortal life? And leave the Underworld forever?

Leave *Evander* forever?

No. She shoved that thought away. Evander might have intrigued her, but he was only supposed to guide her passage. Their alliance was temporary.

That was how it was always meant to be. He was a shepherd for her soul. Nothing more.

"This is going to happen, Mona," Prue said, her eyes shining with hope. "Are you ready?"

Mona nodded, even though she wasn't. Her eyes felt warm, as if she might cry, but she knew she wouldn't. Not in this form. "I'm ready to be with you again. I miss you so much."

Tears streamed down Prue's face, and her arms twitched as if she wanted to embrace Mona. But, of course, she couldn't.

And the thought was so heartbreaking that it made Mona want to weep along with her.

A faint dizziness spread through Mona's mind, clouding her thoughts. "I'm fading," she whispered.

"No, Mona, *stay,*" Prue pleaded.

"I can't. But I *will* come back on Samhain, Prue. I swear it."

Prue pressed her lips together and nodded, more tears streaming down her face.

Mona blinked, and Prue was gone. And yet... the beach hadn't changed. Mona was still in Krenia, and—

"Oh, no," she whispered, raising her arm to see real and solid flesh before her. She was between worlds.

She turned in time to see Vasileios grinning at her, his hands in his pockets as he strode closer.

Mona backed up a step. "Stay away from me."

"Why so afraid? I'm trying to *help* the Underworld. It's dying. Did you know that?"

Mona stilled, unsure if she should trust his words.

"Together, you and I can restore it to its former glory," Vasileios went on. "We can *heal* it, Mona. Just come and find me. And I'll take care of everything."

"No. *No*." Mona shut her eyes, willing herself to disappear from this place. "Take me back. *Take me back*!"

"Mona," Vasileios warned in a growl.

Her voice was a scream as she roared, *"Take me back now!"*

And then, in a flash of light, Mona was in the Underworld once more, surrounded by trees and the sounds of rushing water. A startled laugh escaped her. It had *worked*! She had traveled between realms at will. Could she do it again? Could she return to Prue in time for Samhain?

Mona's smile slowly faded as she realized this area looked different from what she remembered of the Underworld. The trees were more sickly and gray, the grass less vibrant. The churning waters were slower and murkier than she was accustomed to. Even the air seemed tainted with some kind of plague.

The Underworld is dying, Vasileios had said. Was he right? Was this realm in danger?

In the distance, she could make out the pointed twin pine trees she recognized from Evander's domain. But they were much farther away, perhaps a mile or two from where she stood.

Why had she appeared *here*? Why hadn't she returned to Cocytus, where her soul belonged? A shudder rippled over her at the intense feeling of *wrongness* that surrounded her.

Whatever magic lived here was dark and unnatural. And Mona didn't want to be near it.

But she couldn't move. She was a spirit once more, frozen above this river. Frustration boiled inside her, an echo of the impassioned feelings she'd experienced when she'd temporarily had her body again. Everything was hollow. Distant. Goddess, she missed that *feeling*. It was intoxicating. Enthralling.

And to be with Evander like that...

She didn't want to think of him because it made her confused and chaotic. But she couldn't deny the things she'd felt around him, even if neither of them had been themselves. Evander had certainly been different, and Mona, overcome with the emotions and sensations from her new body, had easily succumbed to those arousing feelings.

And yet... she found she didn't regret it at all. She had never felt more alive than in that moment, pressed up against the tree with Evander's naked body wrapped around hers.

Never in her mortal life had she felt so alive.

The thought made her feel a mixture of excitement and devastation. Had her human life been so unfulfilling that her life as a spirit was more captivating? What had she even wasted her life doing? Reading books and romping through the forest with Prue?

No. She would *never* regret her time with Prue.

But even her sister had found passion and life. She'd sought relationships and adventures... while Mona had not, keeping herself locked away with her books and her solitude.

And now she was dead. Her life had passed her by.

"Mona!" a voice cried, jolting her from her self-pity.

Mona looked around, her heart lifting at the sight of Evander hurrying toward her. He wore nothing but his trousers, his bare and muscular chest on full display. His wings were spread, his claws out, and two small horns rested atop his head.

Just like when they'd almost taken each other in the woods.

The reminder made her insides turn molten.

"Thank the gods," Evander breathed when he reached her, his silver eyes wide with panic. His gaze roved the area, his nostrils flaring. "What—what are you doing here?"

"I don't know," Mona admitted. She couldn't meet his eyes. "I just... appeared here. After I visited my sister." She decided not to tell him about her visit with Vasileios. Not yet. It had been so brief, and Evander seemed panicked enough already.

Relief crossed Evander's face, and she knew she'd done the right thing, omitting the truth.

Mona's eyes fell on the withering trees surrounding the gray waters. "What is this place?"

"We're on the edge of the Undead Wilds," Evander said. "It's a... dying wood. No one often travels here."

A dying wood? "But the river—"

"This is Acheron," Evander supplied. "It's connected to my river, but the waters here are different."

Mona shook her head. "No, Evander, something is *wrong* with these waters. Can't you feel it?"

Evander stilled, his brow furrowing. His gaze traveled to the waters, and he bent on one knee to inspect it. "Yes," he said slowly. "It is a soft echo of what I feel in Cocytus. I thought that was because this isn't my domain." His jaw went rigid. "But yes, something is very wrong here." He stood and looked at her with renewed urgency. "I need to get you out of here. I'm not supposed to be here, and if my brothers find out…"

"I can't *move*," Mona said, frustrated.

"You can," Evander said. "Sing with me, Mona. Please."

The invitation in his voice made her body heat all over again. Goddess, he still looked magnificent with his wings and horns. And whatever he thought he became when he was this creature, he was still Evander.

Her Evander.

She felt suddenly ashamed and nervous, worried her voice wouldn't be as smooth as before. That what they'd shared earlier was an anomaly that couldn't be repeated. Mona wasn't a singer, after all. She joined in with the coven songs occasionally, but her voice wasn't anything to be admired.

And after what had happened between her and Evander, how could she find the courage to do this with him again? To expose this raw part of herself? Before, she had just been a soul, and he had just been a guardian. But now? They were something *else* to each other. And Mona barely had the strength to speak to him, let alone do anything else.

"Please, Mona," Evander repeated, his expression

tense with desperation. "I don't like whatever darkness is creeping into these waters. I fear it might harm you."

The concern in his voice melted away a portion of her anxiety. She took a deep breath and nodded slowly. "You go first. I—I don't know if I remember the melody."

This was a lie. The tune had stuck with her so permanently she knew she would remember it for years. But her insides were too frozen and stiff to respond immediately. If Evander started, perhaps she could find her courage.

You are not a coward, Prue had once told her.

Oh, but I am, Mona thought sadly. *I'm such a coward that I can't even sing in front of this beautiful man.*

Evander opened his mouth, and the sweet, sad melody poured from his lips, embracing Mona with all its potent grief and longing. She closed her eyes, swept away in the sound of it, the tension in her chest loosening from the thrill of the song. In seconds, she joined in, her voice echoing along with his. He found a harmony to compliment her melody, the strands of music flowing up and down, twining and twisting within one another.

Just as our bodies did in the woods, Mona thought, the image of them pressed against each other rising unbidden in her mind.

Her voice stuttered and faltered as she lost her grip

on the melody for the briefest of moments. Then, something solid and warm gripped her fingers, giving her strength. She focused on that warmth, bringing her voice back to the song. The heat of Evander's touch spread through her fingers, up to her wrist and forearm, and then all the way to her shoulder. And still, she kept singing with him. His voice drew nearer, but she kept her eyes shut tight, worried if she looked at him, he would unravel her completely.

The song continued for what felt like hours, but Mona's voice never grew tired. The haunting melody seemed to fuel her, feeding her strength with every note she sang. The energy coursing and swelling through her was so similar to her own magic that Mona found herself aching for it, yearning for her earth magic.

Mona wasn't sure how much time had passed—days, perhaps? It felt like an eternity, but she couldn't bring herself to stop. Finally, at long last, she felt something yank her forward. Her feet splashed into the water, and she fell against Evander's hard chest with a grunt.

Her eyes snapped open, and she looked up at him with wide eyes. His arms came around her easily, pressing her body to his, his gaze soft as he looked down at her.

Behind him, wide and magnificent, were his dark red leathery wings. They had been out earlier, but Mona hadn't realized how *long* they were when completely stretched out like this. Evander's wingspan seemed longer than his entire body—perhaps even twice as long.

Goddess above, he was breathtaking. Dark power emanated from him in rippling waves, making her skin tingle and her blood sing. She found herself leaning closer to him, drawn in by the sheer force of the energy pulsing through him. She wanted to feel his skin against hers, to drink in the power quivering from him.

What the hell is the matter with me? Mona wanted to smack herself. It must've been the shock and over-whelming thrill of being in her body once more. Before, she had nearly taken Evander inside her, right there in the woods. Now, she felt a tingling awareness every-where he touched her, her skin buzzing with life.

She wanted him. She couldn't deny it. Perhaps it was a temporary lust that would fade eventually, but right here and now, she wanted to rip his clothes from him and discover what it would be like to have the full weight of his cock inside her.

She imagined it would be the most exhilarating and intoxicating feeling in the world. And she had never wanted anything more in her life.

"Mona," Evander said, his voice a soft groan. Desire ignited in his gaze, and his wings flared slightly.

Mona's lips parted, her mouth turning dry. His power, brutal and magnificent, would be her undoing.

But she didn't care. She *wanted* to come undone. She *wanted* him to do this to her.

"We—we need to leave," he said, his voice low and husky. But he didn't move. His arms still trapped her against him, his face a mere breath away from hers. And Goddess, his scent... Pine and freshwater and that musky man scent that made Mona's skin heat.

"Yes," Mona whispered, though she made no move to leave, either.

A scream pierced the air, jolting Mona from the hazy fog of her mind. She jerked, glancing around wildly for the source.

Evander's face drained of color. "That came from farther up the river. In Acheron. Whatever is happening to these waters, it's hurting the souls." Urgency and clarity burned in his gaze. "Mona. Come with me *now*. We have to get back to Cocytus." He withdrew from her, and Mona suppressed a shiver at the sudden coldness from his absence. Instead, Evander extended his hand to her, and Mona laced her fingers with his, relishing the small, subtle touch. Not nearly as thrilling as being pressed flush against his chest, but her skin still hummed from the contact.

Evander met her gaze and nodded encouragingly. Then, he led her out of the water and downhill, away from the howling screams echoing behind them.

TRUTH
EVANDER

BEFORE MONA'S RESURRECTION

EVANDER HAD NEVER FELT SO AFRAID IN HIS mortal life. It took him several moments to notice the strange and yet familiar weight of Typhon's wings behind him.

How was Typhon unleashed right now? Evander felt completely in control of his body. Typhon's usually infuriating voice was oddly silent in his mind.

How was this possible? Evander had never shared consciousness like this before. It was always either fully Evander or fully Typhon in control. Never both.

"Are we almost there?" Mona panted beside him, her

palm sweating alongside his. "Sorry... Not used to... being on solid legs."

Evander cast a quick glance at their surroundings. The trees had grown thicker and leafier, widening to the expansive forest just outside of Cocytus. Evander released a heavy breath, grateful they'd escaped the Undead Wilds. Perhaps some darkness had seeped out of the wilds, leaking into Acheron? He would have to check with Cyrus to find out.

"Yes," Evander said, slowing his quick pace. "We are in my domain now. We can rest."

Mona nodded gratefully, still gasping for breath, as she sank onto the ground, stretching out her legs and leaning back to rest her elbows on the grass. She wore the same green dress, which had been mended somehow, as if this realm replaced the outfit every time she took her mortal form. Regardless, it was identical—from the shade of emerald to the silky smoothness of the fabric—to the dress she'd worn before, when she and Evander had almost...

Evander's face heated at the memory. Gods, what had he been thinking? He was mortified, and he owed her an apology.

"Mona," he began, striding toward her.

She shut her eyes and shook her head, a thin sheen of sweat coating her forehead and neck. "Goddess, this body... *feels* everything... so intensely." She pressed her palm to her forehead and breathed deeply.

A sinking sensation settled in Evander's chest. Had their moment of passion simply been a result of her new body?

Then again, how could he blame her? *His* actions had been a direct result of Typhon.

And yet... he had felt *everything*. He had been present for the entire incident, and he remembered it acutely. The heat of her skin against his, the caress of her tongue, the peaked tips of her nipples... He could recall it all with perfect clarity, as if he'd been the one doing those things. And not Typhon.

Gods, he couldn't make sense of this at all. What was happening? Something about his link with Typhon was... *off*. It wasn't functioning the way it was supposed to. The magic binding them together indicated Typhon would emerge only from dusk until dawn.

But lately, he was emerging a lot more frequently. Ever since Mona had arrived.

Evander cleared his throat. "Are you all right?"

Finally catching her breath, Mona nodded and looked up at him with a grateful and slightly embarrassed smile. "Yes. Sorry. I feel... oddly disconnected from myself right now."

"You are newly reunited with your body," Evander

said, extending a hand to help her to her feet. "It's understandable."

Mona took his hand, and he hoisted her up. She gasped as she rose to stand right in front of him, their noses practically brushing. She inhaled sharply, her eyes closing for a moment, before she drew back a step.

"Do you know why?" she asked, her voice a bit strained.

Evander licked his lips, his mouth suddenly dry. "Why what?"

"Why I have my body back? Did you do something to fix it?"

Regret and anger flared in Evander's chest. "No. I wish I had, but no." He quickly explained what he'd learned about Vasileios.

The color drained from Mona's face. "Your—your older brother... has *claimed* my body? What does that mean?"

"A union between a prince of Hell and a powerful witch would grant him a significant amount of magic," Evander said, his tone laced with bitterness. "But if he doesn't have your soul along with it, I'm not sure what he can do."

"So—so why do I have my body *now*?" Mona gestured to herself in bewilderment. "If he's claimed my body, I shouldn't have access to it, right?"

"He's putting some kind of plan in motion," Evander

said, rubbing his chin in thought. "My guess is, he doesn't need you to play your part yet. And whatever magic we've been working together has managed to free you. Temporarily. But as soon as he needs you, I'd wager you would return to your spirit form once more."

Mona took a trembling breath. "Magic? You and I have been using magic?"

"Haven't you felt it? In the song?"

Mona nodded, her expression dazed. "I have. I thought it was an echo of my former magic, though, reminding me of what I'd lost."

Something snapped into place in Evander's mind. Typhon. *Of course.* All this extensive use of magic must have triggered the change earlier than normal. That was why Evander's connection with the creature was so unusual as of late.

"Evander," Mona said, not meeting his gaze. "About what happened before... in the woods..."

"No, you don't need to explain," Evander said quickly, drawing closer to her. "My behavior was appalling and inappropriate. I... wasn't myself."

"But that's just it." Mona drew closer, too, taking his hands in hers. Her skin was warm and soft, and he relished the feel of it. "It *was* you. You were different, but I could still feel you there. You smelled the same. And I saw that awareness in your eyes."

Evander frowned. "Mona, that *wasn't* me." And yet,

he could remember that moment... as if he *had* been there. Suddenly, he wasn't so sure what was real and what wasn't.

"Tell me," Mona pleaded, her eyes traveling to the wings behind his back. Evander waited for disgust or horror to cross her features, but there was nothing but awe in her eyes. "Tell me what happened to you."

Evander sighed heavily. He didn't want to unearth his dark past to her, to have her opinion of him tainted by this secret. But he owed her an explanation. He'd dragged her into this, and now he needed to help her understand it fully.

This was his own damn fault. Now, it was time to clean up his mess.

"As gods, we have our own particular brand of magic," Evander began, pacing in front of Mona so he could avoid looking at her. "But here in the Underworld, it's tainted. Cursed. It's called death magic, and it's much more volatile than the purity of the other gods' magic. It has a mind of its own, and it's *alive*." He shuddered at the memories.

"I've seen what it's done to my brothers," he went on. "It's corrupted their souls. Changed them." He paused for a moment, thinking of Cyrus, the only brother who had been kind to him... until he'd let his magic take over completely.

"Eons ago, when I first ventured to the mortal

realm," he said, "I came across a powerful witch who offered to bind up my death magic so I could be free from it forever. I readily agreed, but I should have been more cautious. I should have known it wouldn't be so easy." He ran a hand through his hair, his breathing uneven. "She *did* bind up my magic, but it became something else. A creature that was a part of me. Something I had to surrender to.

"He's called Typhon. He is the solid manifestation of my magic. I give my body to him every sunset, and he returns it to me every sunrise. But... ever since I met you, that's changed." Evander shook his head, frustrated. "And I can't figure out why. Whatever strange magic has hold of you, it calls to Typhon, beckoning him forward. Neither of us can control it."

He took a shuddering breath and finally turned to face Mona. Her eyes glinted with tears as she stared at him, her expression transfixed and full of concern and affection. Everything about her face was gentle and soft. No horror. No disgust. No hatred.

Gods, did this woman possess an unkind bone in her body? She was too *good*.

And Evander didn't deserve her. He never would.

"The enchantment is bound to this stone." He lifted the moonstone resting on his collarbone. "If I remove it, the spell will be undone, and the death magic will take over my body completely. But for now, we are separated. Two entities. Me... and Typhon."

He approached her slowly, to give her time to withdraw from him. To recoil. But she didn't. He took her hands in his, and she clung to him as if she wanted nothing more than to touch him. The thought sent a coil of warmth through Evander's chest, followed quickly by self-loathing.

I'm not good for her. No matter how much either of us wants this, it can never be.

He closed his eyes before the anguish overtook him. "Mona." He cleared his throat and continued, "Whatever magic my brother Vasileios is dabbling in, it's too strong for me to penetrate. Even with Typhon's help, I worry that meddling in his spell will unleash all manner of horrors in this realm and destroy everything in its path. This is more complex magic than I've ever seen. And... I fear what this means for *you*. Vasileios has bound your body to him in some way. The river Acheron is sick, and I can't fix it. This is all beyond me now. I don't think I have the power to keep you here, like this..." His fingers trailed up her forearms, memorizing the feel of her soft skin against him, the solid form of her here in front of him, her scent of roses and saltwater.

"Evander," she murmured, and gods, the way his name fell off her lips nearly undid him right then and there.

A soft groan built up his throat, and he leaned in and rested his forehead against hers. "I wish I could keep you here with me," he whispered. "But you must do whatever you can to escape Vasileios. What he's doing, it... it could tear your soul apart forever." He drew back, his throat tightening with remorse. "The only thing I can think of to keep you safe is... to send you back to the mortal realm."

Mona stiffened, her eyes widening. "What?"

"I've heard whispers of resurrection spells," Evander went on, his words coming in a rush. "It *is* possible to be brought back from the dead, Mona. And with your frequent visits to your sister, she can help you do this."

Mona's face paled, and she pressed her lips together, her gaze dropping. "I, uh, have already talked to my sister about this. I've given her instructions on what to do just in case... just in case..." She didn't finish.

A heavy stone sank in Evander's stomach, though he wasn't sure why he felt so disappointed. *Of course* she had a backup plan. Could he really blame her? Right now, Evander was the only thing grounding her here, in this body. He wasn't strong enough to do this on his own. He knew that, and apparently, she knew it, too.

He couldn't fight Vasileios for her. He was too weak. The thought made him feel hollow and empty inside.

But perhaps she *wanted* to part from him. Maybe she didn't long to be here with him. Not like he did.

"Good." He wasn't sure why his voice was so strained. "That's good."

"Evander," she said again, drawing closer until their chests were flush against each other. He could feel her heat pressing into him, beckoning him closer. Behind him, his wings shuddered from the violent thrill of yearning coursing through him. She lifted a hand and pressed it against his cheek, her warmth thawing some of the chill swelling inside him. "All I want is to remain here with you. To finish what we started in the woods."

Evander's eyes snapped to hers. A bolt of scorching heat seared through him, fierce and merciless, and he had to physically restrain himself from shoving her up against a tree and taking her right here and now.

Mona's own cheeks flamed as if she couldn't quite believe she'd been bold enough to say that. "But I've known something was wrong since the moment I arrived here. That's why I was making plans with my sister. Not because I don't want to be with you, but because, like you, I fear what is happening here. What might happen to my soul if we fail." She leaned in, pressing her lips against the base of his throat. A riot of desire burned through Evander, and he had to clench his fists before the beast took over and did something he regretted.

But *would* he regret it? Evander wasn't so sure anymore.

"Come with me," Mona whispered, her breath tickling his neck.

Evander blinked, stunned. "With you? To—to the mortal realm?"

Mona drew back and nodded, gazing up at him with longing in her eyes. "You said you've been to the mortal realm before. You can come with me. Be with me there, where it's safe for you. Whatever is happening here, Evander, it makes me worry for you." She took his hands in hers and squeezed. "Please. Come with me." Her eyes turned pleading, and it nearly split Evander's chest in two.

He couldn't hold back any longer. He cupped her face in his hands and brought his mouth to hers. She leaned into him eagerly, as if she'd been waiting for him to kiss her. Her lips were smooth and soft and sweet. His mouth claimed her again and again, coaxing her tongue out as their kisses went from gentle to demanding. She moaned against him, her hips meeting his. His hands found her waist, snaring her against him until their bodies were fit perfectly together, her curves meeting his muscles. His wings expanded to cocoon them in a shade of privacy as his mouth trailed down her jaw and to her neck, his tongue flicking against the hollow of her throat.

"Goddess," she cried out, her fingernails digging into his shoulders.

A low growl rumbled from his lips, and the beast inside him yearned to coax even more desperate sounds from her.

In that moment, Evander knew he and Typhon were one. Typhon may have been a manifestation of his magic, but it was still a part of Evander. A part he longed to keep hidden, to keep shut away from the world.

But Mona, she drew him out. She unleashed the feral side of him he pretended didn't exist.

Because Typhon yearned for her, just as Evander did. Because they were one and the same. Two sides of the same coin. Wild and tame. Beast and man.

Evander's mouth met hers again, his tongue sliding between her lips. Her teeth scraped against his lip, and he growled again.

He knew if they continued like this, they wouldn't stop. They *would* finish what they'd started before. This was so much more than a goodbye kiss. It was an admission of what they both tried not to feel; what they both could no longer ignore.

The desire burning between them became an intoxicating, tangible thing, growing more insistent and irresistible. Evander couldn't hold back much longer, and as she writhed against him, rubbing directly against his arousal, he nearly shouted from the dizzying torture of it all.

A piercing scream echoed in the forest, ringing in

Evander's ears. He and Mona froze, springing apart in alarm as they both looked around for the source. Mona's cheeks were pink, her eyes dark with lust and her mouth swollen from their passionate kisses. But as awareness crept into her gaze, her form started to flicker.

Whatever had been keeping her body here was fading.

"More tormented souls?" Mona asked breathlessly.

Wordlessly, Evander nodded. The scream hadn't come from his river—he would have sensed it—but it did feel closer. Was the darkness of this realm spreading? How long before it reached Cocytus?

"I can't come with you, Mona," Evander said. The words caused him physical pain, wrenching from his throat. "My dark magic—Typhon—will not allow me to survive in other realms. The witch who cast the spell ensured I could never return to the mortal realm. The power of the enchantment was born of the Underworld and will destroy me if I leave." He closed his eyes, agony consuming him. Gods, what he wouldn't give to be able to leave with her, right here, right now.

"Go," he pleaded, stepping away to resist the urge to grab her and keep her here forever. "Reunite with your sister."

"Evander," she sobbed, her body no longer corporeal but a transparent spirit once more.

"You can reach me," he promised. "I am your soul's

guardian. Summon me with one of your spells, and I will be there. I swear it, Mona. We *will* see each other again."

"Embrace it, Evander," she said, her voice growing distant. "Typhon is a part of you. He *is* you."

Emotion tightened in his throat. Though he had come to the same realization, it still felt too *real* hearing her say it. Even as she disappeared, he croaked, "I know."

And then she was gone.

QUEEN
PRUE

PRUE SAT ATOP THE THRONE, WEARING A VIBRANT crimson gown nearly as revealing as the violet one she'd worn before. She had learned in her short time in the Underworld that the standards of this realm were far more lax than in the Realm of Gaia. Apparently, other demons often wore just as scandalous outfits without batting an eye.

She still felt naked wearing it, though. The silk fabric clung to her like a second skin, revealing all her curves.

Her insides quivered with unease, her gaze often darting to the throne room doors, afraid Cyrus would burst in and unleash Kronos's fury at the sight of her on the throne.

But he didn't.

Her cheeks heated as she remembered the last time

she'd been in this room—straddling Cyrus as they took each other with a raw, feral desire that consumed them both.

Now, it was completely different. The throne room was full of subjects, and Lagos stood alongside the throne. Prue wanted to fidget, to wring her hands together or shift her weight, but she forced herself to remain still.

The doors opened, and Prue stiffened, alarm racing through her. Trivia led a crowd of several armed demons. Behind them was a chained creature Prue had seen once before: on the day of Mona's death. It had emerged from the Book of Eyes, unleashing its death shadows on Prue's village. To stop the carnage, Mona had given her life to seal the Book of Eyes once more.

The creature had the face of a boar with tusks protruding from his snout. Two ram horns were atop his head, and his entire body was naked, the skin rough and coarse and bumpy like the hide of an alligator.

Screams filled Prue's mind as the memories of that day in Krenia threatened to consume her. To jerk her free from the trauma, she rose to her feet, the motion jolting her and awakening her senses. "Is this the wraith?" Her voice boomed in the throne room.

"It is, my queen," Trivia said, bowing deeply, a smirk forming on her face. Prue knew the goddess was teasing her with the elaborate bow, but she said nothing, knowing the subjects before her might not recognize it as sarcasm.

"Bring him forward," Prue commanded.

The armed demons shoved the chained wraith forward. His long tail slid along the marble floor, the chains clinking as he moved forward.

Prue lifted her chin, glaring down at the creature. "Why are you terrorizing Erebos?"

The creature emitted soft grunting noises. After a moment, Prue realized it was laughter. Seething, Prue gritted her teeth and gestured to the closest armed demon. "Stab him, please."

What she wouldn't give for her own magic. She would unleash hell on this foul beast.

The demon obliged, jerking his spear forward until it pierced the creature's side. The laughing stopped, and a feral howl echoed in the chamber.

"Answer the question," Prue snapped.

The throne room was deadly quiet, everyone holding their breath in anticipation of the wraith's response.

At long last, in a gruff voice, the creature said, "It is not just Erebos I will consume... but this entire realm."

"Why?" Prue bit out. "You serve the crown. You serve the Underworld. Why would you turn on your own kind?"

"I only serve *him*," the wraith growled. "My master. The father of my death shadow."

A chill snaked over Prue's skin. Somehow, she sensed what his next words would be just before he uttered them.

"I serve Kronos."

Long after the wraith had been hauled off to Tartarus, Prue was still shaken from the entire ordeal. She had to redirect her mind often, trying not to dwell on that awful day in Krenia, but the memories kept flooding her thoughts.

She couldn't stop, though. There was still work to be done. This evening she had the blood bargain ceremony where she would officially induct Lagos as a member of her court.

Trivia had taken it upon herself to be Prue's lady's maid, at least until her official coronation. Prue didn't object; for now, she only wanted to surround herself with those she could trust. And despite her reservations about Trivia's motives, the goddess had proven herself helpful.

Trivia helped Prue into a gleaming silver gown that shimmered with each movement. The fabric itself was sheer and magnificent and reminded Prue of starlight.

"Be careful," Trivia murmured after she finished

twisting Prue's hair into an elegant knot. "Blood bargains are serious and very binding. If there's anything in the agreement you don't consent to, *don't* go through with it."

"I know." Prue had learned her lesson with Cyrus in the mortal realm. He would've slit her throat immediately if she hadn't forced him to swear in his blood he wouldn't harm her. She found herself smiling as she remembered how much they had loathed one another.

Thank the Goddess we didn't kill each other, she thought, *or we never would've fallen in love.*

A hollow sadness filled her chest as she thought of her husband and how much she missed him. She yearned to track him down, even if just for another quick dalliance atop his throne.

But she had to give him space. He promised he'd fight for her, and she believed him. Seducing him had broken the enchantment once before, but Prue had a feeling Kronos would only let her get away with it so many times. She had to save the strategy for when she truly needed it. Or for when Cyrus truly needed her.

"You seem lost in thought," Trivia observed.

"Just nervous," Prue said, her hand immediately going to the pomegranate necklace around her throat. Trivia eyed the necklace, something dark stirring in her gaze.

This wasn't the first time she'd looked at the necklace like that—as if she *knew* what power it held.

"Do you like it?" Prue asked, holding it up for her to see.

Trivia's expression went taut, her eyes flashing before she schooled her features into something neutral. "It's a bit plain for my taste." She dropped her gaze, smoothing her palms along her skirts.

Prue pressed her lips together. *Interesting.* Trivia was pretending to dislike the piece of jewelry, but Prue knew better. She would just have to work harder to get the truth out of the goddess.

Rising to her feet, Prue adjusted her dress, ensuring one of her breasts wasn't exposed, before facing Trivia. "Do I look queenly enough?"

Trivia looked her over before smiling deviously. "You look perfectly regal."

Prue nodded, steeling herself as Trivia led her from the chambers and into the hallway. The corridor was completely empty, and Prue distracted herself from her anxiety by scrutinizing the intricate carvings on the vases lining the walls.

You can do this, she told herself. *You are the queen.*

And yet... she felt like an imposter. Someone assuming the role of ruler when she didn't deserve or earn it. She had *tricked* Cyrus into marrying her. It didn't seem fair that now she shared the throne of his domain.

You're all this realm has left, she thought. *With Kronos in control of Cyrus, these people need you to protect them.*

The thought sobered her, melting away her fears, and she lifted her chin as Trivia led her down the grand staircase and toward the throne room.

A crowd of demons stood before the throne, which was empty. Prue's heart sank. A small part of her had been hoping Cyrus would be present, though she knew that would've been disastrous. What if Kronos had been in control?

No, it was better that Prue represented them both at this ceremony.

In front of the throne, on bended knee, was Lagos. He wore an immaculate suit, and Prue had to admit it made him look quite handsome. Even the bull's face did not taint his elegant persona. His head was bowed as if in reverence. In some ways, he seemed more suited for the throne than Prue did. He looked like he *belonged* here.

Stay calm, Prue thought. *You can do this.*

She took a steadying breath, her steps echoing in the vast chamber. She sent a silent prayer of thanks to the Goddess that Trivia had found flat slippers for her to wear instead of those high-heeled death traps she'd worn before. Prue was accustomed to running around Krenia barefoot, so the more complex shoes would surely make her trip.

Trivia peeled away from her and vanished in the crowd. At Prue's entrance, the crowd hushed and immediately parted to form an aisle toward the throne. Prue kept her hands at her sides, willing herself not to tremble. Instead, she reminded herself she was the Maiden of the coven of Krenia. She had played a role of authority before.

She could do it again.

Summoning that same courage and confidence, Prue stepped firmly down the aisle, her head held high as she met the curious gazes of the demons closest to her. Several bowed their heads to her in respect, but most of them looked at her with wary hostility.

This transition certainly won't be easy, Prue thought.

When she reached the throne, she turned and sat on the edge of it, her back straight and her chin still lifted. Her mouth felt completely dry, and she knew she should speak. But she had no idea what to say.

A resonant clapping sounded from the back of the crowd. Prue stiffened and found Trivia applauding her wildly. Gradually, several other demons joined in, offering polite applause for Prue's entrance.

Trivia's show of encouragement bolstered Prue's confidence once more. She took a deep breath and said loudly, "Welcome. I thank you for joining us today on this momentous occasion. Not only is it the first instance of a blood bargain forged between demon and goddess... but it is also my first act as Queen of the Underworld."

Someone scoffed in the crowd, and Prue went rigid. She knew she would have to handle this carefully. What was it Lagos had said to her? *Some of the more rebellious subjects need a firm hand.*

Her nostrils flared as she stared hard at the crowd. "Would someone like to object to that?" She put as much ice into her tone as possible.

A few demons shifted uncomfortably. One cleared their throat. In front of her, still kneeling, Lagos merely blinked, his dark eyes fixed on the crowd. But Prue could tell by the stiffness of his shoulders that he was uneasy.

"Well?" Prue snapped. "Don't be shy. Please make your grievances known."

"This realm has never had a queen," said a voice. "And it doesn't need one now."

A few demons shouted their assent.

"I'm sorry, but where is your king?" Prue said, her voice rising. "Is he here to make the same claim that I am not *needed* here?" She spread her hands, waiting. "*Well?*"

Utter silence filled the room.

"I am bound to Osiris as his wife and mate," Prue said, rising from her throne. The dais granted her a few feet of height above the crowd, and she relished the feeling of towering over them. "You can ask him yourself. We have sealed our bond in the most permanent manner—in flesh *and* blood."

Several demons gasped, and Prue found herself smirking. *Yes, let them talk.*

"Now, those of you who object to my being here: can you honestly say there is nothing you wouldn't change about this realm?" Prue challenged. "Is all well here? Is this truly the utopia you desire?" Her eyebrows lifted.

No one said a word. As the silence stretched on, Prue felt her courage mounting.

"I thought so," she said. "Now, as demons, I would think you would be happy for this occasion. One of your own is being elevated in rank to work alongside me. Isn't that cause for celebration? Imagine what this could do for your people! This is one of the many changes I hope to inspire as queen of this realm."

Someone started clapping again, but it wasn't Trivia this time. It was a demon standing in front, his eyes shining with delight. Several others joined in until, once more, the room was filled with raucous applause, though much more enthusiastic than before. Prue found herself beaming at the crowd, counting this as a small victory. She raised a hand as the applause died down, calling for silence once more.

"Your hand, Lagos," Prue said, fixing her gaze on the demon still bowed before her.

Lagos extended his hand to her. Prue reached for the ceremonial dagger resting on the small table beside the throne. She unsheathed it, then pressed it into Lagos's finger until a bead of blood welled up.

"State your terms, Lagos." Prue's heart thundered madly as she waited for him to speak. Would he insert something new into the agreement? What would she do if he did?

Would he try to trick her? To trap her in a bargain that would enslave her?

Her head was buzzing with nerves, and she swallowed hard in an attempt to clear her thoughts.

"I, Lagos, warden of Tartarus and citizen of the Underworld, pledge myself and my services to Prudence Donati, Queen of the Underworld, as her advisor to serve in whatever capacity she requires. In exchange, I humbly request for her protection and loyalty for myself and the demons of this realm."

Prue raised her eyebrows. A humble request indeed. He didn't indicate payment or status. He didn't even demand a residence in the palace.

Her insides still quivered with unease as she tried to detect something hidden in his words. But as Lagos fell silent, Prue struggled to find anything sinister in his side of the bargain.

Clearing her throat, Prue pressed the dagger into her own finger until blood trickled down her hand. "I,

Prudence Donati, Queen of the Underworld, accept Lagos, former warden of Tartarus and resident of the Underworld, as my advisor and pledge to protect him as one of my subjects." She glanced at Lagos, who inclined his head in agreement.

They pressed their hands together, their blood mingling. Power thrummed in Prue's veins, and she sucked in a breath from the intensity of it, her insides quivering. Goddess, she had missed the feeling of magic in the air. Even if it wasn't hers, she savored the sensation. Her skin prickled and her blood sang as energy swirled between her and Lagos, twining around their joined hands.

The audience gasped as they no doubt felt it, too. Several demons stared wide-eyed at Prue and Lagos.

"The bargain is complete," Prue said with a smile, releasing Lagos's hand and placing the dagger on the table. "Rise, Lagos, the first member of my court!"

Scattered applause sounded across the chamber as Lagos stood alongside Prue, the corners of his mouth lifting in a smile.

With a loud crash, the doors to the throne room banged open, and Cyrus strode inside, wearing a blood-red cloak and a crown of bones atop his head. His eyes were all-black as he surveyed the room.

"Well, well," he said. "Isn't this nice? A ceremony

held behind my back." He flashed his teeth in a cruel smile.

Prue inhaled sharply at the sight of him, instantly stepping away from Lagos. "Cyrus," she whispered.

Except it wasn't him at all; this was Kronos.

"Wife," Cyrus spat. "It was quite rude of you not to extend an invitation to your husband."

Prue's mind roared, but she willed it to be silent. She had considered this a possibility, and she had a plan. She met Cyrus's glare head-on and challenged, "What will you do, oh great king? Will you clap me in irons again? Throw me in the dungeon and keep me as your prisoner? I'm sure many here can attest that you've already done that."

Shocked murmurs rippled through the crowd. Several looked abashed, including Lagos.

Cyrus's jaw went rigid. "You are trying to usurp me. To take my throne from me. This realm has *never* had a queen, and here you are, turning my subjects against me."

"You're already doing a fine job of that yourself," Prue spat. She gestured to Cyrus. "Look at his eyes! Does he not look different to you?"

The crowd shuffled as several demons turned to get a better look at Cyrus.

"This creature is not the god I married," Prue went on. "He's been taken over by another presence. Can you not deny that *something* is sweeping over this realm? The wraiths? The death shadows?"

The whispers of the demons intensified as several of them nodded in agreement.

"I am here to protect the people of the Underworld," Prue said, "because *you* will not." She jabbed a finger at Cyrus.

Cyrus's eyes burned with all the power of his fury, and Prue had to physically restrain herself from flinching.

It's not really him, she told herself. *It's not.*

But that didn't stop the agony from slicing through her. She was betraying him, right here and now. She truly *was* turning his people against him.

"When your eyes glow silver once more," Prue said, her voice growing soft, "then I will gladly rule by your side, darling."

For the briefest of seconds, a flash of silver ignited in Cyrus's eyes, followed by an anguish so potent it cut Prue to the core. In an instant, it was gone, as Kronos took control once more.

He's still in there, Prue thought. He needed a reminder of his promise. "Fight!" she urged. "Fight, Cyrus! I know you're still there. Your people need you."

Cyrus unleashed a terrible roar, and several demons screamed from the intensity of it. Before anyone could react, Cyrus grabbed the nearest demon by the throat—a tall, skinny woman with antler horns—and twisted sharply until her neck snapped. Her body crumpled to the floor, and a stunned silence fell in the room. Prue could only stare in horror, the blood draining from her face.

"I am the sole ruler of this domain," Cyrus hissed, his teeth bared. His face was so contorted with rage that he looked almost feral. "And everyone here will suffer my wrath."

The ground began to tremble. The crowd gasped, shifting about to search for the source. But Prue's eyes remained on Cyrus, whose hands emitted inky black flames. Those all-black eyes were bright with fury and hunger, his mouth curling into a sinister smile.

Pebbles and dust rained from the ceiling. Several demons screamed. Prue's body went tense as she glanced upward to find several cracks splitting through the marble ceiling.

Goddess above, he's going to tear down the entire palace, she thought in a panic. Without thinking, she stretched out her arms, calling to life the earth magic within her...

But of course, nothing happened. She was powerless to stop him.

"Cyrus!" she screamed over the cacophony of the terrified demons and the rumbling of the palace walls. "Stop this, *now!*"

But Cyrus didn't move. The black flames spurting from his fingertips intensified, jetting toward the palace walls.

Prue snatched the dagger from the table and descended the dais, shoving her way past demons until she stood before him, her heart pounding painfully in her chest. What did she expect to do? He was too far gone for her to reach him. And she couldn't stab Kronos without also hurting Cyrus.

"Osiris, god of the Underworld," Prue said in a loud voice, attempting the only strategy she could think of, "as your wife, mate, and Queen of the Underworld, I *command* you to *stop immediately*." She pressed the dagger into her palm. "I command you with my own flesh and blood." A single droplet trickled down her hand.

Cyrus went perfectly still, his lethal eyes fixed on her. Then, a tremendous shudder rippled through him, making his arms and shoulders quiver just as the ground had. He groaned, hunching over, his flames dying and the earthquake ceasing. With an anguished cry, Cyrus fell to all fours, choking and gasping. Prue knelt by him, her hand on his shoulder.

"Don't touch me!" he hissed, flinching away from her.

Prue froze, eyes wide. Was this really Cyrus lashing

out at her? Or was Kronos still in control? She peered closer, trying to get a better look at his eyes...

But Cyrus whirled from her, staggering to his feet and fleeing the throne room. The demons gasped and cried out, some calling for him to be hunted down.

Prue watched him leave, unable to keep her body from shaking. He had just killed one of his subjects. He had almost torn down the entire palace. How could he possibly gain his people's trust after this? How would anyone believe he had truly changed?

And how could Prue free him if Kronos had such a violent hold on him?

When Prue rose to her feet and turned, she found the demons staring at her, their eyes wide with fear. She was all they had left. And as much as Cyrus's attack had rattled her, she had to pull herself together.

Her voice shook as she said, "You all are dismissed. Return to your duties. If anyone sees him repeating these actions, report to me immediately. Do *not* fight him."

The demons bowed before scrambling to leave, no doubt eager to put as much distance between themselves and Cyrus as possible. Prue stood there, barely keeping her emotions in check as she watched them exit the throne room. Her mouth trembled, and tears filled her eyes.

I can't do this, she thought numbly. *Why did I ever think I could?*

Lagos lingered, looking uncertainly toward Prue, but she nodded, unable to speak. Thankfully, he understood her dismissal and followed the others out the door.

Soon, it was only Prue and Trivia left. The goddess gave Prue a gentle smile and offered her arm. "Shall we?"

Prue knew the situation was dire because Trivia wasn't smirking or cracking a joke. But she accepted Trivia's arm and let her lead her from the throne room.

FREE

CYRUS

CYRUS'S VISION KEPT SHIFTING FROM DARKNESS to light, confusion to clarity. One moment he saw nothing but the black void that normally consumed him, and the next he could see Prue's frightened face with crisp precision, every tear clinging to her lashes, every freckle on her nose.

Kronos's hold on him was altered by her presence.

No, by her *command.* She had used the magic of this realm to command Cyrus.

Clever witch. *His* clever witch. Pride and terror mingled in his chest. She could free him. But at what cost?

What would Kronos do to her? Already, he felt the dark presence inside him roaring with fury and indignation, plotting his revenge.

Cyrus wouldn't allow it. As he staggered down the hallway toward the staircase, he gritted his teeth against the magic raging within him.

I will not let you have her, he thought. His fingers curled into fists.

He descended the staircase and burst through one of the side entrances, storming toward the labyrinth of caves. He intended to disappear, to plunge himself so deeply into the chambers and passages that no one could find him. It was better this way. Safer for everyone.

Including Cyrus.

His breathing turned ragged as he stumbled forward, intent on putting as much distance between himself and the palace as possible. He couldn't risk that again. He couldn't ever go there again.

I almost destroyed the castle and everyone inside it. Horror mingled with rage, making his insides twist.

He couldn't take this anymore. He would *not* stand by while Kronos used his body to slowly destroy this realm, one piece at a time. Everything he loved... Kronos would turn it all to ash.

"I will stop you," Cyrus snarled, darkness pressing in on him as he made his way through the caves.

A low laugh rumbled inside him. *I'd like to see you try. Your attempts thus far have been pitiful. You are nothing compared to my power.*

Cyrus's anger rose like a tidal wave, becoming a

tangible presence in his chest. He clung to it, letting it fuel him, letting it stoke the fire that had faded to mere coals. The burn of that anger felt foreign and familiar all at once. It had been so long since he had let fury drive him; he had relied on the death magic for what felt like an eternity.

No more. He would be a slave no more.

Cyrus retreated within himself, finding that hidden store of power he rarely touched. Soul magic. It gleamed, lighting his way, beckoning him closer. Gold light encompassed him, bleeding through the dark haze of Kronos's power.

What are you doing? Kronos whispered.

"I'm ending you," Cyrus growled. He crushed his reservations and fears, burying them until he felt nothing but his rage.

And then, he unleashed his soul magic on Kronos.

A scream filled the cave, bouncing off the walls and reverberating against Cyrus's ears. The gold light scorched him, igniting amber flames that consumed his flesh and blood. A deep, slicing pain cut into Cyrus's chest, carving through his heart and soul. The magic of the gods—the magic he rarely used—was tearing him apart.

He'd only used this particular brand of magic twice before. The most recent occasion was to save Prue's life. To Cyrus, nothing warranted the usage of this power because it was directly linked to the mortal realm. It ate up his soul with every spell he used with it, draining his immortality one drop at a time.

But here and now, he would gladly sacrifice his own soul, his very existence, to end Kronos. If it meant keeping his realm—and his wife—safe, he would do it.

Without another thought, Cyrus succumbed to the pain and the light flowing from within him. The scream intensified, and Cyrus realized it was Kronos. The dark creature was being torn apart, just as Cyrus was.

A savage satisfaction crept through Cyrus, bringing a weak smile to his face just before he lost himself to the soul magic.

MERGE

EVANDER

BEFORE MONA'S RESURRECTION

EVANDER HAD CHANGED.

Mona's departure had ripped him to pieces, leaving nothing left. And now, Cyrus was gone, called to the mortal realm.

His younger brother's plea still rang in his ears. *I am begging you for help now. Please. Watch over Acheron in my absence and do what you can to keep Father and the others at bay.*

Cyrus never begged. *Never.* He normally encouraged begging from others; relished it, really. But he never stooped so low himself.

If that wasn't proof enough that something was wrong in the Underworld, Evander didn't know what was. But he had long since suspected a strange darkness was taking over his home. Ever since Mona had arrived, something had been different. Off. *Wrong.*

It couldn't be just Aidoneus and his brothers. They were cunning and devious, but even they didn't have the foresight for such an intricate and lengthy plan. The changes in the realm had been happening for ages now.

No, Evander's brothers didn't have that kind of patience. Whatever means they would use to destroy the realm would be quicker. More violent.

Even so, Marcellus was a good place to start. He'd been plotting with Vasileios from the beginning. But no one had seen or heard from Vasileios in a long time, and Evander didn't feel like tracking him down.

Marcellus's presence was easier to track anyway. He was always obnoxious about showing off his skills in battle and looking down upon those weaker than himself.

Rage quivered inside Evander, igniting Typhon's presence. For once, Evander didn't resist it.

Go ahead, he urged. *Tear my brother to pieces. I'll be glad for it.*

Typhon roared his assent, hungry for a fight.

Evander's wings expanded behind him. A low growl rumbled in his throat.

And for the first time in his existence, he was not afraid of Typhon.

A searing heat scorched his collarbone. Something cracked and splintered, then shattered on the ground before him. He glanced down to find his moonstone necklace had fallen and broken into pieces.

The enchantment separating himself from Typhon had broken. By merging himself with the darkness, the moonstone necklace was no longer needed.

And he had never felt *freer.*

He crouched, stretched his wings, and took off into the sky. The brisk wind whipped at his face, awakening him to a new sense of himself. His magic. His darkness.

Typhon is a part of you, Mona had said. *He is you.*

Evander trusted in Typhon's strong sense of smell, sniffing out his older brothers and recognizing their stench almost immediately. They were in Oceanus—Leonidas's former domain. Currently, Leonidas was tasked with overseeing Acheron. But, given the state of Acheron, he was likely hiding elsewhere.

And with Cyrus gone, it made his scheming much easier.

Evander arced to the left, his wings beating with another burst of speed that sent him soaring. The euphoria of being in the air, surveying this great kingdom, was like nothing he'd ever experienced before. He had no fears. No anxieties.

It was just him and the sky.

Eventually, his keen ears picked up on low murmuring. He descended slowly, vanishing under the trees to avoid being spotted. When he landed, he treaded softly through the forest, his wings brushing against branches and leaves.

Let his brothers see how terrifying he could be. Let them stare in horror at his wings and his horns and his claws.

Let *them* fear *him*.

The thought of finally having power over his brothers sent a strange spark of exhilaration through him. He'd never craved power; he'd vowed to never travel down that path, especially after seeing what it had done to Cyrus.

But this felt different. The magic was still separate, still a part of Typhon. It was available whenever Evander wished, but he could also part from it at will. His mind was untainted.

How long would that last? How long before he wound up just like Cyrus?

Evander shook these questions from his mind. Now was not the time.

His footsteps were silent as he crept closer. The babbling river masked most of their words, but he could barely make out the hushed voices of Leonidas and Marcellus as they muttered urgently to one another.

Oh, yes. His brothers certainly *were* busy plotting.

But where was Vasileios? Evander hadn't seen him in ages. Perhaps he'd gotten himself killed with the dark magic he was dabbling in.

The thought gave him a swell of satisfaction.

His rage fueled him as he emerged from the trees, spreading his wings wide so his older brothers could behold them in all their glory.

Marcellus noticed first, ever the soldier aware of his surroundings. His beefy, muscular frame had once intimidated Evander.

Not anymore.

Leonidas turned then, his silvery eyes fixed on Evander. Already a look of amusement played along his face.

And then his gaze snapped to Evander's wings, and his face drained of color. His mouth slackened in shock, his eyes going wide.

"Evander," Leonidas said numbly, still gaping at him.

"What in the ever-blooming *hell* is that?" Marcellus boomed, facing Evander fully. His eyes narrowed, taking on that hungry glint he often got when faced with a fight.

Good. Evander wanted a fight, too.

"Tell me what you've done to Acheron," Evander said, his voice low and deadly. "To this entire realm. Tell me how to stop it or I swear on all the mighty gods that I will tear you apart." He flexed his fingers, allowing his claws to elongate.

Alarm flickered in Leonidas's gaze, but Marcellus boomed a laugh. "Do you really think we'd fear *you*, Evander? You're like a kitten; you couldn't possibly harm us."

"Marcellus," Leonidas warned.

But Evander only offered a cold smile, eager to wipe that smirk right off Marcellus's face. Typhon took control, and red burned into the corners of Evander's vision. In a flash, he darted forward, slamming into Marcellus's chest and pinning him to the forest floor. Marcellus cried out as Evander plunged his claws straight into his throat.

Leonidas rushed forward, but Evander swept his wings sideways, knocking him off his feet. Marcellus wriggled under his grip, but Typhon's force was unrelenting. He pushed further, burying his claws deeper.

Marcellus went still, his eyes wide and his face ghostly pale.

"Tell me," Evander urged, his voice still low.

Marcellus choked on his words. Silver blood bubbled on his lips.

"Evander, *stop!*" Leonidas roared. Black magic shot forward, spearing straight into Evander's back. But his wings curled inward, absorbing the attack.

"Holy shit," Leonidas breathed, staggering back a step. "What *are* you?"

"I am death," Evander growled. "And I've come to deliver your sentence. This is your final chance. *Tell me* what you've done to the Underworld or I will end you right here and now."

Marcellus's chin was now covered in blood, but he nodded fervently, granting his assent. Evander eased the pressure, but only a fraction. His eyes never left Marcellus as he said, "Leonidas. Answer my question before I sever our brother's head from his body."

"I—I—it was Aidoneus!" Leonidas sputtered. "It wasn't us."

A roar burned in Evander's throat, and he spun around, wrenching his claws from Marcellus's throat and slashing them toward the other brother.

Leonidas jumped backward just in time, but one of Evander's wings swept forward, obscuring Leonidas's vision for long enough for Evander to sink his claws into his leg.

Leonidas fell to his knees with a scream that echoed in the forest.

For good measure, Evander slashed at the other leg, too, just to ensure he couldn't hobble away. It was the least he deserved, after centuries of bullying and assaulting Evander.

"Explain," Evander snarled.

"It was a lie!" Leonidas screeched. "It—we didn't poison anything. The river was *already* poisoned. Some—some darkness has been seeping into the realm for a while now. Aidoneus only took credit for it to make Cyrus panic."

Evander frowned. "So you did *nothing*?"

"Nothing," Leonidas insisted. "We would never knowingly destroy our home. It was all a bluff."

Evander turned his head to stare at Marcellus, who was climbing to his feet. The older brother wiped blood from his chin and nodded slowly. "He speaks the truth." His voice was a low rasp.

"So what is happening?" Evander demanded. "What is this darkness you speak of?"

"Aidoneus said he recognized it from eons ago but wouldn't tell us what it was," Leonidas said quickly. "He only said it came from Tartarus and must've been unleashed when Cyrus bound himself to the Book of Eyes."

Evander's brows knitted together. That was *ages* ago. Had this darkness been creeping through the realm since then, merely biding its time before it struck?

And why now? Why was *this* the opportune time to take over the Underworld?

"Many souls escaped Tartarus when Cyrus went to the mortal realm," Marcellus said. "Aidoneus speculates whatever *thing* is attacking this realm must've escaped during then, too, and was too powerful for Cyrus to send back."

Gods above, Evander thought, his body stiff with horror. What the hell could've escaped from Tartarus and escaped their notice for so long?

How long before it devoured this realm entirely?

"That's all we know," Leonidas said, pressing against the wounds in his legs. "I swear it on my life."

"I believe you," Evander said, though it wasn't completely true. He wouldn't put it past Leonidas to withhold vital information. He was always far too cunning for his own good.

"Please, Evander," Marcellus said, his palms raised. "We don't have any quarrel with you."

Evander raised his eyebrows. Marcellus was practically *begging.* The thought made him want to laugh. "No quarrel with me? Is that why you tormented me for eons, beating me and belittling me?" He shook his head, his eyes narrowing. "I should rip your limbs apart." He cocked his head as he considered doing just that, if only to hear their screams. "But unfortunately, I have more important things to do... like clean up this mess everyone seems content with ignoring." He shook his head in disgust, for once seeing his brothers for what they were: cowards. They were over here, hiding and scheming, instead of doing whatever it took to save their home.

Evander was finished with it. He was done with hiding and cowering, avoiding others out of fear. No longer would he succumb wordlessly to their cruelty. He was power and vengeance now.

He felt nothing but grim determination as he spread his wings. Before he could take off, leaving his brothers to lick their wounds, the ground began to quiver.

Evander froze, his gaze flicking to Leonidas and Marcellus, who both looked equally bewildered. The trembling intensified, causing the trees to shake. Several branches snapped, landing with a loud crash among the brush. The earth cracked with an ear-splitting boom that made Evander's ears ring.

Pebbles and dust rained from above. Evander squinted up at the sky, baffled by the flecks of dirt falling from... where?

"Gods above," Leonidas breathed. "The enchant-ment. *Look.*"

Evander followed his gaze and felt bile climb up his throat.

The sky was no longer blue. It was a cold gray, the color of storm clouds. It had a roughened texture to it as if it were made of stone instead of magic.

The sky had never been real; Evander had known this. And yet, there was something about seeing the enchantment die that cast a horrifying light on his home.

It wasn't real. None of this was real; the trees, the grass, the smells... It was all an illusion.

And now, that illusion was falling apart.

"What the hell is happening?" Marcellus bellowed.

A shrill scream tore through the realm, echoing and reverberating in Evander's bones. He trembled, overcome with an icy sensation of dread and despair.

He recognized the voice ringing in his ears. It was Vasileios. Judging by how pale his brothers looked, they heard it, too.

"What in the gods' names is he doing up there?" Leonidas murmured, exchanging a dark look with Marcellus.

Evander's insides turned frigid as he pieced everything together. Vasileios... *up there.*

His oldest brother was in the mortal realm. And whatever dark magic he was conjuring was impacting *this* realm as well.

A piercing pain stabbed through Evander's chest. He groaned, hunching over, as his brothers mimicked the movement. All three of them collapsed, writhing in agony.

Vasileios's screams intensified, along with the pain coursing through Evander's body. And when all went still and silent, he knew with a solemn surety that Vasileios was dead.

PART TWO

> "SHE BOTH TORMENTS AND IS TORMENTED AT THE SAME MOMENT, AND IS EVER HER OWN PUNISHMENT."
>
> HENRY THOMAS RILEY, *METAMORPHOSES*

RETURN
MONA

PRESENT DAY

CHARYBDIS'S POWERFUL VOICE STILL RANG IN Mona's head, echoing through her bones and her soul, resonating with her as she finally came to. Her mind was a spinning array of chaotic thoughts, and she couldn't make sense of anything. Where was she? *Who* was she?

She vaguely remembered the beastly creature of the sea, the spinning whirlpool she had leapt into. But as she conjured these thoughts, they slipped from her mind like water droplets in her hands, leaving an aching emptiness in her head that frightened her.

What's happening to me?

She sat up, then winced, bringing a hand to her temple. Her fingers came back coated in blood. She must've slammed into something hard when she fell... where? Where was she?

Darkness surrounded her, and she blinked as her eyes adjusted. Rushing waters met her ears as she finally processed her surroundings. She sat in the damp grass, the midnight sky stretched above her, the moon providing her only source of light. As she rose to her feet, she found the source of the churning waters:

A whirlpool.

It was small—smaller than she would've thought—and spinning restlessly. On its other side was a wide, expansive river that the whirlpool fed into.

Something hummed in Mona's chest, and she gasped as her right hand started to glow. She lifted her hand, turning it over, and realized she wore an emerald ring on her finger. When she tried to touch it, it scalded her, and she yanked her hand away with a hiss of pain.

Okay, she thought uncertainly, *so the emerald ring is staying. For now.*

She may have had no memories, but the magic roiling inside her told her this was no ordinary ring. It was bound to some sort of magic keeping her here. And until she knew more about it, she didn't want to meddle with it. Who knew what kind of spell she might undo?

Mona glanced around the wide stretch of grass surrounding the whirlpool. A few sparse trees stood nearby, and on the other side of the river were rolling hills that disappeared from view. She wracked her brain, trying to make sense of all this.

One thought blared, loud and clear: *Prue.*

In a rush, a flood of memories burst in her mind. Prue and Mona, sitting together on the beach. Prue and Mona, casting spells together. Prue and Mona, embracing and laughing.

"My sister," she whispered, her body numb with shock. "I have a sister."

Mona looked around more urgently this time, as if she might find Prue standing there, waiting for her.

But no. That was why Mona was here. She had to help her sister. Prue was in trouble, and Mona was the only one who could save her.

Determination filled her, and she exhaled in relief. Thank the Goddess she could remember *something.* Now she had a purpose. A mission.

She was here in the Underworld, which was where she last saw Prue disappearing to. Mona would do everything she could to find her.

She strode forward with resolve coursing through her, only to halt at the sight of a figure standing next to the whirlpool.

"Prue?" Hope rose in Mona's chest, and she almost

ran to her until she realized it wasn't Prue. It was a woman with long hair, just like Prue, but her golden eyes glowed, even in the darkness.

Mona took an uncertain step backward. "Who are you?"

"You don't remember me?" The woman's voice rang with power.

Mona faltered. She knew something had altered her memories, erasing everything except Prue. But was this woman lying? How could she know for sure?

"No," Mona finally said, knowing she wouldn't get answers if she pretended to know this woman. "Who are you?"

"My name is Hecate. But your people call me Trivia."

Mona's mind strained, her thoughts painfully scraping at nothing. There was *nothing* in her head right now. "You are... a goddess?"

"That's right."

"What do you want with me?" Mona's body was tense with alarm, and the woman seemed to sense it, because she laughed.

"Relax. I'm only here to help you. I've met your sister, Prue."

Mona straightened, hope blossoming in her chest. "Prue? Where is she?"

"I will tell you where she is, but you will owe me one

favor in the future," Trivia warned. "Do you accept this bargain?"

Mona hesitated. Even with her memories gone, the prickle of awareness skittering along her skin made her cautious of bargaining with this strange goddess.

Could she take her chances and find Prue on her own? The idea was just as horrifying; Mona had no idea what waited for her here in the Underworld, and even if she had studied before arriving, she would've forgotten everything.

She was completely helpless here. Even her magic seemed stifled in this new realm.

"What kind of favor?" Mona hedged.

"It will cost you nothing," Trivia assured her. "And it won't hurt you or anyone you love."

Mona bit her lip, still considering. Could Trivia lie to her? What if this favor *did* harm others?

Did Mona really have a choice?

With a heavy sigh, Mona nodded. "I agree to your terms."

Something hot burned in Mona's chest, twining around the magic growing inside her. She gasped, realizing this had been a binding agreement. Something she could not get out of. Her magic told her that much.

Trivia smiled, the expression almost predatory. "Very good. You'll find your sister in Tartarus." She pointed behind her, toward a narrow bridge barely visible on the other side of the whirlpool. "That way. In the caves." Her eyes glinted, and Mona suppressed a shiver.

"But how—" Mona froze, looking around in alarm.

Trivia had vanished.

CONFRONTATION
PRUE

PRUE WAS GRATEFUL TRIVIA HAD ALREADY pointed out Aidoneus's penthouse to her. Though the goddess had been particularly helpful to her already, Prue didn't trust anyone here in the Underworld, and the last thing she wanted to do was alert enemies to her visit with the former god of the dead.

There was something unsettling about Trivia. Prue didn't believe in favors from strangers. Especially from a goddess. Discovering the truth about her mother, Gaia, and her deception still left a foul taste in her mouth.

Prue had been lied to. Manipulated. For *years*.

It made it hard to trust *any* god.

Trivia had to have a good reason for helping Prue, and it made her all the more suspicious. She trusted

Trivia with court affairs, but not something as serious as this: plying Aidoneus for information about Kronos.

But Prue couldn't wait any longer. After Cyrus's display in the throne room, she was desperate for answers.

Desperate enough to seek out his father.

The potent, woodsy smells surrounded her as she ventured through the Forest of Thanatos and toward the impressive peak of the penthouse. When Prue reached the clearing with the building in its center, she paused, craning her neck to gaze up at the massive edifice. A single, pointed spire reached toward the sky, the sharpened tip reminding Prue of a deadly blade. The building itself was cut from marble, glistening in the sunlight, giving the overall effect of a metal prong. Impenetrable. Indestructible.

"A little much, don't you think?" she muttered to herself. Then again, was she really that surprised? Cyrus had spoken nonstop of the grandeur of his realm and how the mortal realm paled in comparison.

Her fingers instinctively clutched the pomegranate necklace around her throat as she approached the building's entrance, trying to quell her mounting anxiety.

She didn't have her magic. How would she defend herself if Aidoneus attacked her?

I'll just have to be pleasant and diplomatic, she thought, *to ensure things remain civil.*

She almost laughed at her naive thoughts. No matter how polite Prue was, if Aidoneus was determined to despise her, she couldn't stop him. She only hoped he wasn't in a hostile mood today.

To her surprise, the front door slid open easily for her. She lifted her chin and strode inside, uncertain what to expect.

The lobby was sleek and elegant, with large windows and marble floors and a sweeping spiral staircase. Plush sofas surrounded a fireplace, and glass statues lined the walls.

Ostentatious was an understatement.

Prue glanced uncertainly at the staircase. Judging by how high the building was, there was no way she could climb all the way to the top on foot. Then, her eyes fell on a metal grate built into the wall. She arched a single eyebrow as she approached it. Power thrummed from the contraption, swelling around her like tendrils of smoke.

There was magic on this device.

Feeling bold, Prue slid the grate open and squeezed herself into the small space. As soon as the grate slid shut, the small box surrounding her shuddered to life. Coils of magic filled the air, tickling her nose until she almost sneezed. The ground shifted underneath her as the contraption rose higher and higher. Prue gazed downward in awe, watching the floor sink farther and farther below her.

"Fascinating," she murmured, trying to ignore the sickening way her stomach dropped the higher she climbed. She forced her gaze upward to avoid looking down, placing her hand on the wall next to her for support.

When the machine finally came to a stop, Prue exhaled, giving herself a moment for her stomach to settle. The grates slid open, and Prue stepped out, adjusting her dress and straightening her spine.

I am the queen of this realm, she reminded herself. *I cower before no one.*

She scrutinized her surroundings. It looked like the grandest suite she had ever seen, the large space nearly two times the size of her tiny home in Krenia. A grand piano stood on one side of the room, and on the other side was a wide and ornate set of bookshelves. Prue fought back a smile at the thought of Mona's face if she could see such a collection of books.

"Who dares to disturb me?" thundered a voice.

Prue stiffened, her nostrils flaring as she stepped closer to the sound of the voice. Footsteps drew nearer until she found herself facing Cyrus's father. His jet-black hair fell to his shoulders, and a scruffy goatee lined his chin. His eyes were bloodshot and red-rimmed, his steps unsteady. He held a glass of amber liquid in one hand and gazed at Prue through half-lidded eyes.

Wonderful, Prue thought. *He's drunk. This will not end well.*

"My name is Prue," she said, her voice firm. "I'm Cyrus's wife." She thought it best not to provoke him by referring to herself as the queen of the realm.

Aidoneus spat at her feet, his mouth curling into a foul sneer. "*Cyrus.* You think I care about that little shit? He took *everything* from me."

"He is the ruler of this domain."

"Not for long." A sinister smile spread across his face. "From what I've heard, he's not been himself as of late."

Prue narrowed her eyes and cocked her head at him. "Does the name Kronos mean anything to you?" She figured it would be best if she got right to the point. Perhaps, in his drunken state, he would reveal something helpful.

Aidoneus went perfectly still, his eyes flashing with recognition.

"It does," Prue said, before he could brush off her question. "Do you know who he is? What he's capable of?"

Aidoneus swirled the contents of his glass before taking a sip. "Kronos was an ally who turned against me. Just like everyone else."

"So you threw him in Tartarus."

Aidoneus glared at her. "I did what I had to to save my home."

"And now? Do you still want to save it? Or do you want to watch it burn?"

Aidoneus only scowled, refusing to answer.

"What happens to *you* if this realm perishes?" Prue drew closer to him.

"I don't care," he said bitterly. "I've lived long enough. My life has been nothing but sorrow and betrayal."

"So that's it? Since you're done with your life, you're going to subject all the lives in the Underworld to your destructive quest for revenge? *All* of your sons? All the souls that live here? Is your bitterness *really* worth that much?"

Anger flashed in his gaze. "Who are you to come in here and presume to know *anything* about me? All you know are the lies my son has fed you."

"Your son hasn't told me *anything* about you except that you despise him and want to destroy his home. Is that not the truth?"

Aidoneus's jaw went rigid, but he said nothing.

"You may think you have nothing left," Prue said. "But you have a *choice*. You can sit here and waste away, letting your home and everyone in it perish at Kronos's hand. Or you can tell me how to defeat him and do one last decent thing before you wither away."

Aidoneus's dark eyes pinned her in place, his expression somber and surprisingly clear, given his inebriation. Something cold and calculating filled his eyes, and he smirked at her. "I can sense my son's magic around you. Pity he has you so chained and docile." His eyes fell on the pomegranate necklace around her throat.

"I am not *chained*."

Aidoneus laughed, the sound harsh. "Don't lie to me. I may be a shadow of the god I once was, but my magic is strong enough to sense that much. He's caged your powers. It's a shame, really. I sense there is great potential in your magic. Far greater than that of an ordinary witch." He cocked his head at her, his eyes assessing. "What *are* you? You are not fully mortal."

Prue's blood ran cold. The last thing she wanted to do was give this man leverage and reveal her divine heritage. "Will you help me or not?"

Aidoneus chuckled again, finishing the contents of his drink before hurling the glass at the floor. Prue flinched as the glass shattered into thousands of pieces. "Here's what I think." He inched closer to Prue, and she found herself drawing away from him. "I think my son's magic has tainted your perspective. It's poisoned you, and you can't see clearly." His eyes darkened with fury. "Allow me to open your eyes."

He lifted a hand, and Prue gasped as phantom fingers curled around her throat, tightening, cutting off her breath. She clawed at her neck, trying to free herself from his grip, but her fingers met nothing. It was like a ghost was strangling her.

"My magic may not be what it once was," he hissed. "But I still have some power left. Much more than *you*."

Aidoneus bared his teeth as he curled his fingers together, and the force on her throat tightened. Black spots floated in her vision, and she swayed on her feet. Desperation pulsed through her, and she tried to summon her magic, to unleash the fury of her power against him.

But the fire within her sputtered and died, a feeble attempt to free her powers. She was helpless. Defenseless. He would kill her right here.

No, she thought with renewed determination. She would not fall to this weak and pathetic man. She was more than some frail damsel with no power and no hope.

Aidoneus's words rang in her mind. *He's caged your powers. I can sense his magic around you.*

The bond. Aidoneus was referring to the bond between them.

The bond Prue had forged.

She thought of the way Trivia and Aidoneus had both looked at the pomegranate necklace with hunger in their eyes... as if they could sense the power emanating from it.

The necklace. The power of our bond is in the necklace. When Prue had first summoned Cyrus, she had bound him to her using the magic of the pomegranate seed.

Kronos's control of Cyrus was stifling her magic. But if she severed her bond with him, her magic could return.

The realization broke through the haze of darkness clouding her mind. But with that realization came a tendril of uncertainty. *If I break this bond,* she thought, *what happens to Cyrus? Will Kronos have complete control of him? Will Cyrus have anything to hold on to?*

Darkness crowded her vision again, and she felt her mind slipping away. She was out of time.

And she couldn't help Cyrus without her magic.

I'm sorry, she thought to him. *I'm so sorry. But I swear on my life, I will come for you and I'll do anything to bring you back. We will be bound together once more.*

Prue snatched the necklace around her neck and tugged until the chain snapped. The enchanted pomegranate fell to the floor with a clatter. In a burst of white light, energy exploded within her, burning her flesh and boiling her blood. Her bones quivered from the sheer intensity of it, and she cried out, her throat now free of Aidoneus's assault.

Her magic swelled within her, so powerful it brought tears to her eyes. A heavy weight had been lifted from her chest, and she could finally *breathe.* Goddess above, she could feel *everything*. The pungent smell of alcohol filled her nose, along with Aidoneus's dark and smoky magic. She could see the wisps of black power surrounding him, a dark aura of death magic.

He has it, too, she thought in horror. *He has a piece of Kronos's magic. And he has no idea.*

With a thrust of her hands, she sent her vines forward, snaring around Aidoneus's ankles and rooting him to the floor. He yelped, struggling to free himself to no avail. Prue's vines trapped his wrists behind his back, then snaked around his mouth to gag him. He stared at her in part fury, part shock.

"Here's what I think," Prue seethed, her throat still raw from his attack. "I think you're a sad, pitiful man who's too much of a coward to do anything while his realm slowly dies. My bond grants me access to Cyrus's death magic, which is lethal to everyone, even gods. I could end you, right here and now, without a drop of remorse. If that's your greatest wish, I will oblige. But not before you give me the information I seek."

Aidoneus growled something unintelligible, and Prue released the vines on his mouth. "Foul witch," he spat.

Prue flexed her fingers, and Aidoneus howled in pain as her vines tightened around his hands and legs. "I can bring you pain, or end your suffering," she said. "It's your choice."

"How?" Aidoneus groaned, his voice strained. "How can you possess this much power? The only way—" He faltered, clarity burning in his eyes as he stared at her in horror. "It can't be."

No, Prue thought, her mind spiraling into a panicked haze. *He knows. He knows I'm Gaia's daughter.*

"Tell me how to defeat Kronos," Prue commanded, trying to ignore the flicker of fear in her chest.

Aidoneus started laughing again, but it sounded manic and uncontrollable, like he was losing his sanity. "What the hell has my son brought here, in *my* domain? Gods, this realm truly *is* doomed with you here. Your efforts are wasted. This place is already lost." He shook his head, his eyes crinkling with amusement. "Even the darkest of curses in Tartarus wouldn't be able to keep out your power. I wish I'd met you sooner; together, we could end this place far quicker than I could on my own."

Even the darkest of curses in Tartarus. So... Tartarus had its own magic? Was this Kronos's magic, too?

Was that how Kronos was imprisoned before: through a curse?

"Why is Kronos afraid of Tartarus?" Prue asked.

"Go ahead and venture down there, little witch," Aidoneus said, choking on his laughter. "See what happens when you open it. I'd love to see the look on your face when you unlock the darkness waiting for you down there."

Prue snarled in frustration before curling her hands into fists. The vines tightened, and Aidoneus wheezed as the breath was squeezed out of him.

Prue waved her fingers in the air, tying the vines around the pillars supporting the ceiling. "Stay here and rot for all I care," she growled before turning on her heel and leaving him there, struggling against her vines.

FORGOTTEN
EVANDER

Evander sensed the moment she entered the realm. The air quivered from the intensity of her aura, her essence. His soul was so tethered to hers that he would recognize her presence anywhere.

Mona, the beast inside him rumbled, and Evander nodded his assent. After checking to ensure Cocytus was flowing normally, Evander spread his wings and took off into the sky, allowing his bestial senses to take over as he tracked the witch he had been waiting for.

In Mona's absence, he had busied himself with investigating the information his brothers had given him. But Tartarus yielded no clues, and Evander had faced dead end after dead end. Whatever had been unleashed from Tartarus was too well-hidden for even Typhon's senses to pick up on.

Besides, the Underworld was still broken from the devastation of Vasileios's death. Whatever chaos he'd caused in the mortal realm had reflected in the Underworld as well, and it had never recovered. Sections of the realm were empty of all magic, and Aidoneus's powerful enchantments weren't working.

Evander steered clear of those areas. Each time he ventured near one, a chill snaked across his body, making it difficult for him to breathe. The rocky gray nothingness of the sky and the absence of trees and grass created this numbing void of nothingness that made Evander want to tear his brains out.

He couldn't stand it.

Everything here was an illusion, yes, but he needed that illusion for a sense of normalcy. Without it, he'd go mad.

Those empty spaces weren't the only repercussions of the incident in the mortal realm. Evander didn't know exactly what happened with Cyrus in the human world, and he was too afraid to ask. Cyrus had trusted him to watch over the Underworld, and he'd failed.

Now, the realm was in shambles. Because Evander hadn't been strong enough. All of the Underworld had been affected. Plants dying, rivers drying up, earthquakes rending the ground in two... Half the rivers weren't functioning as they should, and when Cyrus returned from the mortal realm, he had tripled the guard surrounding Tartarus. When Evander asked him why, Cyrus had practically spat in his face, telling him to mind his own business.

It was quite clear Cyrus wasn't himself. And that he knew something was wrong with Tartarus.

But now that the god of the Underworld had returned, and with his new bride, Evander couldn't thoroughly investigate without raising suspicion.

I should have sought out Cyrus the instant he returned, Evander lamented. *I should have found out what happened before this darkness took over.*

And with Mona here, she was in more danger than she knew. Evander had no doubt she would be targeted immediately by the dark presence that was poisoning the realm. In addition, he had no idea how Cyrus would react if he discovered her presence. Mona and Prue were sisters, yes, but Evander wouldn't put it past Cyrus to declare Mona a threat to the realm.

As Evader flew, the wind whipped against his face and hair, tickling his horns and making his tunic billow around him. His chest constricted with a combination of anxiety and longing. What would Mona think of him now? Would she be pleased that he had embraced the beast inside? Or would she be revolted?

It doesn't matter, he thought. *She's here. I'll see her*

once more. Whether or not she desires me as I desire her is irrelevant.

His life of immortality was desperately lonely, and it always would be. He would take this as the small gift that it was: one last goodbye with Mona.

Because she certainly could not stay here. As much as Evander wanted her to, it wasn't safe.

The slow destruction of his home was a painful reminder of how fragile things were. Immortal beings could still be destroyed. And if Mona lingered too long, Evander wouldn't be able to keep her safe.

A whiff of roses and saltwater met his nose, and his wings adjusted, allowing him to dive. Mona was close. He could feel her aura draw nearer. The leaves atop the trees tickled his arms as he descended, the fresh pine smell overwhelming his senses, nearly drowning out Mona's scent.

He landed hard, his feet slamming into the ground, his wings spread wide behind him. His breaths came sharp and fast as the exhilaration of flight slowly wore off.

Since merging with Typhon, Evander hadn't fully exposed his transformation to his brothers. Only Marcellus and Leonidas had seen his true form. His one encounter with Cyrus had been brief, and as soon as Evander had detected the strangeness surrounding his brother, he fled immediately, not giving Cyrus the chance to see Typhon in his full glory.

But now? He was reluctant to withdraw his wings. They were a part of him now.

Let his brothers judge him for his new appearance. They couldn't fly like he could. The thought sent a slow smile spreading across his face.

A soft gasp sounded in front of him, and Evander straightened, folding in his wings just enough to allow him to see better.

There was Mona. She wore a plain gray dress, torn and stained. Her hair was a tangled mess of dark waves around her face. Her complexion was paler than he remembered, and she looked thinner, as if she hadn't been eating.

Concern washed over him as he drew nearer, noticing a bloody gash on her temple. Rage boiled inside him. Who had done this to her? He would tear them apart, limb from limb.

Mona's eyes grew wide as she drew away from him, clearly alarmed by the fury on his face. Evander schooled his features into something gentler, not wanting to frighten her. She still hadn't said anything. She was only gaping at him in shock and horror.

Gods, she hates me. She despises me. She can't stand the sight of me. Uncertainty clouded his thoughts, and

Evander stepped away from her, giving her the space to flee if she wished.

"Who—who are you?" she whispered.

He faltered at that. Of all the reactions he expected from her—joy, anger, disgust—*confusion* was not one of them. "It's me, Evander." Perhaps his new appearance was so alarming that it made him unrecognizable. Or perhaps it had been so long that she'd forgotten what he looked like. He had no idea how much time had passed in the mortal realm.

It could've been years. Though Mona essentially looked the same. Still the most beautiful young woman he'd ever seen.

Mona only frowned, her gaze traveling up and down his body as she took in his appearance. "I don't know you. I'm sorry. My—my memories, they're gone." She grimaced apologetically.

Evander's stomach sank like a stone, his insides going cold. *Oh no.* His eyes took in her damp hair, and he sucked in a sharp breath.

She'd gone through the Pool of Forgetfulness. *Shit.*

"You don't remember anything?" he asked, afraid of what her answer would be.

"Just my sister, Prue. Have you seen her?"

Anguish twisted in his chest like a knife, and he had to turn away from her for a brief moment. He scrubbed a hand along his face, resisting the urge to groan in utter agony.

She'd traveled through the whirlpool. She'd been allowed a single memory to hold on to.

And she'd chosen Prue.

Of course she had. How could Evander have expected anything different? Mona loved Prue more than anything.

Even more than Evander.

He shoved his tormented thoughts down deep before turning to face her, adopting a pleasant expression, as if she were merely an acquaintance he had come across during his stroll through the woods. "Forgive me. I, uh— it's only caught me by surprise, is all."

How could he have forgotten? It had been centuries since he'd last visited the Pool of Forgetfulness, and he had completely overlooked its link to the whirlpool in the mortal realm.

Gods could pass through freely. But for mortals, there was a price to pay if they wanted to travel to the Underworld. And Mona had paid that price.

"I knew you the last time I was here," Mona said, squinting at him. "Didn't I?"

"Well, I—yes. Yes, you did. I was the guardian of your soul. I helped you find a way to return to the mortal realm."

"Guardian of my soul? Wait... Was I—" Her face paled. "Did I die?"

Shit. How had she not known? "You remember your sister, correct?"

"Yes..."

"What do you remember of her? When did you last see her?"

"Well, it was in Faidon. She cast a powerful spell, and she—she—" Mona's eyes grew round, her hand flying to her chest. "Goddess above! You're right! Prue *resurrected* me. Oh, how could she have been so reckless? A spell like that could have *killed* her!"

"It had to be done," Evander said solemnly. "This realm wasn't safe for you. Your soul and your body were unbound. It would have unraveled you completely if you'd stayed."

Mona chewed on her lower lip as she scrutinized him, her eyes guarded. "And you... helped me? We were allies?"

More than allies, Evander wanted to say. *I am intimately familiar with every curve of your body. I know exactly how your breaths sound when you are aroused.* The thought sent a bolt of heat directly into his stomach.

This line of thinking certainly wasn't helping anything.

"Yes," he said, realizing she was waiting for an answer. "I was the only one you met in this realm.

Well… besides my brother." He winced. "Do you remember him? Vasileios? Was he in Faidon with you?"

Mona's gaze clouded in confusion and alarm. She stared at the forest floor, her eyes unfocused as she considered this. "There was someone else there. Two others. But… I can't recall their faces." She shook her head, gritting her teeth in frustration. "Dammit! I can't remember *anything*."

"It's all right." Evander lifted his hands to placate her. "Don't strain yourself. If you fight against the magic of the Pool of Forgetfulness, it could rebel against you. Just accept it. We don't want to alert anyone to a foreign presence in this realm."

"Foreign presence?"

"Mortals don't generally come here. It's forbidden, actually. Which is why I gave you explicit instructions on how to travel here safely." His eyes fell to the emerald ring around her finger, and he smiled. "You followed my instructions perfectly."

Mona followed his gaze, lifting her hand to inspect the ring. "This gem allows me to stay here, doesn't it?"

Evander nodded. He wasn't sure exactly what kind of magic emeralds possessed, but he knew it was essential to keep mortals alive down here.

Mona lifted a finger, her brow furrowing. "Wait. You said I didn't meet anyone else when I was here before? What about Trivia?"

Evander cocked his head. "Who's Trivia?"

"Hecate. She's a goddess. She was waiting for me when I arrived."

Evander's anger returned as he instinctively drew closer to Mona. He lifted a hand to the injury on her head, just barely brushing against it. His fingers came back sticky with her blood. Mona shivered from the contact.

"Did Trivia do this to you?" Evander growled, a low rumble rising in his throat.

"What? No. I must've hit my head when I arrived." She gazed up at him, her lips parting and her emerald eyes glowing. Evander could sense her pulse quickening. Did he frighten her? Or was it something else?

"Um." Mona cleared her throat, dropping her gaze. "She said she'd met me before. When I was here the first time."

"The name Hecate is vaguely familiar," Evander muttered. "But if she's a lower goddess, she would've served my father and Cyrus, so I wouldn't know her personally. I tend to keep to myself most of the time." Alarm pulsed within him. "What did she say to you?"

Mona hesitated, only fueling Evander's panic. "She— she told me where Prue is. In exchange for a favor from me."

Shock bolted through him, swift and merciless,

jolting his very bones. "You made a *bargain* with a god? Mona..."

She shook her head. "I had no choice! I had to find Prue!"

"Why didn't you come to *me*? I would've helped you without extracting a dangerous bargain from you."

She blinked. "You would have?"

"Yes! I would do *anything* for you, Mona."

A blush bloomed across her cheeks, and she averted her eyes once more. "I—I don't know what to say."

Dammit. Evander had gone too far again. He'd frightened her. He was essentially a *stranger* to her.

"I'm sorry," he said quickly. "I just—it concerns me that this goddess would manipulate you into bargaining with her. She didn't tell you what the favor would be?"

"No."

Oh, hell. That was even more dangerous. The favor could be *anything*. And it could be called in anytime. The endless possibilities made Evander's head spin.

"Don't trust her," Evander warned. "If you see her again, get away as fast as you can. She is *not* your friend."

"And you are? How am I supposed to believe that?"

Evander tried not to let her words sting. Of course he would need to prove his loyalties again.

Mona didn't know him. She didn't remember anything.

That truth cut through him so deeply his insides throbbed.

"I'll take you to Prue," he promised, then smiled. "Free of charge." He had never officially met Prue, but he was certain she would be near Cyrus, who was never hard to find.

"Trivia said she's in Tartarus."

Evander's head reared back. "*What*?" That couldn't be true. Could it?

Was Evander a fool for not seeking out Prue earlier? He knew she'd traveled here with Cyrus, and that she was now the queen of this realm... and a small part of him had wanted to meet her, to see how similar she was to Mona, to learn more about the woman he had fallen in love with.

But since merging with Typhon, he didn't trust himself around anyone. Especially someone mortal like Prue. What if he accidentally hurt her?

Besides, what if she despised him? What if he disgusted her so much that she vowed Mona would never love him?

Regardless of what Prue thought of him, Evander didn't imagine she would've gotten herself in trouble so quickly. If he *had* tracked her down, perhaps he would know for sure if Trivia was telling the truth about Prue's whereabouts.

But if she wasn't, it was a trap for Mona. No mortal

was safe in Tartarus. Even souls didn't survive the trauma lurking in its depths.

Gods, Mona was so fragile and delicate. If he left her here to go searching, what if Trivia found her again? What if one of the demon overseers came across her?

She was human. Mortal. She could die. It wasn't like before, when she was only a spirit, a transparent soul who couldn't be harmed.

Evander couldn't afford to leave her side. He would *not* lose her again.

But the mistrust in her expression hurt him, cutting him deeper with each passing moment.

"I don't know if Prue is in Tartarus," he admitted. "I highly doubt it, but my... enhanced senses will be able to track her down. I *can* find her, and I can take you to her. But only if you'll allow it. If I frighten you or if your magic is warning you away from me, then you are free to leave. I won't chase you or follow you. But gods, Mona, all I want to do is keep you safe. If you'll let me, I can protect you." He took a solid step away from her to give her space to think. "But the decision is yours. I won't force anything on you. I know I need to earn your trust once more."

Mona's mouth opened, her eyes wide with surprise. Her gaze roved over him again, but this time her expression changed into something thoughtful. "If my magic warns me away? You know about my magic?"

He nodded. "Earth magic. Your grace is roses. Or at least... it *was*. The last time you were here, you made thorns spring up from the ground." His face heated at the reminder. It had been when they were both naked together, his body pressed up against hers, her hips writhing against him.

"Thorns? Really?" Mona lifted her hand, inspecting it thoroughly. "I feel *something*. But it's like my powers are muted down here."

"They are. All magic comes from the heart of this realm. Anything else is dampened, quelled by the powerful energies here. The magic of the Underworld is too potent for other magicks to thrive."

"Which means Prue won't have her magic, either," Mona said, her eyes full of panic.

Evander frowned. "Prue is bound to Cyrus. They are connected, so his magic *should* protect her, too." But he was uncertain of this, especially given Cyrus's altered behavior.

Mona seemed to read the unease in his tone. "Take me to her. Please. I... I give you my permission, Evander."

Relief spread through him, and he found himself smiling. "As you wish." He drew closer to her, then paused. "May I?" He stretched his arms toward her, his wings flaring behind him.

Mona looked like she might faint, but she nodded

slowly. Evander wrapped his arms around her, bringing her against his chest. He could feel her rapid heartbeat, the warmth of her skin, and oh gods, she was so solid and *real* in his arms.

She's really here. She's really alive.

"Hold on to me," he whispered.

Her arms tightened around him, and with her gathered close to his chest, Evander took off into the sky.

FAMILIAR
MONA

MONA WASN'T SURE WHAT TO MAKE OF THIS horned, winged prince of Hell next to her. Upon first meeting him, something warm and... *familiar* had sparked to life in her chest. But it faded so quickly, she couldn't be certain if she was imagining it or not.

Immediately following that was fear and unease.

How could she not be afraid? Evander's appearance was terrifying. He looked exactly like the kind of demon Mona had nightmares about.

And yet... when she looked at him, when she heard him speak, she found herself wondering why she should be afraid of him. His voice was smooth, soft, and gentle. His gaze, while intense, was careful and hesitant. He seemed almost... *shy*. Which was absurd for someone as powerful as him.

When he'd approached and wrapped his arms around her before taking flight, there had been a solid sense of *rightness* between them. As if Mona's body belonged to him and yearned to touch him. His warmth, his strong arms around her...

She couldn't forget the look of tormented longing in his eyes when he'd first seen her. Before he knew she'd lost her memories.

What had happened between them before? What was he to her? What was *she* to *him*?

Frustration crept into the corners of her mind as she wished for the hundredth time that she still had her memories. Her encounter with Trivia had proven that not everyone in this realm was honest. Trivia claimed to know Mona before. But Evander claimed the opposite.

One of them was lying. And for some reason, Mona was inclined to believe Evander. Was her instinct correct, or was he manipulating her, too?

A million dizzying thoughts circled Mona's mind, but everything was silenced as soon as Evander took off into the sky. His great wings beat behind him, and Mona wrapped her arms more securely around him as the wind whipped at her, tossing her long hair wildly about them both. Her stomach dropped with each movement, and she forced her eyes open to witness the sights below her. As nauseating as it all was, how often would she get to see this?

Below her stood a great expanse of trees and shrubs. A wide, glistening river cut between the forest, winding as far as she could see. But as her gaze followed the river, an odd grayness took over the forest, creating a strange, hazy fog in the sky. Evander flew in the opposite direction of this murkiness, but Mona still squinted at it over his shoulder.

"What is that?" she asked.

Evander didn't follow her gaze, but the darkening of his expression indicated he knew what she was referring to. "There are... decaying sections of this realm, where magic cannot exist. The enchantments do not work there."

Mona frowned. "Why is it decaying?"

"Whatever happened in your realm at the time of your resurrection affected this realm as well. Something is... broken in the Underworld. It has been for a long time, even before your resurrection. There were small signs, mere hints of it. It's why your soul was unbound when you first came here. And now, after the incident in your realm with my brother, things are so much worse."

Mona's chest tightened with apprehension. "Can anything be done?"

Evander met her gaze, and they were so close that she could see flecks of gray and white burning in his silvery eyes. She felt she should withdraw, but she couldn't. Even if she *wanted* to, she had to cling to him to avoid falling from his grasp.

"I'm doing everything I can," Evander said at last. "But my abilities only reach so far. Whatever is causing all this is lurking in the shadows, undetected."

Mona pressed her lips together, thinking of the earth magic Evander had told her about. She *did* feel a swelling presence inside her, waiting to be unleashed. Could she help?

But that was ridiculous—why would she help? This realm meant nothing to her. She needed to find Prue and get out. That was all.

The thought sent panic and anguish roaring inside her, though she couldn't explain why. She shut her eyes to block out the pain.

"Are you all right?" Evander asked.

Mona took a deep, shuddering breath. "I *feel* things that I can't explain. Things my body remembers but my mind doesn't. It's very frustrating."

She opened her eyes to find Evander smiling. "You always did like a puzzle to solve."

Mona blinked at the warm familiarity of his tone. Before she could respond, Evander inhaled deeply, his brow furrowing. "Her scent ends here."

"What?"

"Prue. I can't smell her anymore. Hold tight while I land."

Mona obeyed, gripping his neck more firmly as he circled low, ducking below the treetops to land on a patch of decaying grass. Ahead of them, another strange mist obscured most of the forest. When her feet met the ground, Mona swayed, suddenly dizzy. Evander's arms were around her in an instant, steadying her. She leaned into him without thinking, her body growing hot from his close proximity.

"This isn't Tartarus, is it?" Mona asked.

"No." Evander gazed around, his eyes solemn.

"Another decaying area?" she guessed.

He nodded. "I call them voids. And they're spreading. I don't know how to stop it." He sniffed again, his brows furrowing. "I'm catching snatches of her essence in there, but my senses can't penetrate the barrier. The void is impeding my abilities."

Mona looked up at him, then glanced to the wings still outstretched behind him. "You have a heightened sense of smell?" Was he part animal? Somehow, the idea didn't frighten her as much as it should.

Evander met her gaze. "Yes. A part of me is tethered to the dark magic ingrained inside all of us. It would make sense that this magic wouldn't be able to function properly in a void."

"All of us?" Mona asked. "You mean you and your brothers? Or your father?"

Evander stared at her, stunned, his mouth opening slightly.

Mona felt the blood drain from her face as she realized why he was so surprised. He had only mentioned *one* brother to her. So how had she known about his other brothers, or his father?

"I—I—" She faltered, unable to form words.

"Yes," Evander said quickly, as if to spare her from her bewilderment. "I'm referring to anyone with my blood. Our magic manifests itself differently in all of us."

Mona nodded, still shaken. As she searched within herself, she *knew* Evander had five brothers, though she couldn't explain how she knew this. She also knew his father lived here, but not his mother. The further she dug into the recesses of her mind, the more the memories faded away like smoke.

"Mona." Evander gently grasped her elbow. "We can rest for a moment before we go in."

Mona's gaze darted to the strange fog awaiting them. Her insides quivered with anticipation. What would this void do to *her*, a mortal? Would it kill her?

Evander seemed to read the unease on her face. "It's harmless. Your magic doesn't work down here anyway, so the void has no concern with you."

"You speak as if it's a living thing," Mona whispered, her eyes never straying from the mist.

"It is. It's growing and multiplying like a living

organism. I just don't know what—or who—is causing it."

Mona suppressed a shudder.

"I wish you hadn't come back," Evander murmured, his voice barely above a whisper.

Mona whirled to face him, stung by his words. "What?"

"That's not—I didn't—" Evander gritted his teeth, his eyes closing in exasperation. "I didn't mean it like that. I'm overjoyed to see you again. I only meant this realm is dangerous. And I fear what it will do to you. You aren't just a spirit anymore—you're flesh and blood, and you can be harmed. The thought... terrifies me."

Mona's lips parted as she gazed at him in wonder. He was terrified of seeing her harmed? Tendrils of heat coiled in her chest at the look of conflict and yearning in his expression. Without thinking, she lifted a hand and pressed it to his cheek. His skin was surprisingly warm, and he leaned into her touch.

"I'll be all right, Evander." She found herself smiling. "I have you to protect me."

He huffed a short laugh. "I'm not invincible. I can't protect you from *everything*." His eyes darkened. "I couldn't before."

"Vasileios," Mona whispered.

Evander nodded. "Yes."

"Well, he's dead. He can't hurt me anymore."

Evander's head reared back. "How do you know that?"

"I was there. I—" But as Mona tried to reach those memories, they, too, faded away from her. She blinked, finding herself lost once more. "Dammit. As soon as I focus on it, it vanishes."

"The memories must be returning to you on instinct," Evander breathed, his gaze distant. "Remarkable. I've never heard of this happening before."

"Really? How many mortals have come through the whirlpool?"

"Well, it isn't usually humans who make it through. Sometimes gods or goddesses, or even demons." Evander's brows knitted together. "But I wonder if it has more to do with your magical heritage than your mortality."

"You think my *magic* is helping me retrieve memories? But I thought my powers didn't work down here?"

Evander's silver eyes bore into hers. "You're a witch, Mona. A powerful one. You got your powers to work before, so I wouldn't be surprised if it happened again."

A witch, Mona thought. *But not just an ordinary witch...*

She drew in a sharp breath as another memory formed in her mind. *A goddess.* Mona was a goddess.

Gaia's daughter.

A splitting pain seared through her temples, and

Mona groaned, hunching over with a gasp. Evander's hands were on her again, but she barely felt his presence through the agony sweeping over her.

In a flash, it was gone, leaving her trembling with fatigue.

"What's happening to me?" Mona panted, cramming her eyes shut against the echo of pain still rippling over her.

"The magic of the Pool of Forgetfulness," Evander said, his hands rubbing gentle circles on her shoulders. "The magic is fighting against yours." He swept his thumb down the length of her jaw. "Gods, please be careful, Mona. The power of that magic could tear you apart."

"What if my magic is stronger?" Once she was certain the pain wouldn't return, she straightened to look him in the eye. "What if my magic can win?"

Evander shook his head. "You are talking of the magic of the *gods*, Mona."

"And I'm a goddess," she said firmly.

Evander stilled, staring at her in shock. "A *goddess*?"

"Gaia is my mother. I remember it clearly."

His face drained of color. "Gods above, I..." He broke off, shaking his head in disbelief. "That explains *so much*. I knew you weren't just an ordinary soul."

Mona smiled. "You have the magic of the dead down here. But I have the magic of life. Whatever you destroy,

I can bring back to life." Her gaze turned to the void behind them. "Perhaps there's more I can do here than just rescue my sister."

Evander's grip tightened on her shoulders. "Mona, listen to me. This realm has existed for *millennia*. You can't alter the ancient powers here in just a day. You are powerful, yes, but your magic is no match for this. Even gods can be destroyed. It is more difficult to kill them, but it can still be done."

Mona looked at him, registering the panic and fear in his eyes, the desperate need to keep her alive. The plea in his gaze was almost too much for her. It unraveled her completely, leaving her bare and vulnerable before him.

Naked. His gaze left her naked before him.

In an instant, an image bloomed to life in her mind: Mona and Evander, naked together in the forest, his body pressed up against hers as they both moaned with pleasure. Mona's eyes closed, remembering the pure rapture and thrill of that moment. Her insides churned with an intoxicating heat that made her toes curl.

"Mona..." Something deep rumbled in Evander's voice.

Her eyes flew open, and she found his nostrils flared and his gaze burning with desire.

"I can... smell your arousal." His voice sounded pained. "What—what—" He seemed unable to form words. He swore under his breath and shook his head. "I think—"

A roar shook the ground. Mona stiffened, leaning into Evander and clinging to his tunic in alarm. Evander straightened, scanning the forest for the source of it.

"Evander!" Mona screamed, pointing at the void behind him. A tendril of black smoke emerged, curling like a large tentacle, before winding around Evander's ankle. Mona dug her fingernails into him, gripping him tightly, determined to keep him with her.

He noticed when she did. He bent over, trying to extract himself from the darkness. The smoke tugged at him, yanking his feet out from under him.

"No!" Mona screamed, grabbing his arms as she tried to keep him from the dark magic's grasp. "Let him go!"

But the dangerous presence kept pulling insistently, and Evander cried out, his face contorting. Mona's hands were slippery with sweat. She was losing her grip on him...

With one final tug, the magic yanked Evander from her grasp, pulling him into the mist, the fog obscuring him. Mona gasped as his screams echoed before he vanished entirely.

PANDORA

PRUE

PRUE'S MAGIC SWELLED INSIDE HER AS SHE MADE her way back to the palace. She felt alive for the first time in months. Every breath brought a renewal of energy to her body, a new awareness and clarity she didn't realize she lacked.

Her first instinct was to find Cyrus, to use her magic to *force* Kronos out of him.

But no. If she lost, she would have nothing left.

And Kronos didn't know she had her magic back. She needed the element of surprise. She needed to save her magic and use it to find whatever was hiding in Tartarus—the key to freeing Cyrus once and for all.

Prue found Lagos poring over maps in the throne room, a row of demon soldiers lining the wall behind him.

"Leave us," she ordered the soldiers, who bowed and exited the room without hesitation.

Lagos looked up and straightened. "My queen."

Prue hesitated, uncertain of how to approach this. Could she ask him questions about Tartarus without arousing his suspicions? Or should she be forthcoming and tell him *everything*?

The latter made her insides shrivel with terror. Could Lagos be trusted? He had pledged his blood to her, yes, but how much did Prue know about him? How much did she know about the laws of the blood bargain they had forged?

Even so, Lagos was a better option than Trivia, who had *not* sworn anything to Prue. And Prue still didn't trust her completely.

"You know there's something wrong with my husband," Prue began slowly, fingering the edges of the map closest to her. "A dark presence has taken hold of him. I... I've heard rumors of a curse in Tartarus that could possibly rid us of this presence. Do you know anything about this?"

Lagos went perfectly still, his impassive face revealing nothing. Not for the first time, Prue wished he showed facial expressions like mortals. But his animal-like facade remained unreadable.

"You speak of Kronos," he said in a hushed voice.

Prue nodded. *Yes, let him put the pieces together*

himself. She wouldn't reveal all the secrets she'd learned, but she knew Lagos would be able to guess many of them.

Lagos took a step closer to her. "My queen, are you telling me Kronos has escaped Tartarus?"

No point in denying it. Lagos was too clever to see through any of her lies. "Yes."

A shudder rippled over his form, and a low growl resonated in his throat. "I knew something had shifted in Tartarus. For ages, the air there has felt *different.* But I attributed it to the shift in power between Aidoneus and Cyrus."

"How was Kronos trapped before?" Prue asked, her pulse racing. She resisted the urge to fidget or wring her hands together. Goddess, she was so desperate for answers... It took all of her restraint not to grab Lagos by the shoulders and beg him for a solution.

"He was overcome by the darkness in Pandora's box," Lagos said. "The only thing powerful enough to overcome Kronos's power... is the magic inside that box."

Prue froze, her blood chilling. *Pandora's box.* She had heard of the legend from bedtime stories. Her mother had told her of the dangerous box that held all manner of horrors inside.

How much of that had been fiction? How much had been true? Knowing her mother was Gaia, did that mean *all* of her stories had been true?

"Pandora's box resides in Tartarus," Lagos went on. "No one has seen it since."

Prue remembered what Aidoneus had said to her: *Go ahead and venture down there. See what happens when you open it.*

Aidoneus had been speaking of the box. He *knew* it was the solution to stopping Kronos.

If he wanted Prue to open it, then surely it *did* contain the horrors Prue had heard about as a child.

"What's inside it?" Prue breathed.

But Lagos was shaking his head vehemently. "No one knows. The box draws in anything surrounding it. The last one to open it was trapped inside."

Prue's stomach dipped. *Oh, Goddess.* "Aidoneus didn't open it himself?"

"No. He sent one of his soldiers to do the deed."

Of course he had. Prue groaned and rubbed her forehead. What the hell was she supposed to do? Whatever could free Cyrus was inside that box, but if Prue opened it, who knew what would happen?

"My queen." Lagos drew closer and gently touched her arm. "Please tell me you aren't considering opening this box. It would require you to venture into Tartarus yourself, which is already a daunting task. But... the contents of that box could destroy this entire realm."

"The realm is already dying," Prue argued, letting her arms fall against her thighs. "Either I let Kronos take over completely, or I open this box and unleash an unknown darkness that *could* destroy everything." She shrugged. "I'd rather take my chances. We *know* Kronos will destroy us. But we don't know for sure what will happen if that box is opened."

"In your realm, the unknown is far less terrifying," Lagos said solemnly. "But down here, the unknown is the most frightening. The magicks that exist here are far more deadly and dangerous than you are accustomed to. There is a *reason* Pandora's box can only be contained by Tartarus."

"Yes, the same reason that Kronos was imprisoned there as well."

Lagos said nothing.

Prue placed her palms against the maps on the table, bracing her weight and leaning against the sturdy piece of furniture. She felt like crumbling. Everything around her was falling apart.

With Cyrus possessed, she was all this realm had left. How could she decide the fate of the Underworld?

"What would you do?" Prue asked, her voice barely above a whisper. "You've lived in this realm for far longer than I have. What would you do?"

Lagos remained silent for a long moment as he considered this. After a moment, he said, "I would learn as much as I could about either option. Kronos and the box. Find out any information that could be of assistance. Observe them as closely as I can without endangering myself. Then, make a decision from there."

Prue frowned at him. This was solid advice. But how could she learn more about the box without risking her own life? She was still half-mortal, after all.

Lagos bowed low, startling Prue from her thoughts. "It would be an honor to serve you and seek out the answers you need, my queen."

Prue gaped at him. "No!" she cried, her voice much louder than she'd intended. More quietly, she went on, "Lagos, I would *not* ask you to do this. It's far too dangerous."

"You aren't asking. I am offering. Besides, you cannot go yourself. You are the queen of this realm. If something happens to you, who will rule?"

Prue flinched. She still hadn't adjusted to the idea of her being the sole ruler of this place. *No,* she thought firmly. *It's only temporary. Cyrus will join me on the throne soon.*

"Who in this realm knows about Kronos and Pandora's box?" she asked.

"Besides Aidoneus? No one. Some other demons may have heard whispers, as I have. But the only ones who truly know of the origins of such darkness are the gods and goddesses who reside in Elysium."

"Can I reach them?"

Lagos huffed a dry laugh, which sounded more like a

snort, his large nostrils flaring. "No. There is a single portal to Elysium, but it requires a powerful amount of magic to pass through it. Even Aidoneus doesn't use it often. I fear this realm is too sick to even fuel such power anymore."

Damn. That didn't give Prue many options.

Kronos and the box both originated from Tartarus. It was becoming more and more clear that this was the place that held the answers.

Despite how her insides chilled at the thought of visiting such a place, she turned to face Lagos and said with determination, "We are going to Tartarus."

ALLIES

CYRUS

Cyrus's eyes flew open, his breaths coming in short gasps. His head throbbed with piercing intensity, a shrill scream echoing in his ears. Darkness pressed in on him, crowding him.

Slowly, he sat up, his head spinning. He raised a hand to his forehead to quell the pain. As his eyes adjusted, he realized he was in the caves of Styx. He recognized this particular chamber.

But... *why* was he here?

He carefully climbed to his feet, gritting his teeth against the ache in his bones. He took one hesitant step. Then another.

Nothing happened.

He waited for Kronos's presence to assault him as it

usually did, particularly when he was alone and vulnerable. But there was nothing but absolute and utter silence in his mind.

Hope bloomed inside him, but he squashed it down, focusing instead on his unease. Was Kronos truly gone? Or was this a trap? Was Kronos merely biding his time, waiting for Cyrus to expose his secrets?

Nothing about this felt right.

Cyrus strode forward, navigating effortlessly through the tunnels and passages until he emerged in the clearing that housed his palace. A surge of regret and longing filled him at the sight of the gleaming chrome walls and pillars. *His home.*

And gods above, what had he done? He had nearly destroyed it...

If there was any chance Kronos would come back and possess him again, Cyrus couldn't risk it. He had to know for sure.

He moved toward the palace, then froze as his gaze snagged on something on his arm. He lifted his right hand, stunned at the display of inky flames along his flesh. When he raised his left hand, he realized it matched it completely.

Holy gods. He glanced underneath his tunic, then tugged at his trousers to check his legs.

Every inch of him was covered in ink. Before, it had

only been the left side of his body. But the soul magic he'd used to vanquish Kronos must have conjured the remaining tattoos.

Cyrus wasn't sure what to make of this. His tattoos had always been a mark of his power. But was it *Kronos's* power? Had that magic *ever* truly belonged to Cyrus?

He thought of what Prue had said when he'd told her of his tattoos. *I like them.* The way her fingers traced over the curling flames on his skin... His insides warmed from the memory.

No, it didn't matter. What *did* matter was the proof this provided. These tattoos meant his soul magic had successfully extracted its price from him.

He tried not to think about what this meant for his soul. If he used more soul magic, what would happen? His body was already covered in ink; there was no more space left. Would one more instance render him mortal... permanently?

He shook his head. He could worry about this later.

Kronos was gone. He *had* to be. If Cyrus hadn't succeeded, wouldn't Kronos be exacting revenge by now? Wouldn't he have been waiting to ambush Cyrus?

Was it possible Kronos was only wounded? That he had fled before Cyrus had finished him off?

Cyrus set off with renewed determination. Instead of entering through the palaces front doors, he took the servants' doors and descended to the dungeons. This part of the palace was rarely used; if anyone needed to be imprisoned, they were usually sent straight to Tartarus. No need for a prison here when there was a much more effective one nearby.

For that reason, Cyrus kept some of his most valuable possessions here, knowing they wouldn't be disturbed. The air grew more chill with every step he descended. When he reached the bottom, the blue glow of his reflection bowl cast a gentle light about the empty space.

Except... it *wasn't* empty. A figure stood hovering over the bowl, peering into its contents.

Rage and indignation roared up inside Cyrus as he hissed out a low breath. "What are you doing here?"

The figure turned, and Cyrus took a step back in shock.

He had expected Aidoneus, perhaps even Marcellus or Leonidas. But he *hadn't* expected to see Romanos—the brother he rarely encountered. The brother who remained obedient, keeping his head down, never attracting too much attention.

Had it all been an act? Had Romanos been plotting against him, too? Cyrus had thought Romanos had been sensible, but perhaps he'd been wrong.

With a roar of fury, Cyrus stormed toward him,

prepared to rip out his throat. But when he noticed the glimmer of tears in Romanos's eyes, he stopped, his anger cooling.

Romanos cleared his throat and shifted his weight, casting his silver gaze downward. His dark hair fell into his eyes, obscuring his expression.

But Cyrus had seen enough. Whatever Romanos had been looking at in the pool had devastated him.

"Romanos," Cyrus said quietly. "What are you doing down here?"

"I haven't told the others about this place," Romanos said in a low voice. "I swear it. I—I only come down here to—to—"

This isn't his first time down here, Cyrus realized. He glanced around the room as if he could unearth any clues about Romanos's intentions. But the room remained empty, save for a few boxes and items covered in sheets.

"You best explain yourself," Cyrus said in a growl, "before I have you thrown in Tartarus."

Romanos sighed and lifted his gaze to meet Cyrus's. His expression was more guarded, but the lingering anguish still burned in his eyes. "There is a woman. In the mortal realm. I use the reflection bowl to see her every now and then. I just need to know what she's doing. How she fares."

Cyrus cocked his head. "You come down here to spy

on a mortal woman? How? Surely she would be dead after long."

Romanos shook his head. "Not this one. She's been cursed by the gods. She lives an immortal life, like we do."

A chill swept over Cyrus. When Romanos said *the gods,* Cyrus knew he didn't speak of anyone here in the Underworld.

He was referring to those in Elysium.

"Why?" Cyrus asked. "What is she to you?"

"Nothing. Not anymore. I met her during my one journey to the mortal realm. But I was cursed, too, and now I can never return to her."

Romanos is cursed? Cyrus stared at his brother in bewilderment. How had he not known any of this?

Romanos smirked at the shock on his brother's face. "It isn't something I want others to know. Can you imagine what our other brothers would do with this information?"

Cyrus found himself nodding. Yes, Leonidas and Marcellus would have used this information to their advantage. Cyrus didn't know the extent of Romanos's curse, but he was certain it came with weaknesses that others could easily exploit.

"Why are *you* down here?" Romanos asked, his tone more curious than demanding.

Cyrus bit back a snarl. How dare Romanos question

him? Ordinarily, Cyrus would insist he was the ruler of this realm and didn't need to explain himself. But his past actions—whether by Kronos's hand or not—made him feel inadequate. Like he didn't deserve to call himself a king anymore.

"I need to search for someone," Cyrus said, drawing closer to the bowl. "There is... a presence here that has managed to escape me. I need to know if I destroyed it or not."

Romanos frowned but asked no further questions. He stood back to let Cyrus approach. As Cyrus stood over the bowl, the blue glow burned against his eyes, bathing everything in a cool light. He took a deep breath, then glanced at Romanos.

Romanos crossed his arms and smirked, indicating he would *not* be giving Cyrus any privacy.

Cyrus sighed. *Fine.* It was no secret that Kronos was wreaking havoc in this realm. Perhaps Romanos could help.

"Show me Kronos," Cyrus commanded the bowl, ignoring the way Romanos stiffened next to him.

The liquid in the bowl rippled and shimmered, and Cyrus held his breath, waiting for it to conjure the one being he loathed more than any other.

His blood chilled as the bowl revealed a forest. But no... it shifted to the mist obscuring the forest. Within the mist were tendrils of black flame. *Cyrus's* black flame.

"Gods above," Cyrus whispered. Kronos was controlling the mists of the realm—the dark sections of poison slowly spreading throughout the Underworld.

"He's not corporeal," Romanos mused.

"His body must still be in Tartarus," Cyrus said, piecing it together. "He needs a vessel."

Romanos stared at him. "You. You were his vessel."

Cyrus nodded, not bothering to deny it. "But I vanquished him. So what is he after now? A new vessel? Or is he moving on to something else?" He frowned. "I know he wants to devour this realm, but how?"

The contents of the bowl rippled, showing an overhead view of the entire realm. Patches of gray mist were spreading along the Forest of Thanatos, as well as Lethe and Acheron.

Kronos's power was overtaking everything. And it would keep going until it obliterated the realm.

"If I find his body," Cyrus said, "maybe I can destroy it. Perhaps that would sever his power."

"It's a gamble." Romanos rubbed his chin thoughtfully.

"But when he was controlling me, he kept increasing the security around Tartarus," Cyrus said. "He was *terrified* of something there. At first, I thought he was afraid to go back. But now I'm wondering if he's worried someone will find his body."

Romanos's eyebrows lifted in surprise. "You would venture inside Tartarus to find it? Have you ever been down there before?"

"No," Cyrus admitted. "Have you?"

Romanos shuddered. "Once. I'm not eager to return."

"Romanos." Cyrus turned to face him. "You must help me. Our home is at stake. If you are cursed and cannot leave, think of what this would do to *you*. It would destroy you, too."

Romanos pressed his lips together, then scratched at his dark goatee. "You really trust me with this?"

"I don't have any other choice," Cyrus said. Honestly, Evander would've been his first choice, but he likely hadn't ever been to Tartarus, either. None of his other brothers or even his father would be of any help.

Romanos sighed, rubbing the back of his neck. "You're right. I don't particularly want to be devoured by Kronos. So, yes, I'll help you."

Cyrus breathed a sigh of relief, but Romanos raised a hand.

"On one condition. You help me break my curse. Help me *leave* this place."

Cyrus's brows furrowed. He had no idea how to break a curse cast by the gods of Elysium. But he would do anything—*anything*—to save his home. To save Prue. Even if it meant seeking an impossible cure for Romanos's curse.

Cyrus stuck out his hand, and Romanos shook it. "Agreed."

REMEMBER
MONA

MONA ACTED ON INSTINCT WHEN SHE DOVE INTO the mist, not caring for her own safety or the dangers that might be lurking within. She thought of only one thing: Evander.

She couldn't let the darkness have him.

The fog momentarily obscured her vision, and her body tensed, expecting that dark tentacle to wrap around her, too. But nothing happened. She took a deep breath, but it shook everything inside her. Fear clamped down on her, freezing her in place.

You are not a coward, she said to herself. She might be afraid, but that wouldn't stop her from moving forward. When fear existed, it only made way for courage.

"I can be courageous," Mona whispered before plunging onward.

As she entered the fog, it slowly parted to reveal a rocky wasteland of dust and stone. Towering boulders surrounded her. The sky was nothing but murky gray nothingness, an empty expanse that threatened to swallow her whole.

No magic, Evander had said. The trees, the sky, the grass... It had all been an enchantment.

Mona focused on her breathing, struggling not to faint from dizziness. "An illusion," she whispered. "The forest was just an illusion. This is the same place, just without magic."

An anguished shout echoed nearby, and Mona started sprinting without thinking. "Evander!" she shrieked.

The shouts continued, and she followed them, dodging large rocks and broken statues. She stumbled, her foot catching on a boulder, but righted herself and kept going.

Evander's cries subsided to low moans, but the sounds grew closer. Mona was almost there.

Then, she saw him. He was huddled behind a boulder, gripping his ankle and hissing breaths through his teeth.

Mona rushed over to him, crouching to inspect his foot. She froze when she noticed the tendrils of black shadows creeping up his skin, making their way up his leg.

"Oh Goddess, no," she breathed, her insides chilling as a memory surfaced. Inky blackness climbing up and up until it consumed the body entirely. The eyes going completely black before the life was extinguished from them...

This was the same darkness that had attacked her village. The same darkness she had given her life to stop.

But how could she stop it *now*?

Her own words echoed in her mind: *I have the magic of life. Whatever you destroy, I can bring back to life.*

She touched Evander's leg, and he growled in pain. Ignoring him, Mona closed her eyes, searching within herself for that powerful presence.

The presence of a goddess.

"Come on," Mona urged when nothing happened. "*Please.*"

She gritted her teeth, her head throbbing from the effort of drawing on her power. Her third eye quivered, as if it *wanted* to open. It *wanted* to help Mona.

"Come on!" Mona cried.

Evander's clammy hand grasped her arm, and she opened her eyes. His face was covered in sweat, and he shook his head. "Just leave me," he groaned. "Before it takes you, too."

"No," Mona snapped, rising to her feet. "I'm not

abandoning you. We just need to get you out of this void so I can conjure my magic."

"Mona—"

"Be quiet." She grabbed his arm and hauled him to his feet. He barked out a cry of pain. "Can you use your wings?"

"I—I don't know."

"Well, try, dammit!"

Evander grumbled something unintelligible, his wings flaring to life beside him. He shuddered, his form threatening to crumple, but Mona caught him, straining against his weight.

"Come on, Evander, I can't carry you," she said. "Get us out of here."

Evander nodded, his wings flaring. A brisk wind tickled Mona's back as his wings kept flapping until he was able to rise a few inches off the ground.

"Let's go," he said.

With her arm around him, Mona helped him navigate through the fog, occasionally tugging sideways to keep from crashing into boulders. He grunted when his wings dipped and his injured foot brushed the ground, but he kept pushing onward.

At long last, they emerged from the void, and Mona laughed in relief at the sight of the lush green forest before them. She walked Evander over to a stump and helped him sit on it. By now, the shadows had made it to his kneecap. Mona remembered the shadows moving much more quickly before, but perhaps his divine blood was keeping it at bay.

Mona took several deep breaths, still panting from holding Evander's weight. She gently pressed her hand against his leg, then closed her eyes.

I plead for help from the Triple Goddess, Mona thought. *Grant me power. Bless me with the magic of life.*

Her third eye blinked open, then closed. A burning fire churned to life inside her. Something hot prodded at her hand, and she hissed in pain.

"Mona," Evander said in warning.

Mona's eyes flew open, and she stared at the emerald ring on her finger. It was glowing white, and it *burned*. It was scorching her skin as if it would melt the flesh from her bones.

Of course, she realized. Without a second thought, she tugged the ring off her finger and tossed it to the forest floor.

"Mona, *no!*" Evander roared.

But it was too late. An explosion of light burst from her hand, bathing her and Evander in a warm glow. Power flared to life inside her, blossoming into a beautiful and overwhelming flow of energy. Her third eye flew open, observing everything.

Mona pressed her hands to Evander's leg and channeled her power against the shadows writhing against it.

"Use the magic of life to end this destruction," she whispered. "*Sano!*"

Evander howled in pain, his head thrown back, the tendons standing out on his neck. His wings twitched, quivering from his pain. But Mona pressed more firmly against the wound, intent on driving out all the shadows clinging to him.

Cracks split the ground, and thorny brambles spread from the gaps, snaking toward Mona as if summoned. Even the mist behind them seemed to shift, moved by the very presence of this extraordinary power. A soft wind rustled the leaves of the nearby trees, and dust and ash floated in the air. The thorns continued to rise up, mingling with the particles in the air until it seemed Mona was surrounded by a whirlwind of thorn and ash.

Be gone, foul magic, she thought angrily. *Leave him. Now.*

Sweat dripped down her face as she poured all of her magic into Evander, determined to heal him, to save him...

She was thrown backward, and she tumbled on the forest floor, her thorns receding obediently to avoid piercing her skin during her fall. Her limbs throbbed, and her skin was on fire. With a groan, she stumbled to her feet, searching for Evander. He still sat on the stump, gasping, gripping his leg with a shocked expression.

The shadows were gone. His leg was completely healed.

Evander's bewildered gaze flicked from his leg to the thorns spread along the ground. The ethereal wind had stopped, but the rest of the forest floor resembled a chaotic and decaying wilderness.

Mona rushed to his side once more, kneeling before him and resting her hands on his knees. "Are you all right? Is it gone?"

"How—how?" He shook his head weakly.

"I'm a goddess," Mona said. "The goddess of life."

"The ring..." Evander glanced at the ring discarded on the forest floor.

"It's meant to protect mortals," Mona said, the pieces clicking together in her mind. "But I'm not fully mortal, am I?" She offered a small smile.

Evander stared at her, his chest rising and falling with labored breaths. "You—you remember?"

Mona nodded slowly, her eyes never leaving his. She remembered *everything*. Evander's song, his dark demonic presence, her insistence that he merge with Typhon...

And he *had*. He had embraced both sides of himself.

Goddess, he was *here*, he was alive. With her.

Mona clasped his face in both her hands and brought his mouth to hers. He gasped in surprise, but his mouth moved over hers as if on instinct. As if his body wanted nothing more than to mold against hers.

He lifted her so she sat atop him, her legs wrapped around him. He moaned as her tongue slid between his lips, twining with his. She devoured every bit of him, savoring his warmth and his flavor. Goddess, he tasted *so good.*

"Mona," he groaned against her lips, the sound a plea. "Gods, *Mona…*"

Mona silenced him with another kiss, ravishing him with her lips and tongue and teeth. He was *all hers.* And she would claim him right here and now.

His hands were on her hips, hitching her skirt higher and higher until her sex was pressed flush against his trousers. Goddess, she needed all of him. *Right now.*

She tugged at his shirt, struggling to lift it over his head and his wings. Frustrated, she ripped at the fabric until it fell in tatters around him, exposing his bare, muscled chest. He was beautiful. Every inch of him was a masterpiece.

"I'm yours, Mona," Evander whispered, brushing loose strands of hair away from her face. "From here to eternity, my soul will always find yours. No matter where you are."

Heat and desire burned in her chest, and tears stung her eyes. How could she convey to him what he meant to her? How could she help him understand the gravity of what she felt for him? She pressed a hand to his chest and leaned into him.

"My soul has always been bound to yours," she murmured, her nose brushing his. "And it always will be. No force in all the realms can come between that bond. I love you, Evander. With my whole heart and soul."

His mouth crashed into hers with such violence that her bones quivered. He feasted on her just as she had feasted on him. His hands wound around her, ripping the dress and shift from her body until it left her naked atop him. Mona stepped off him only to tug his trousers free before she straddled him once more, gasping from the hardness pressing against her.

She had never felt such clarity and vibrancy, not even in that brief moment when she and Evander had almost taken each other before. Now, with her memories, with her magic, she felt more alive than ever.

She felt like a goddess.

Her hips ground against his, and he growled, his eyes flashing. His hands snaked up her back, tangling in her hair. He tugged, angling her face so he could kiss her more fervently. She thrust, rubbing against his cock mercilessly as he moaned into her mouth. His lips lowered, trailing down her neck, his tongue flicking against her skin and making her tremble with need.

Then, his mouth captured her breast, his tongue

circling her nipple. She groaned, shaking against him, pushing and demanding more of him, *more…*

"Please," she begged.

"Please what?" His tone was teasing as he licked her breast again.

"*Please*, Evander. Take me."

His hand cupped her rear as he shifted underneath her, his hard arousal rubbing against the moisture in her center.

Oh Goddess, she would die right here and now if he didn't take her.

Her fingers grasped his cock and squeezed. His hands clenched tightly around her as he roared, his voice echoing in the forest.

"*Now,*" she commanded.

He looked at her with ragged desire in his gaze, and she knew in that moment he would do *anything* for her.

She shifted, widening her legs around him, her core throbbing with anticipation. His cock nudged at her entrance before entering her fully. She cried out, her sex burning, her eyes pricking with tears from the intensity of him filling her. Pain coursed through her, but it was almost as intoxicating as her arousal. She clung to it, fingernails digging into the muscles of his back as he plunged into her, deeper, more firmly. She threw her head back from the sheer pleasure of it, of him wholly inside her.

His mouth found her neck, his tongue gliding along her skin. She rocked against him, relishing how she could clearly *feel* his cock moving inside her. Mona's insides melted, cascading into waves of arousal and desire, leaving no coherent thoughts behind. Evander thrust again, his hands pressing into her sweat-slicked back, bringing her more firmly against him.

"Harder," she commanded, her voice a low rasp.

Evander obeyed. He withdrew, then drove into her, the movement violent and eliciting a scream from her. He pulled out, then slammed in again. And again. Each movement had her moaning and crying out his name, her body on fire, the tension inside her coiling and mounting, soaring higher and higher. Her body jolted with each thrust, his hips moving in time with hers like a blissful rhythm that united them both.

Just like their shared song. The melody had them moving as one, like dancers. He pushed, she followed. He gasped, she moaned. Back and forth, they continued their routine until it felt as if their souls had joined together as one.

After one final thrust, Mona closed her eyes, crying out one last time, her throat raw from screaming as pure release flooded her, an explosion of pleasure and intensity so violent that her fingernails cut into Evander's skin. He buried his face in her neck, whispering her name again and again as he came, his body shuddering from his climax.

They clung to one another, both covered in sweat, both refusing to extract themselves. Mona's head was a muddled mess, her insides nothing more than a puddle. She could barely move. Barely *think*. All she knew was Evander, the feel of him inside her, the way their bodies aligned perfectly.

She didn't want to move. She wanted to preserve this moment forever. But already, they had wasted too much time. Mona still needed to find Prue.

Reluctantly, Mona shifted atop him, but Evander stopped her, his hands tightening around her waist. Exhaustion and satisfaction filled his face as he gazed at her, his eyes shining with delight. She had never seen him look so at peace. So at ease. He always carried this tension, this weight about him, as if the secrets he carried were a heavy burden.

But now, he looked… *free.*

Mona's hands found his face, her palms framing his cheeks. Her fingers traced the line of his jaw, down to his chin, then stopped at his collarbone. Only then did she realize his moonstone necklace was missing.

A slow smile spread across her face as she took in the wings behind him. "You merged with Typhon, didn't you?"

Pride glinted in his eyes. "I did. Because of you." He

brushed his lips against hers, the motion so chaste compared to what they'd just done that Mona found herself grinning wider.

Several minutes of blissful silence passed between them as their bodies cooled. Mona's stomach growled, her limbs aching with fatigue. She didn't want to think about how long it had been since she'd eaten.

"I'm sorry I don't have food for you," Evander lamented. "We don't eat much down here."

"It's all right." Mona closed her eyes and summoned her magic. From the cracks of the earth grew a vine of grapes. Mona slid off Evander's lap and popped a few grapes in her mouth.

Evander raised his eyebrows, clearly impressed. Mona bit back a smile, trying to ignore how drained she felt from using so much magic without resting.

But she didn't have time to rest. Who knew what Prue was enduring all this time? Mona *had* to find her.

She gestured to the mist. "So Prue isn't in there?"

Evander shook his head, grabbing his trousers before pulling them on. "When I was being dragged in there, I caught a whiff of Cyrus, too. It mingled with Prue's scent. I have a feeling whatever power is lurking inside was using Prue and Cyrus's scents to lure us in. To trap us."

Mona shuddered. What dark and dangerous thing lived in the fog? And why did it want to lure them in?

"So, what do we do?" Mona asked. "Do you think it's possible Prue *is* in Tartarus? Like Trivia said?" She found her shift, which was too torn for her to reuse, but her dress only had a few small rips in it, so she slid it on.

Evander was silent for so long that Mona turned to look at him, apprehension rising in her chest. After a moment, he said, "Mona, if that... *thing* has your sister's scent, it probably has her, too."

Dread coiled inside her, and she found herself shaking her head. "No. It can't be."

"I need to go to Tartarus. Even if Prue *isn't* there, this darkness is taking over the realm, and it originated from Tartarus. Perhaps if I can find the source, I can destroy it and free us all."

"Then, I'm coming with you."

Evander drew closer to her, alarm flaring in his gaze. "Mona, you can't. It isn't safe."

"You think I'm just going to sit here while you go to Tartarus? While my sister is probably suffering? Forget it." When Evander opened his mouth to object, Mona added, "Besides, I have my magic to protect me. I'm not helpless."

Half Evander's mouth quirked in a smile. "No, you aren't." He sighed, running his hands up and down her arms. "All right. We'll go to Tartarus together."

Mona grinned, standing on her toes to press a kiss to his mouth.

Evander's eyes shone with affection, but he gazed down at her somberly. "But you must be careful. And let me lead the way."

Mona nodded. "I promise."

Evander stepped back, then opened his arms. Mona stepped into them, wrapping her arms securely around his torso. His wings spread wide, and Mona braced herself as they took off into the sky.

TARTARUS
PRUE

PRUE SUPPRESSED A SHIVER AS LAGOS LED HER through the network of caves, her mind returning to those awful days when she'd been chained as a prisoner. And that whole time, she'd never realized Tartarus was so close...

Lagos seemed to know exactly where he was going, so Prue stayed close to him, knowing she could easily get lost in this labyrinth if she were on her own.

"How long were you a warden here?" Prue asked, her voice echoing in the caves.

"I lost count of the days." Lagos's tone was low and rough with emotion. "It helps if I lose myself down there. Detach myself from the tasks and from any concept of humanity. I simply... existed."

Prue's chest tightened, her stomach coiling with

dread. What horrors had her friend faced down here? "I'm sorry you had to endure that for so long."

"I wasn't the only one. The area has to be guarded by someone. If it wasn't me, it would've been someone else." The edge in his voice told her all she needed to know: *all* the people here were suffering.

Prue thought of the villagers of Erebos, poor and starving. If Lagos hadn't served in Tartarus, would he have lived in Erebos? Would he have been suffering no matter where he resided?

"We'll trap Kronos," Prue vowed. "Heal this realm. And start anew. I swear things will be different, Lagos."

He glanced at her over his shoulder but didn't stop. "They already are, my queen. You may not realize it, but you are already changing things. Starting with me."

A tendril of warmth worked its way into her chest, and she suppressed a smile as they continued walking.

After a moment, Lagos sniffed deeply, then grunted, his hand flying up to signal they should stop. Prue froze, her limbs rigid, as she listened carefully.

Then, she heard it. Footsteps. Low voices.

Alarm raced through her. Who could it be? Other demons? Or something else?

A whiff of something soft and flowery reached Prue's nose, and she stiffened. She would know that sweet earthy scent anywhere.

"Mona?" she whispered.

But no, that was impossible. Prue had resurrected Mona and left her in the mortal realm. She was safe. Happy.

The scent of her sister's magic grew stronger as the voices drew nearer. And Prue couldn't stop herself from moving forward, hurrying toward those voices. Lagos hissed a protest, but Prue ignored him, following the sounds, her heart pounding with anticipation and dread and hope and longing.

She rounded a corner and nearly collided with a pair of figures. The first had great wings tucked behind him and silvery eyes that matched Cyrus's—one of his brothers, no doubt. The second was—

"Mona!" Prue gasped, surging forward to crush her sister in a tight embrace.

Mona cried out in surprise and delight, clinging to Prue desperately, half sobbing and half laughing. "Goddess, Prue! I thought I'd never find you!"

Prue immediately withdrew and fixed a firm expression on her sister. "What are you *doing* here? I brought you back so you could *avoid* this place!"

"I'm here for *you*! This whole realm is in trouble, Prue. It isn't safe."

Prue blinked, stunned by this. Mona had come... to *rescue* her? "I made this bargain with Cyrus," she said softly. "I knew what I was doing."

Mona scoffed and crossed her arms, her doubtful

expression so familiar to Prue that she couldn't help but laugh.

"I guarantee you did *not* know what you were doing when you summoned Cyrus and bound yourself to him through marriage," Mona said in a flat voice.

Prue snorted, then covered her mouth. "Okay, you're right. *But* I knew what I was doing when I followed him here. I love him, Mona. I want to live with him in this realm." It surprised her how much the words rang true. She had never given it much thought, having been so consumed with finding a way to free Cyrus. But now that she considered it carefully, she *did* want a life here with her husband. She wanted to be queen. She wanted to create a better place for the people of the Underworld.

"The realm is dying," the winged man next to Mona said in a soft voice. "It isn't safe for anyone, let alone a pair of mortals like you."

His voice wasn't at all accusing, but Prue still raised her eyebrows at him. "And who are *you*? What are you doing with my sister?"

"I'm Evander," he said. "I'm... the guardian of your sister's soul. I've been her guide in this realm."

There was warmth and heat in his voice that made Prue shoot a dubious look Mona's way. Indeed, her sister averted her gaze, her mouth thinning. It was too dark to see clearly, but Prue would wager her sister was blushing right now.

"And who's *your* friend?" Mona asked, gesturing behind Prue.

Prue turned to find Lagos staring stoically at the pair of newcomers. She smiled and waved a hand in his direction. "This is Lagos. My advisor. And *my* guide to locating Tartarus."

Mona sucked in a sharp breath. "So, you *are* going to Tartarus?"

"Yes." Prue forced courage into her voice.

"No, you aren't," growled a familiar voice.

Prue's blood heated at the sound. Slowly, she turned to see another pair of figures approaching from behind Lagos. The first was Romanos, the prince of Hell who guarded the River Styx. And the other was Cyrus, his eyes gleaming in the darkness. They were all silver. Not a trace of black.

"Goddess above, *Cyrus*!" Prue sidestepped Lagos to rush to her husband, pressing her hands against his cheeks to inspect him thoroughly. She frowned at the sight of the tattoos now covering his entire body. But in a way, it only made him more alluring. She had always liked his tattoos. "What happened to you? Are you—Is Kronos—"

"I'm free," Cyrus said. "But so is Kronos. He's taking over the realm."

"Kronos?" Evander asked, his brow furrowing. "He's behind the darkness spreading here?"

Cyrus nodded.

"I've read about him," Mona said thoughtfully. "He was cast into Tartarus for betraying the gods. But... how did he escape?"

"Rumor has it he escaped when Cyrus bound himself to the Book of Eyes," Evander said. "He's been hiding, biding his time ever since."

A stunned silence fell between them, and Prue sucked in a sharp breath. That had been *ages* ago. Long before she'd summoned Cyrus. Kronos had been free that entire time?

At long last, Romanos murmured, "Well, there is strength in numbers, I suppose. Perhaps we can help each other."

"No," Cyrus snarled. "My wife isn't setting foot near Tartarus."

"Excuse me?" Prue crossed her arms. "Who has been ruling the Underworld in your absence? I'm the queen of this realm, and I'm doing this *with you*. Whether you like it or not."

Cyrus's mouth twitched as if he were holding back a smile, but he sighed heavily.

"How are we to believe you are truly free of Kronos's influence?" Evander said in a tight voice.

Cyrus straightened, his nostrils flaring from the challenge in his brother's voice. "Look at my skin, brother. It has been marked by the very soul magic I used to push him out."

Prue's heart hammered painfully in her chest. *Soul magic.* He had used it once to save her life. The price was a piece of his own soul.

How much had he given in order to vanquish Kronos? How much of his soul was left?

"We aren't accomplishing anything by standing here arguing," Mona said firmly. "We're all going to Tartarus. So, let's do this before Kronos poisons more of this realm."

Without waiting for a reply, she strode forward. Evander muttered a curse and hurried after her. Slowly, the group crept farther down the cave. Prue found Cyrus immediately, and his hand twined with hers. She exhaled in relief, relishing the warmth of his skin against hers, the solid *rightness* between them she had missed for so long.

Yes, this was truly him. Not Kronos. Her very soul could sense it.

"I missed you," she whispered.

He squeezed her hand. "I missed you, too." His words had an edge of anguish that twisted her heart. What manner of horrors had he endured while under Kronos's control? Was he reliving those horrors right now?

"We'll get through this," she promised him. "Together."

He nodded but said nothing, his gaze distant. Prue knew it would take time to get past whatever he'd gone through. But she vowed to stay by his side and help him through it. No matter what.

After a while, the tunnel opened up to a vast chamber. Nearby, the babbling waters of Styx echoed against the cave walls. But Lagos led them away from the river and toward the darker end of the chamber. Prue's magic rioted inside her, rebelling against the darkness she felt seeping into her bones.

Tartarus. Its power was strong; strong enough to frighten her own magic. But Prue swallowed down her unease and pushed forward, relying on Cyrus's steady grip on her hand to keep her grounded.

Lagos stopped short, and Prue glanced around him to find out why. Ahead of them was a large, gaping abyss, a well of darkness that resonated with power. But standing above it was a figure she recognized: Trivia.

Prue stepped forward, alarm rising inside her. "What are you doing here?"

Trivia turned, her eyes wide with concern. Beside her, a small creature bounded forward—Cerberus. His tongue lolled happily as he panted, his tail wagging behind him.

"Same as you, I'd wager," said Trivia. "I'm trying to save this realm."

Prue narrowed her eyes, doubting her words.

Trivia sighed. "I know you know about Pandora's box. That's why I'm here."

Prue stiffened, and she felt the others shifting uncertainly behind her.

"I've been researching the palace archives," Trivia went on, drawing closer. "The box is a magic repellant. It will *drain* all magic within seconds. That's why it was trapped; the gods here wanted to keep their powers and their magic. But if the box is opened, *all* magic—whether of the gods or of Kronos—will be pulled in and caged inside that box."

Prue stilled, her skin prickling as realization set in. The box would take *her* magic, too. And Mona's.

But if it meant trapping Kronos and freeing this realm...

"Is there any way to close the box?" Prue asked. "Once it's been opened?" She thought of the innocent citizens of Erebos. She couldn't doom them to whatever destruction would be unleashed if she opened the box.

Trivia frowned in consideration. "My research indicates only a powerful god or goddess can trap the magic inside the box once it's been opened. Aidoneus managed to do it once. And... you're the daughter of Gaia. You're powerful enough to close the box, too. I'm sure of it."

The certainty in Trivia's voice sent a bolt of confidence shooting through Prue's chest. "I'll do it," she said. "Even if it means giving up my magic, it's worth the price."

"Prue," Cyrus objected.

"But my sister has to leave," Prue went on. "I want her back in the mortal realm before the box is opened."

"No!" Mona cried. "Absolutely not."

"Mona—" When Prue turned to face her sister, she faltered, noticing Mona's hand clasped in Evander's. His frame was tense, his gaze fierce with a protectiveness Prue knew too well.

"I'm not leaving," Mona insisted. "I'm willing to give up my magic, too."

"I can help you find the box," Trivia said. "But—"

A low boom echoed from within the cave, and the ground began to tremble. Prue teetered, finding Cyrus at her side in an instant, steadying her. The walls quivered, and pebbles rained from the ceiling. Somewhere, a distant crash sounded.

"What is that?" Mona asked.

"It's going to cave in," Evander warned. "We have to get out."

"Not without the box." Prue surged toward the gaping pit, prepared to dive in, but Cyrus jerked her arm.

"Prue, *wait*—"

"It must be Kronos," Trivia said, glancing toward the

ceiling while Cerberus trotted in circles around her. "He knows we're here. He knows what we're about to do." She gritted her teeth, her gold eyes flashing with determination. "I'll head him off. Pull his attention away from here as long as I can."

"Trivia..." Prue said.

"I'll be fine. You all need to find the box as quickly as you can, understand? It's the only way to save this place."

Before anyone could reply, Trivia hurried away, vanishing into the shadows. Cerberus bounded after her, his clacking paws and her light footsteps echoing in the tunnel with their departure.

The walls shook again, and more dust fell from the ceiling. Panic burned in Prue's chest, and she knew if they waited too long, the ceiling would collapse on top of them.

They were out of time.

Prue slowly approached the gaping abyss, but she stopped when she heard her sister's panicked voice.

"Oh no... Where's Evander?"

Prue faltered, glancing around to find Evander had, indeed, vanished. Cyrus's gaze darkened as he scanned their surroundings, no doubt searching for a threat.

Mona wrung her hands together, shifting her weight. "I—I have to go find him. What if something happened to him? What if Kronos grabbed him again?"

"Again?" Prue said, alarmed.

Mona jabbed a finger at her. "I'm going to go look for him. Don't you *dare* go in that pit without me, Prue."

Prue almost laughed. *Of course* she would go without Mona, if it meant sparing her from the horrors of Tartarus. But if Evander really *was* in trouble, she had to let Mona track him down.

And so, even though the words tasted foul on her lips, she told the lie. "I'll wait for you, Mona."

Relief crossed her sister's face as she clasped Prue's hands in hers. She turned to face the tunnels, then hesitated.

"I'll go with her," Romanos offered. "I can lead the way."

"Thank you," Prue murmured.

Mona glanced at Romanos and nodded before they both darted away, their footsteps echoing in the tunnels.

Prue swallowed down her guilt and regret and turned to Lagos, who stood obediently next to Cyrus. "Lagos, I need you to get back to the castle and secure everyone inside. Prepare for the worst, in case we can't find Pandora's box or Kronos attacks."

"My queen," Lagos began, but Prue cut him off.

"You're the only one left who can warn everyone. Do what you can to protect everyone."

Lagos stiffened, clearly conflicted. After a moment,

he bowed and said, "Yes, my queen." He made to leave, then turned to face her. "Please be careful."

Touched by his concern, Prue nodded, trying to stifle the tears welling in her eyes. "You, too."

And then Lagos was gone, leaving Prue with Cyrus. He fixed a fearsome look on her, as if he knew exactly what she was thinking.

"I'm doing this, Cyrus," she said. "You can't stop me."

"I know," he said. "But you think I'll let you jump in there alone? I'm going with you, Prue."

Prue drew in a breath and looked at him, the clarity in his gaze, the fierce longing in his expression. She pressed a firm kiss to his lips, relishing the feel of him, solid and here with her. When she withdrew, they clasped hands and leapt into the pit together. Prue screamed from the fall, but the sound was lost as darkness overtook them both.

REVEALED

EVANDER

EVANDER'S MIND WAS ELSEWHERE AS HE DARTED through the cave tunnels, his mind only on one thing: Trivia

How did she know so much about Pandora's box? There was next to nothing in the palace archives. Evander knew that firsthand.

She was hiding something. Every inch of him quivered with unease, his instincts screaming that she was *not* who she claimed to be. After all, she had manipulated Mona into bargaining with her. But to what end? There were too many questions unanswered, and he couldn't just let her disappear.

The ceiling rumbled again, raining down more pebbles on his head. Evander hastened his pace, hurrying to catch up to Trivia.

The walls continued to tremble, and heavier rocks began to shower from above. It wouldn't be long before the entire structure caved in completely.

What would happen to the river? What would happen to Tartarus?

To Mona? To Prue and Cyrus?

Evander didn't want to consider it. If the horrors of Tartarus didn't destroy them, the collapsed cave certainly would. Cyrus, being a god, might survive, but Prue and Mona...

They are goddesses, too, Evander thought. *Not fragile mortals. They'll be okay. They have to be okay.*

He tried to ignore the small part of him that thought, *But goddesses can still be killed.*

He finally emerged just as a cluster of boulders crashed to the ground behind him. His wings spread wide, and he took off, trusting his bestial sense of smell to locate the mysterious goddess he was looking for.

It didn't take long for him to track her scent. She smelled of oak trees and woodsmoke. He easily tracked her across the river Styx, his gaze snagging briefly on the glistening Pool of Forgetfulness before he landed just north of it. Ahead of him, the glowing portal to Elysium gleamed and thrummed with power.

What the hell was Trivia doing *here*?

"I thought you seemed too quiet back there," said a voice.

Evander's eyes narrowed as the red-haired goddess came into view, her golden eyes glinting like a predator sizing up its prey. Beside her was that same black dog from before, its ears twitching as it watched Evander curiously.

"Who are you, *really*?" Evander demanded. "You aren't just some lesser goddess. No one knows that much about Tartarus or Pandora's box."

Trivia wagged a scolding finger at him. "Someone is too smart for his own good. That won't do, Evander."

Evander snarled, his wings stretching wide. Claws extended from his hands, and red burned in his gaze. If this traitor had anything to do with the destruction of his realm, he wouldn't hesitate to end her existence.

Trivia merely raised her eyebrows. "Impressive. But no match for me, I'm afraid." She spread her arms, and the ground rumbled and cracked, forming great fissures around Evander.

His wings flapped, raising him from the ground before it could swallow him whole. But from within the cracks sprang thick roots, winding around him. He frowned, his eyes widening as he remembered how Mona's brambles had done the same thing...

Earth magic. This goddess possessed *earth magic.*

The roots tightened, constricting around him, the bark grating against his skin. His blood boiled, raging from the restraints. He thrashed against them, struggling to break free, but the roots held fast, gripping him like chains.

"You—" Evander's words were cut off as a long root snaked around his mouth, gagging him. He choked on the bark, the damp and earthy taste filling his mouth. Gritty and bitter. Tough and unyielding. The taste of it was everywhere, drowning his senses. He struggled to free himself, but the roots had hold of his arms and legs now, too. They were inescapable.

Trivia had essentially created a brand new forest here, blocking them from view. No one knew Evander was here. No one would know if she obliterated him. He stared at the dog, hoping he would bark or make some noise to alert someone to their presence... but the creature was sitting happily on the ground, scratching behind his ear with one paw, oblivious to the grimness of the situation.

Thank the gods Mona hadn't followed Evander... He regretted sneaking off like that, but this was exactly the reason why he didn't want her with him.

Trivia drew closer to him, all smugness gone from her face. Only pure rage remained. "I am Pandora," she hissed. "My magic has been trapped for far too long, and I plan to unleash it. I *will* have my revenge. Starting with this wretched realm."

Evander stared at her with wide, disbelieving eyes. It couldn't possibly be true...

Trivia—Pandora—laughed at the bewilderment on his face. "I know. I've hidden my identity well, haven't I? But the gods will pay for what they did to me. They were angry with Gaia for trying to replicate the Triple Goddess's power with triplets."

Shock rippled over him, and for one stunned moment, he stopped struggling against his restraints.

"Oh, yes," Pandora said, delighted by his reaction. "There are *three* sisters. Prudence, Pomona... and me."

No. She had to be lying. She *had* to.

But the evidence was all around him. Earth magic, so potent it could only be born of a goddess.

Pandora. How? Pandora was an ancient being; her magic had been trapped eons ago. There was no way she could have been living among them for so long without anyone knowing.

"When the gods found out, they punished Gaia. She tried to protect her children, but she could only save two. The third one was captured by Janus himself. As punishment, he imbued the child with the soul of Pandora, bringing all her pain and misery to life in a newly born vessel."

Gods above. That was how she'd done it. Pandora had been reincarnated as Mona's sister. Now, this goddess before him had all the anger and resentment and anguish of the original Pandora, whose essence had been trapped within that box.

"Evander!" shouted a voice.

Evander stiffened. *Mona.* She'd gone looking for him after all. His chest swelled with part relief, part horror. What would Pandora do to her?

"Shit," Pandora muttered, glancing over Evander's shoulder. "I was going to simply destroy you, but it looks like we're out of time, handsome. You'll have to come with me. Can't have you telling the others my secret, now, can we?"

Evander's protests were muffled by the roots in his mouth. He choked and gagged, struggling to breathe. Red bled into his vision, his demonic side thrashing and desperate to be unleashed. And, oh, how he wished to release all of Typhon's terrible power on this goddess before him.

But her magic was too strong. Far stronger than Evander had anticipated.

Pandora knelt next to the dog, scratching behind its ears. "Sadly, you can't come with me, sweet thing. Go home, Cerberus." As she stood, the dog obediently bounded off, disappearing between the trees.

Pandora waved her hand, and her roots slid Evander forward. The golden glow of the portal of Elysium burned against his gaze.

Realizing what was happening, Evander thrashed more intensely, screaming against her hold on him.

She was going to take him through the portal.

"Evander!" Mona's voice grew closer.

Evander writhed, managing to get one arm free. He used his hand to tear the roots away from his mouth. "Mona!" he yelled. "Stay back! She's not—"

An explosion of power slammed into his head, making him see stars. Dizziness overcame him, and he slumped over. He barely registered Pandora loosing her branches on him. He fell over, dazed from whatever she'd struck him with.

She caught him under the arms and whispered, "Let's go for a ride, shall we? See how well your demonic nature survives..."

I'm going to die, Evander registered faintly. Demons couldn't survive in Elysium. And now that he had fully merged with Typhon, the two were inseparable. Without the moonstone necklace to cage Typhon, there was no escaping it.

The realm of the higher gods would tear him apart.

He would never see Mona again.

I love you, he thought, unable to say the words. *I love you with all my soul.*

He caught a glimpse of her wild mane of hair, her panicked eyes, just before Pandora pulled him through the portal. A flash of gold light enveloped him, followed by a slicing pain cutting straight to his bones. He screamed as everything went dark.

DARKNESS
CYRUS

Cyrus's hand was still linked with Prue's, his grip firm and unyielding as the darkness consumed them. He would *not* let her go. Even if this prison ripped him to shreds.

He would never let her go again.

"Cyrus?" she whispered.

"I'm here."

Prue drew closer to him, her warmth soothing against the icy chill of Tartarus.

Gods, they were really here; in the deepest pit of Hell. The torturous prison reserved for only the vilest of souls.

"How do we find the box?" Prue asked. Even though her voice was faint, it still echoed in the vast cavern.

"Follow the magic," Cyrus said. "It should leave a trace of its power."

Prue trembled in his grasp. "I can't feel anything but darkness."

"That's what this place wants you to feel. Don't give in to the fear, Prue. Everything here is an illusion."

"Even you?"

Her attempt at humor was feeble, but Cyrus smiled all the same. He pulled her flush against his chest, letting his hands roam up and down her ass. He leaned in, relishing her floral scent, his lips brushing along her throat. "Does this feel like an illusion?"

She shivered, but he knew it wasn't from the cold. Her skin heated against his touch, her body arching into him. "How would the gods react if we made love right here in Tartarus?"

Cyrus's blood thrummed at the prospect, and he laughed. Gods, the look on Aidoneus's face would've been priceless. To defile such a place would be the worst offense.

It almost made him tempted to try.

But the ground rumbled again, reminding them they had little time left.

"Come on." Cyrus withdrew, taking her hand once more. "Tell me if you sense anything unusual."

He led Prue through the darkness, stepping carefully to avoid tripping over loose rocks or boulders. The blinding darkness around him threatened to swallow him whole, making him feel helpless and weak. But he searched within himself for his magic, his power. There was only a fragment remaining, with Kronos gone from inside him. But his soul magic still lingered, as well as a remnant of the death magic ingrained into his blood.

He wasn't powerful anymore. Everything he had sacrificed to be the strongest in the realm... It was all for nothing.

And yet, as he clutched Prue's hand in his, he found he didn't regret any of it. He had his queen. He had his mind free of Kronos's influence.

Yes, this was worth it. The certainty of it surprised him. Power had been his goal for so long... It seemed like an impossible ambition to let go of, and yet, he knew what it felt like to be separated from Prue, to have a dark presence come between them.

He would never risk that again. Never.

"Tell me," Prue said suddenly. "What is Erebos? You said you'd never heard of it, but..."

Cyrus sucked in a breath. "I did some research after you mentioned it. There *was* a village created... in my absence. Someone organized a city of demons and mortals while I was in the Realm of Gaia with you. They did it behind my back, and when I returned, I knew nothing of this new civilization."

He could almost feel the confusion rippling off her. "But why? To what end?"

Cyrus shook his head. "I don't know." His thoughts were already in turmoil, but they continued spinning with the idea that there was a cluster of his people living in this village and *suffering*.

Who would want to create something like that? Who would organize a village only to abandon it?

Silence fell between them, and Cyrus had to focus on something else. Unless he wanted Tartarus to prey on his fears.

"This place toys with your mortal senses," he explained in a low voice. "You have to trust your *immortal* senses."

"I don't know how."

"I know. I'll help you." Cyrus found himself smiling again. Prue had only just found out she was the daughter of a goddess. Her skills were untrained.

But Cyrus had been practicing his magic for eons. Even if he had very little power left, he knew how to use it. Already, he could sense the dampness, the cold familiarity of these caves. They were different from the ones above; these were deeper. A gaping abyss waiting to devour him. Each step brought a suffocating darkness, a blinding shroud of inky blackness that could utterly devour him.

That was what Tartarus did. It consumed its victims from the inside out.

Cyrus focused on the chill, the coldness that his magic recognized. It was easy to be swept up in the empty nothingness that surrounded him, so instead, he focused on what else he knew. The ground against his feet crackled with each step, the stones and pebbles reminding him that there was something real and tangible to be felt here. Not just fear and uncertainty.

"Search for that place within you that houses your magic," Cyrus said as he did the same. "Find the light inside you. Allow it to illuminate your surroundings."

Prue tensed beside him, and he knew she was focusing, her thoughts intent on her task. After she huffed an exhale, she said glumly, "Nothing is happening."

"You have to dig deeper. This isn't just your witch magic you're conjuring. This is the power of the Triple Goddess. You have it in your blood."

Prue sucked in another breath, her grip on his hand tightening. Cyrus closed his eyes and dug deep within his reserve of magic until he found the gold light of soul magic.

How much of his immortality was left? He had used so much of this magic already...

But he didn't have a choice. It was his only weapon down here.

Light gleamed in the darkness, burning against

Cyrus's eyes. He winced against the intensity of it, expecting the gold glow of his soul magic.

But this light was white. Ethereal. Divine.

And it was coming straight from Prue's chest. Her eyes were still crammed shut in concentration. The glow spread to her arms and hands until her entire body was alight with power.

"Gods above," Cyrus murmured, awestruck by the angelic presence of his wife.

She truly *was* a goddess.

Prue's eyes flew open as she looked at him, her shocked gaze taking in the glow before her. Her face split into a wide smile.

"Hold on to it," Cyrus warned. "The magic here will try to fight back."

"I'll try." Prue scanned their surroundings, squinting against the brightness of the light.

"What do you sense?" Cyrus asked. He conjured his feeble soul magic and felt the glow burn within him.

Something thrummed just ahead of them. Cyrus stilled, his eyes drawn to that dark corner of the cave. The air churned with power, a warm current that washed over him with a familiar smell. Something ancient and powerful.

Prue turned before he could speak, her senses no doubt drawn to the same thing. "Over there. Something powerful is over there."

Cyrus nodded, clutching her fingers in his as they drew closer. Prue's magic lit the way as they approached. Cyrus expected—hoped—to find the box, but of course it wasn't that simple.

Instead, he found a prone figure lying on the ground, eyes closed and long, dark hair spread around him like a mane.

Prue gasped, her hand flying to her mouth. "It's a *man*."

Cyrus narrowed his eyes, crouching as he inspected the figure. The man had a mustache and beard, his tunic and trousers finely crafted. There was *power* about this figure. He wasn't a mere mortal.

"Kronos," Cyrus growled.

Prue's eyes widened. "This is his body?"

"It has to be. His power smells the same." Now that Cyrus was close enough, he knew for sure; it reeked of the same icy coldness that had overtaken him before.

"We have to destroy him," Prue said. "But how? Isn't he a god? How do you kill a god?"

Cyrus swore, running a hand along his face. "I *could...* with my death magic. But that—"

"Belongs to Kronos," Prue finished.

"Yes."

"And my magic only creates life," Prue said. "It was never meant to destroy."

Cyrus nodded absently. He would never ask Prue to

end a god's life like that. His own soul was tainted enough; one more murder wouldn't make much of a difference. But Prue? Her soul was much more pure. And he intended to keep it that way.

Frustration boiled his blood, and Cyrus hissed out a low breath. Of course he would find the one thing he hoped to destroy... only to be unable to destroy it. It was torture.

He froze as something occurred to him. Slowly, he approached Kronos before prodding the god's arm.

Cyrus's hand passed right through it.

"Damn. It's an illusion." Cyrus straightened. "The place is toying with us."

"But the magic," Prue protested. "I can smell it, too."

"Tartarus has the power to manipulate all the senses. Even smells. Come on, we have to keep looking."

They continued onward, hand-in-hand, both of them tense with apprehension at what they would find next.

Then, a strangled cry poured from Prue's mouth. She broke her grip on Cyrus and surged forward.

"Prue, *wait—*"

Cyrus hurried after her, but the darkness had already swallowed her completely. His steps faltered, and a single light appeared in front of him. Alarm and suspicion crept through him. This light wasn't coming from his magic—or Prue's.

It was from Tartarus itself. Which meant the darkness had something to show him.

This couldn't be good.

A prone figure lay on the ground before him. For one moment, he thought it was Kronos again. But as he drew closer, his chest constricted, cutting off his breaths and plunging him in icy horror.

Prue lay on the ground, her wide, unseeing eyes fixed on the ceiling. A trickle of blood oozed from her lips. Her arms and legs jutted out at odd angles, as if every bone in her body had been broken. Bruises spotted her arms and neck.

"Prue," Cyrus choked out, his throat closing. Gods, he couldn't breathe. He stumbled forward, crashing to his knees. A distant part of his brain chanted, *It's not real. It's not real.*

But her body was here. She was so real in front of him. The anguish on her face, the despair and fear... The sight of her like this twisted Cyrus's insides until he thought he might unravel completely, leaving his own body alongside hers. Deformed. Useless. A soulless, empty shell.

Some distant cry echoed in the caves. Ordinarily, Cyrus would dismiss it as another tortured soul in Tartarus. But he knew this voice intimately.

It was Prue. She was *alive.*

That bolt of clarity burned through his haze of

misery. He climbed to his feet, legs shaking, and blinked fiercely at the sight of Prue's dead body. Squinting, he stared hard at it, trying to conjure his magical senses, trying to remind himself to see past the illusion.

The image of Prue flickered. Cyrus breathed a sigh of relief.

In a flash, her body vanished, and a new one took its place. Prue's sister, Mona. She lay on the ground, a jagged, bloody gash covering her head, exposing her skull. Beside her was Prue, on her knees and sobbing.

Cyrus lunged for her, his hands pressing into Prue's shoulders. She was solid and warm and *real* in his grasp. Thank the gods.

"Prue." He squeezed her shoulders. When she didn't respond, he shook her slightly. "*Prue.*"

"Mona," Prue wept. "I—I couldn't save you. *Mona!*"

"It's not real!" Cyrus told her. "Prue, come back to me. It's just an illusion. Trust your magic. Break free. You're stronger than this."

Prue trembled, her shoulders shaking with more sobs. Cyrus gathered her mass of curls together, tucking them over one shoulder and exposing the back of her neck. He crouched down, dragging his lips up and down the column of her neck.

She shuddered, then gasped, and Cyrus knew the touch of him jolted her from her grief.

"Breathe," he murmured against her skin. "Find yourself. Assess your surroundings. You can do this."

Her breathing turned ragged and then slowed. She exhaled, long and deep. Eventually, her body stopped shaking, and she turned to face him, her red-rimmed eyes swimming in tears.

"You t-told me it was an illusion," she whispered. "How did I still fall for it?"

"This place captures your first impression and clings to it," Cyrus said. "If you see an illusion and immediately know it's false, you are safe. But... if for even one moment, it claims you, convincing you it's real... then Tartarus has you."

Prue gripped his arms tightly in hers, and he helped her to her feet. For a moment, she buried her face in his chest, and he wrapped his arms around her, still shaken by the illusion that had deceived him, too. They held each other, clinging to reality and the support of each other. For the first time, Cyrus was glad she was here with him. He hadn't wanted her to jump into the pit, but it was such a comfort that they had one another to depend on.

For what felt like hours, Prue and Cyrus crept forward, pausing often to assess their divine powers, to seek with the one sense Tartarus did *not* have control over. It was difficult to trust in these new instincts, especially with Cyrus's magic so depleted. He had spent enough time in the mortal realm with Prue to easily rely on his human needs and senses. And now, with his magic drained, he was starting to rely on them once again.

Prue struggled, too. She'd spent her entire life living as a mortal witch.

And she and Cyrus both had many, many fears for Tartarus to play on.

At one point, the illusion they found was a different version of Mona dead on the ground—this time, her throat slit and blood coating her body. In another illusion, it was Evander, his wings shredded and his eyes open and empty.

In one instance, Cyrus found himself in a cage, his body withering away, the skin barely clinging to his bones. Kronos had control of him once more, leaving his eyes all black as he roared like an animal.

Each vision broke them more and more, but each one reminded them they couldn't trust their mortal eyes.

It took them several tries, several attempts at locating a powerful source of magic only to discover it was an illusion, before they could fully rely on their immortality to lead the way.

Cyrus knew exactly when it happened. His forehead was covered in sweat from the mental exertion of retraining his mind. But once he tapped into that source, the source of his powers and magic and immortality, the air changed. The darkness fled from the cave, revealing a wide and nearly empty chamber.

Screams echoed around them, causing bumps to rise on Cyrus's arms. A chill snaked over him as he realized he had finally pierced through Tartarus's illusion.

All that remained were the tormented souls that were already down here.

"Prue—" He turned to face her, and his blood ran cold.

She no longer stood next to him.

OPEN
PRUE

PRUE WAS WORKING SO HARD AT SUMMONING HER goddess magic that she didn't realize when Cyrus's hand had slipped from hers until it was too late.

She reached for him, only to find an empty space. Panic bloomed in her chest. "Cyrus?"

No answer.

Oh Goddess, no...

"Cyrus!" Her voice bounced against the cavern walls, reverberating in her ears. Darkness pressed in on her once more, and she focused on her shallow breathing. Her eyes closed as she searched for her magic again.

Don't panic, she told herself. *Trust your magic. Don't let the fear take over.*

She counted each breath until she reached ten. Then,

she started again until her heart rate slowed and her body stopped trembling.

A white light burned against her eyelids, and she opened her eyes to find her body aglow again.

And this time, the darkness of Tartarus had faded completely. It was now illuminated as if sconces lined the walls. There was no darkness, no magic pushing against her. It was just... an empty cave.

Screams echoed in a nearby tunnel, and Prue jumped, her pulse skittering. The cries were faint, but they still tugged at her heart, drawing her in.

The tormented souls of Tartarus.

Sympathy swelled within her, but she pushed it down. She couldn't do anything for them. Not right now.

No, she needed to find the box first. That was the priority.

Clinging to her new and solid sense of power, Prue strode forward with purpose, entering the first tunnel and winding her way through it. She paused frequently to smell the air, to sense any power lurking nearby. If she sensed nothing, she turned back around until she reached the wide chamber once more, then took a different tunnel.

When her body was covered in sweat and her legs ached from her constant walking, Prue finally sensed it. A deep hum that made her bones quiver. The smell of oak and embers met her nose, and she frowned. The scent was somewhat familiar, but she couldn't quite place it...

Even so, her curiosity had her following the source, eager to find what magic emitted such intense power. She wiped her sweaty palms along her skirts, her steps eager as she followed a tunnel, turning at a fork and continuing onward. The power grew, making the walls rumble. Prue's blood sang with awareness. She felt... a *connection* to this magic. Something she couldn't deny. It bonded with hers in a way that—

She stopped short. She had only ever felt this way with Mona's magic.

Was her sister down here?

"Mona?" Prue hurried forward, determined to find her. She rounded a corner and froze, her mouth falling open.

A small, square black box rested on the ground in front of her. It seemed small and insignificant, but with the power emanating from it, Prue knew it was anything but. Wisps of smoke floated from the box, tickling her nostrils.

Then, she realized why it smelled so familiar.

It smelled like *Trivia*.

The goddess hadn't had such a strong fragrance; it had been muted somehow. But this definitely had traces of her magic.

How? Why? Trivia had seemed to know a lot about

the box, but to have her magic embedded in it? That would mean...

"No," Prue whispered, crouching over the box to inspect it more thoroughly. The powers emanating from it *called* to her. It called to her magic. The energies swelling inside her flowed forward in response, like greeting an old friend.

Earth magic. Whoever had crafted this box possessed a fraction of Gaia's power.

Just like Prue.

But... what did that have to do with Trivia? Did this mean *Trivia* possessed the same kind of magic as Prue?

Prue lowered her head to sniff deeply, closing her eyes. In a flash, a dozen images flooded her mind. Her mother, the vines springing from the ground when Prue had fought her, Mona's corpse when she'd sacrificed herself, and...

Visions she'd never seen before filled her thoughts. Gaia—her mother—clutching three children against her chest, knowing she couldn't save them all.

Trivia, a young woman with dark red hair, her golden eyes glowing as she lifted her arms. Thick roots poured from the earth at her command. Prue stared in horror as the vision displayed Trivia organizing the village of Erebos, intent on creating a destitute city to prove to Prue how evil the gods were, how they didn't care about the welfare of others.

Trivia had tricked her, creating this suffering village as a ruse for Prue, trying to turn her against Cyrus.

Dread burned in Prue's chest as she watched the vision shift. The buildings and homes rose up from the ground, sprouting new life. Demons poured through the village gates, eager for a new home.

Trivia had created a whole new society with her magic.

Gaia's magic.

The Triple Goddess.

Trivia had the power of the Triple Goddess, just like Prue and Mona.

This was more than just the two faces of Janus. The Gemini twins. Prue and Mona had been powerful as twins, but how much *more* powerful would their magic be if there had been a third sister?

A third facet to the Triple Goddess's powers?

"Mother, what have you done?" Prue whispered, her hand shaking as she covered her mouth in horror.

But no, it couldn't be. The magic within Pandora's box was *ancient.* And Prue and Mona were only eighteen. It was impossible!

And yet, she couldn't deny the familiarity of the magic contained in this box. Was this Tartarus playing tricks on her again?

She glanced around. The tunnel was still illuminated, the icy darkness no longer surrounding Prue. She had broken through the enchantments and illusions.

This was real. The box was really here.

But she had to be sure. She raised her hand, letting it hover above the black box. The tendrils of smoke wrapped around her fingers as if welcoming her, beckoning her closer. She was a kindred spirit.

The earth magic recognized her.

Prue shuddered just before pressing the tip of her finger against the lid. She almost hoped her hand would pass through it; that this was all an illusion to trick her, to make her panic.

But her finger met something solid and warm to the touch. A whimper escaped her as she pressed her lips together to keep the tears from falling.

It was true. Trivia—or whoever she was—possessed earth magic. She, too, was Gaia's daughter. And her powers were a part of the magic embedded in this box.

It doesn't matter, Prue thought with determination. *I still have to open it. It's the only way to end Kronos.*

Had Trivia been telling the truth when she'd said the box would drain away all magic in the land?

If she'd been hiding her identity, what else had she lied about?

Prue shook her head, withdrawing her hand to take several deep breaths.

"I have to do this," she whispered. "For Cyrus. For Mona. For this entire realm."

Prue moved to open the box, but a figure appeared in front of her. She scrambled backward, yelping in surprise as she took in this tall stranger.

She recognized him. It was the same man she and Cyrus had found lying on the ground before.

Kronos. In the flesh.

Prue stared, her mouth open in shock. What was he doing here? What would he do to her? Would he kill her?

Then, she frowned. *Could* he do anything to her? His magic was unleashed, roaming freely across the Underworld. Did this corporeal form of his even *have* any power?

Prue drew herself to her full height, looking him in the eye. "What do you want?"

"I want to stop you from making a grave mistake," Kronos said, his voice low and steely.

Prue scoffed. "A grave mistake would be letting you continue to poison the Underworld."

"I am remaking it. The realm will be born anew, cleansed of the evil that has plagued it for so long. But this"—he gestured to the box—"will erase the realm completely from existence."

Prue's eyes narrowed. *Erased from existence?* "I don't believe you."

"And yet you believe everything your husband tells you? You believed that witch, Trivia. And look where that got you."

The sting of Trivia's deception cut Prue deeply, and she swallowed around the lump in her throat. "You want to *cleanse this realm* of everything and everyone I love. I can't just stand by and let you do it."

"The contents of that box will destroy it all anyway." Kronos's expression remained impassive. "This realm is doomed either way."

Dread sank in Prue's chest like a heavy weight, but she shook her head, refusing to believe it. "No. I can close the box again. The realm will be safe."

Kronos chuckled, offering a patronizing smile. "Oh, child. Do you really think it's that simple? When you've lived as long as I have, you'll learn that sometimes the only way out is to wipe the slate clean and start again."

Wipe the slate clean. He said it so callously, as if this realm weren't full of hundreds of lives, millions and millions of souls who each had their own unique story. Their own personality. Their own desires.

Kronos or Trivia?

Both deceivers left a foul taste in Prue's mouth. But Trivia had never tried to kill her or anyone she loved.

And in the end, the choice wasn't between Kronos and Trivia... It was between what Kronos wanted and what *Prue* wanted.

Prue didn't trust Kronos. But the magic emanating from this box was familiar to her. It shared a kinship with her own magic.

And *that* she trusted.

Kronos didn't want her to open the box. That was all the convincing she needed to know she *had* to.

He seemed to read the intent in her gaze. He lunged for her, but not before she grasped the lid and opened it.

A roar exploded from within, making her ears throb. She screamed, flying backward from the force of it as a river of shapes and images flooded from inside the box, twisting and churning like a tidal wave. Bright lights danced in front of her eyes, her head throbbing from the impact. She struggled to rise, then scrambled away from the box. More magic poured from it, swirling in the air like a funnel of water. Dozens of sounds echoed in the cave—laughter, screams, whispered enchantments, bestial roars and growls... It was like an entire *world* had been trapped inside that box. People and creatures and magic...

The powers contained in the box were rushing *out*... But wasn't the box supposed to draw magic *in*? Prue could only stare, numb with shock, as the flood of power continued churning and gushing with such violence she thought it might rip a hole in the cave floor.

Kronos screamed as the river of magic collided with him, slamming him backward into the cavern wall. His screams turned more anguished, more panicked, rising in pitch until they stopped entirely. Squinting through the haze in the air, Prue tried to make out his figure.

But all she saw was a pile of ash on the ground. Kronos was gone.

The walls quivered again, the earth rumbling beneath her. A boulder shook loose from the ceiling and crashed to the ground in front of her, narrowly missing her foot.

Prue jumped up, alarm flaring inside her. Opening the box hadn't helped at all. The cave was still going to crumble.

She had to close it. *Now.*

With the small black lid still in her grasp, she tried placing it on top of the box once more, hoping the magic would get sucked back inside.

But while the lid was still intact, the bottom of the box had disintegrated, resembling nothing more than a charred husk of melted black sludge.

"No," Prue breathed in horror, trying in vain to replace the lid. But once she set it atop the melted remains, the lid began bubbling and burning in her fingers. She yanked them away, hissing in pain, and watched as the lid, too, melted with the rest of the box.

You're the daughter of Gaia, Trivia had said. *You're powerful enough to close the box. I'm sure of it.*

Trivia had been lying.

"No!" Prue screamed, trying to summon her magic, to draw the dark magic back. She had to put a stop to it. She had to fix this! This wasn't supposed to happen... The box was supposed to take her powers, to take *all* the magic away! What was going on?

The roaring vortex of shapes and sounds was spiraling toward her. From within, she heard a maniacal laugh, as if Pandora's dark magic was eager to devour her...

"Cyrus!" she shrieked, turning and fleeing from the tunnel and the explosion of power that still echoed behind her. She sprinted back through the passageway until she reached the main chamber once more.

It was empty.

"*Cyrus*!" Prue screamed.

More laughter echoed behind her, and she whirled to find the spinning horde of magic trailing after her. Taunting her.

She remembered what Lagos had said: *The box draws in anything surrounding it. The last one to open it was trapped inside.*

The magic of Pandora's box would consume her completely unless she found a way out. *Right now.*

"Trust your magic," she reminded herself, her voice a trembling whisper. She closed her eyes, conjuring the divine power inside her. It rose up willingly, as if it had been waiting. Her eyes flew open. Her hands glowed white, the heat burning inside her. With a shout of fury, she thrust her hands, palms out, toward the dark magic careening toward her.

The magic stopped short, hovering in the air, the great mass faltering from her show of strength.

Was it afraid of her power? Or had it recognized Gaia's magic?

"I am not your enemy," Prue growled. "I am the same as you. Now, leave me be lest you invoke the Triple Goddess's wrath." Her voice was firm, echoing in the cave.

The floating magic quivered slightly. Whispers echoed around Prue in an ancient tongue she couldn't decipher. She shuddered from the power of it. Dark and unstoppable.

"Sister," a voice hissed from within the vortex.

Prue's insides chilled as the voice confirmed what she had suspected. She and Mona had another sister.

Trivia.

"Where is she?" Prue demanded, not entirely expecting an answer.

"She... is... free," the whispers chanted.

The magic surged forward, and Prue yelped, ducking down low to avoid being struck. But the spiral of power merely grazed over her head, funneling toward the ceiling before it vanished from view. Echoes of its laughter still rang in Prue's ears.

Stunned, Prue straightened, her insides churning with unease and horror. What had she just unleashed on this realm?

Whatever it was, it certainly didn't seem like it would help things. If anything, it would add to the destruction and chaos.

Trivia had lied about *everything*. The box didn't drain magic; it *unleashed* all the forbidden magicks of the universe.

And they were forbidden for a reason.

What would happen to the people of the Underworld? Prue thought of Lagos, and panic flared in her chest. She *had* to get out of here.

But Cyrus was still down here. Where was he?

Find him. Use your magic.

Her hand flew to her collarbone, only to realize her pomegranate necklace was no longer there. *Of course.* Their bond was broken; it would be even harder to find him now.

Prue gritted her teeth. Cyrus was her husband, and *she would find him.* She knew his magic, his scent, better than she knew herself. Closing her eyes, she conjured his face in her mind, his musky and dark scent, the icy chill of his death magic, the growl of his voice when he was angry... and when he was aroused.

Each singular feature of Cyrus—his skin, his hair, his tattoos, the way his eyes crinkled with his smile—

came to her mind as she crafted a perfect likeness of her husband.

"Show me where you are," she whispered. Without knowing why, she stretched her arms out, her eyes remaining closed as she blindly reached out for him. "Show me, Cyrus."

She inched forward, her feet scraping against the rocky ground. She didn't know where she was going, but some innate instinct told her to keep her eyes closed, or else the bubble of magic around her would shatter.

So she did. Trusting in the light guiding her, she edged forward. Her hands met the rocky surface of the cave walls, and the light beckoned her to the left. Then to the right. Down a tunnel. Her footsteps echoed in the darkness.

Then, her fingers met something solid and warm. She grasped it and touched fabric. Her eyes flew open, and she found Cyrus standing in front of her, his eyes wide with surprise.

"Cyrus!" she breathed, crushing him in a tight embrace. "Goddess, I thought I'd lost you."

"What happened?" He drew back to inspect her, his eyes fierce. He stroked the hair from her eyes and cupped her face in his hands. "Are you hurt?"

"No. But Pandora's box, it's... I opened it." Sudden comprehension struck her: if Cyrus had been with her, the box *would* have destroyed him because he did not have Gaia's magic. Just like it had destroyed Kronos.

Prue sent a prayer of gratitude to the Goddess for whatever force had pulled them apart earlier.

Cyrus's grip on her tightened, his eyes darkening. "You opened the box?"

Prue bit her lip and nodded.

Cyrus closed his eyes for a moment and exhaled deeply. "I felt it. I felt something powerful strike the realm. What did it do? What was inside the box?"

Prue thought of what she had learned about Trivia, and Kronos disintegrating into a pile of ash... Goddess above, how could she tell him everything? "There isn't time to explain it all, but it's bad. It's *really* bad. Cyrus, I've made a terrible mistake." She broke off with a sob, unable to remain calm for much longer. Panic gripped her, seizing her limbs so tightly she thought she might faint.

Cyrus ran his thumb down her jaw before his hand slid behind her neck as he pressed his forehead to hers. "It'll be all right. We're together. We can figure this out."

Prue swallowed hard and nodded. She had to keep herself from falling apart. Just for a little longer. "How do we get out of here?"

"Come on." Cyrus took her hand and led her away, farther into the tunnel.

Prue followed him through the winding passage,

realizing she hadn't been down this one before. It grew darker and narrower, and Prue had to stay behind Cyrus because it wasn't wide enough for them to stride side-by-side. He kept her hand clasped in his, tugging her forward.

"There!" Cyrus said, pointing.

A thin beam of light shone just ahead of them. As they drew closer, it grew in size, illuminating the tunnel. They hurried toward it, but the ground quaked. The walls shook, and dust and pebbles fell from above. Prue shrieked as heavier rocks began to fall.

"Almost there!" Cyrus shouted over the noise, pulling her more urgently.

A boulder crashed into the ground, and pain flared in Prue's ankle. She released Cyrus's hand, falling to the ground, her foot throbbing. She cried out, trying to free her foot, but the boulder was too big.

"Prue!" Cyrus hurried over to her and struggled to lift the boulder himself. It shifted, but not enough for her to free her foot.

"Just go!" she shouted. "You can get out and come back for me. Please, Cyrus!"

"Like hell," he growled. "I'm not leaving you, Prue. Ever."

Tears streamed down her face as more boulders rained from above. One of them would crush her skull—or Cyrus's. They would both die down here.

She would never see Mona again. She would never be able to save this realm from the destruction of Pandora's box.

"Hold me," she said, her voice trembling.

Cyrus obeyed, kneeling next to her, wrapping his arms around her.

Prue clutched him against her, her fingers fisting the fabric of his tunic. She closed her eyes, weeping into his shirt, as she conjured all the force and fury of her magic. Every last drop. White light burned from within her, but she kept drawing more power. More magic. Her body sagged from the exhaustion of it, and still she fought.

I give it all up, she thought, her third eye quivering from the magnitude of her full power. *Just spare his life. Please.*

A scream ripped from her throat as white light exploded from her chest, ricocheting off the walls. A glowing dome surrounded her and Cyrus. The ceiling caved in above them, boulders slamming into her shield as the cave collapsed. Her scream went on, tearing through her, draining every last ounce of her power and her soul.

She gave up every piece of herself to keep that shield intact. And when the boulders stopped falling, she succumbed to the darkness completely.

PORTAL

MONA

Romanos couldn't stop Mona from hunting down Evander. She knew his scent, his magic, and once they had emerged from the caves, she could track him easily. She flew across the bridge of the river Styx and toward the gleaming portal before her.

And then, she saw him. With Trivia.

She screamed as Trivia hauled him through the portal. By the time Mona reached it, it was too late. They were both gone.

The gold light of the portal flickered and then vanished, leaving nothing but an empty stone archway. Mona slammed her fists against the unyielding stone, sobbing against it.

"Open!" she cried. "Open, *now*! Let me through!"

"It won't work," panted a voice behind her. Mona didn't have to turn to know it was Romanos, finally catching up to her. "It has to recharge. It takes ages to channel enough power to send one person to Elysium—let alone two."

Elysium. Horror washed over her as she remembered what Evander had told her. *My dark magic—Typhon—will not allow me to survive in other realms. This power was born of the Underworld and will destroy me if I leave.*

Evander had fully merged with Typhon. If he traveled to Elysium, he would die.

Mona screamed, her voice echoing in the forest. She pounded her fists against the stone again and again, ignoring Romanos's protests behind her, ignoring the aching pain burning in her hands. Blood ran down her arms, coating her fists, but still she kept hammering against it, unleashing all of her fury and desperation.

Something roared behind her, making her falter. She glanced over her shoulder to find a mass of darkening clouds rising in the sky. Thunder and lightning boomed from within.

"That... that's not part of the illusion," Romanos said.

A fierce wind whipped around them, tousling Mona's hair. Within that wind, Mona could sense an immense amount of power. Dark, ancient magic swelled around her.

"The box," Mona breathed. "They opened it."

"That doesn't look good," Romanos murmured darkly, drawing closer to Prue. "I thought Trivia said it was supposed to *drain* all magic."

Mona gaped at the mass hurtling toward them, then turned to the archway behind her.

It was glowing gold.

Shock and excitement pulsed within her. She grabbed Romanos's arm. The dark clouds loomed closer. Lightning struck the ground directly behind them.

"What are you doing?" Romanos cried, struggling against her grip.

"Do you want to be swept away in that?" Mona gestured to the dark clouds. "The portal is opened!"

"What? How?"

"The box doesn't drain magic; it *adds* magic. Whatever magic was trapped inside is enough to charge the portal. We have to go through *now*."

"I can't go to Elysium! I'm cursed!"

"You're doomed either way!" Mona shouted. "That magic will devour you, Romanos!"

Panic flared in his gaze as he glanced over his shoulder. The storm was on top of them now, the clouds cloaking everything in shadow. Whispers and laughter echoed around them, the magic closing in.

"Shit," Romanos growled, his fingers clasping Mona's as he threw himself forward.

Mona followed after, both of them diving through the glowing gold portal and leaving the darkness and the Underworld behind.

EPILOGUE
PANDORA

PANDORA LANDED IN ELYSIUM, THE GOLD LIGHT of the portal fading to make way for the stone path before her. At the end of the path stood the golden gates of the realm she despised more than anything. Behind her, Evander collapsed, groaning in agony, but she paid him no mind. He wouldn't last long anyway.

Trees lined the path, the sky a creamy white expanse above her. The air smelled sickly sweet, as if a garden had thrown up on her.

"Disgusting," she muttered, shaking her head. But she would have to get used to it. Enduring a sickening smell was a small price to pay.

She strode forward, a satisfied smile spreading along her face. For the briefest of moments, she thought of her two sisters, now wasting away in the destruction of the

Underworld. A shame, really. If they hadn't clung so tightly to their fleeting affection for those princes of Hell, they could have joined Pandora here and risen with her.

Such a pity.

Her feet practically glided along the smooth stones of the path. Her magic flared to life inside her, but she quieted it. For now. She couldn't unleash it yet and reveal her identity. She had to get inside first.

It was all part of the plan.

The Underworld was destroyed. Now, all that was left was to take down Elysium.

The gods would suffer for what they had done to her. Soon, every single one of them would pay.

The gates swung open, allowing her entrance. Pandora's smile widened as she stepped through, prepared to enact the final step to her revenge.

LEARN MORE AT

rlperez.com/oak-and-ember

NOTE TO THE READER

Thank you so much for reading! I greatly appreciate you taking the time.

If you would be so kind, please leave a review to let others know what you thought of the book!

ACKNOWLEDGMENTS

So many amazing individuals helped make this book possible.

Jo, Jenni, Melissa, Tori, and Kari, my incredible beta readers. Your critiques and suggestions really helped make this story shine!

My Tuesday Tribe, for the support during my meltdowns and the brainstorming sessions when I was stuck (which was often!).

My amazing ARC team and your love, kindness, and constant cheerleading! Thanks for being so eager to dive into my novels.

My wonderful friend and colleague, Joss, for your never-ending encouragement, for championing me and my books from the start.

My lovely readers! Thank you for continuing with this series, for always being eager to read the next adventure.

Blue Raven Book Covers for the gorgeous cover art.

Imperiness for the stunning character art.

All the marvelous Kickstarter backers who helped

with the Ivy & Bone project! Your contributions were monumental in bringing this story to life.

Alex, Colin, and Ellie. My greatest loves. Thank you for being a part of this journey, for sharing in the excitement during my successes and for being a comfort to me during the difficulties.

ABOUT THE AUTHOR

R.L. Perez is an author, wife, mother, reader, writer, and teacher. She lives in Florida with her husband and two children. On a regular basis, she can usually be found napping, reading, feverishly writing, revising, or watching an abundance of Netflix. More than anything, she loves spending time with her family. Her greatest joys are her two kids, nature, literature, and chocolate.

Subscribe to her newsletter for new releases, promotions, giveaways, and book recommendations! Get a FREE eBook when you sign up at subscribe.rlperez.com.

9 781955 035255